Gold Coast Detective
Scotty Stephens

Book 3

TARNISED

ANDREW M^cDERMOTT

Tarnished by ANDREW McDERMOTT
www.andrewmcdermott.com.au

First published in Australia by X Press Publishing 2025
P.O. Box 395 Coolangatta
Queensland 4225 Australia
mail@andrewmcdermott.com.au

A catalogue record for this
book is available from the
National Library of Australia

ISBN: 978-1-7638597-0-8 (pbk)
ISBN: 978-1-7638597-1-5 (ebk)

Cover design by X Press Publishing © 2025
Cover background image: © KinoMaster (Shutterstock)

Typesetting and design by X Press Publishing © 2025

For Margaret and Andy

BOOKS BY
ANDREW M^CDERMOTT
(see samples and more details at back of this book)

Gold Coast Detective Scotty Stephens series:
X'posé (X prequel)
Book 1 – X
Book 2 – Mary's Mansion
Book 3 – Tarnished
Book 4 - INSEXT

Detective Joe Dean series:
Hidden Moon (Flirting with The Moon prequel)
Flirting with The Moon

The Tiger Chase

Speculative fiction:
Quest of The New Templars series:
Birthright (prequel)
Book 1 – RESURRECTION

Children's books:
The Last Tiger

1

So long, Freckles.

It's true. Your life really does flash before your eyes just prior to death. Although, if twenty-two-year-old Cory Evans were of a conscious mind, he might have debated the term 'flash'. More like a sequential replay of the key moments.

In a forest clearing close to the New South Wales and Queensland border, the BIC lighter hissed in the stillness of the night, but Cory hardly noticed. As if guided by the flame, his mind shifted through the scenes of an extraordinary life.

Wearing only a pair of boardshorts, he was two years old, sitting cross-legged on a rug, while a make-up artist smeared melted chocolate around his mouth. Next to him sat Sunny, the obedient golden Labrador Retriever. The only reason Cory knew he was two was because he remembered reading it on his Wikipedia page. The Tim Tam commercial was the first gig, the launch pad for the madness that would become the life of Cory Evans—aka Freckles.

Rather than make-up, the young cosmetologist used real chocolate. A brilliant move. What kid couldn't be controlled by the lure of a Tim Tam? But little Cory had had enough. He'd been sitting on the floor for hours. While technicians adjusted the lighting, and the cameraman discussed angles with the director, a photographer snapped shots of the chocolate covered cherub. The name Freckles wasn't coined yet. That came later, after the third commercial. By that time, the dimples, the big blue eyes, the golden hair, and of course, the freckles, would be a registered trademark.

'Action,' the director cried.

The dog moved in and licked chocolate from the kid's face.

'And cut. Let's do it again.'

Little Cory didn't really know what was happening. All he knew was he'd been sitting on that floor for hours while strange people hovered around him, a dog continually licked his cheek, and he was being force fed chocolate. Screwing up his face, he began to cry.

'Somebody see to the kid,' the director called out impatiently. 'We need to get this wrapped up.'

When Mum appeared from nowhere, and leaned down and picked him up, the lack of motherly concern was of little comfort. 'Now you behave yourself, Cory, and do as the man says.'

The flame flickered.

He was a year older. The Vegemite commercial was set in a family kitchen. Like the Tim Tam ad, it featured a cute kid smeared with product. There seemed to be a growing theme.

Among the hive of busy workers, Cory spotted his parents standing just offset. Dad was in an off-the-shelf suit and Mum was in a sparkly cocktail dress. Of course, three-year-old Freckles wouldn't have been so analytic at that age. All he wanted was for them to pick him up, cuddle him and take him home. But the twenty-two-year-old whose life was about to end, was tuned in to every detail. His parents' clothes were inexpensive at this time. The Rolex watches, Brioni and Louis Vitton would come later when the 99.9% share in their investment began to pay dividends.

But the kid knew none of this. A wave towards his parents was countered with a stern scowl from his father. Short, dark-haired and with the hint of a receding hairline, Barry Evans was all about business.

The figure leaning in through the window of the late model MINI watched in silence as the young man, bound and gagged in the driver's seat, began to shiver.

The flame, hovering in the petrol doused interior, escorted Cory to the next period of his life.

Freckles was four years old. He was sitting on a couch, looking extra cute in his little suit and tie. The studio audience applauded as chat show host Roy MacDonald took his seat.

'So, Freckles …' Roy said as the applause died down. 'What's it like to be so famous?'

The little boy twisted shyly in his seat and blushed. 'Good.'

'I bet it is. Here are some shots of how good it is.'

The screen was filled with images of Freckles appearing around the country. Posing in front of Uluru. Climbing the Sydney Harbour Bridge. Snorkelling the Great Barrier Reef. These were followed with a series of group photographs of the boy posing with local townsfolk around the country: Longreach, Broken Hill, Darwin, and Tasmania. The last shot was in Canberra. It was a photo of the lad and his beaming parents with the Prime Minister of Australia.

'So, how old are you now? About twenty-six?' Roy asked.

'No …' Cory said, delivering the mischievous giggle that would melt the nation.

'How many commercials have you done so far?'

The boy shrugged, which once again brought waves of sympathetic *God-I-love-that-kid* laughter to the studio audience.

'Well, you've done eight commercials in two years. How does that make you feel?'

The shrug again, this time with a blushing grin. This kid didn't even have to speak. Everyone loved him.

'I hear you're going into acting.'

The boy nodded.

'Would you like to tell us where we're going to see you next.'

'... Ramsey Street!'

The audience jumped to their feet, clapping and whistling.

When the applause finally subsided. Roy continued. 'So, you'll be appearing in *Neighbours*?'

The nodding again, this time with the over excited enthusiasm of a four year old.

As always, Barry Evans was standing just off camera, his scowling eyes fixed firmly on his son.

Freckles, ignoring his father, kept his attention on Roy. Roy was good fun.

'So, you're going to be an even bigger star than you are now?'

The boy shrugged and nodded in a cheeky, matter-of-fact way.

'Ladies and Gentlemen, let's hear it for Freckles.'

The applause echoed and swirled until a dark silence hung over the small clearing like an invisible fog. A henge of trees looked on like a congregation of elders waiting in witness. With the absence of the moon, the only light was from the flame.

It wasn't the set of *Neighbours* where the five and three quarter year old found himself standing. He was on a beach. Unlike most of the commercials, he did have recollections of his one season on *Home and Away*, and of the season with *Neighbours* the year prior. He remembered this as a happy time, working with other young people who treated him like a normal kid.

'Action!'

A middle-aged woman was running, somewhat awkwardly, on the loose sand. Just before she reached the child, she threw her arms out. 'Oh goodness, there you are, Stevie.' Dropping to her knees, she reached out, grabbed the boy, and pulled him close. 'We thought we'd lost you.' Then, pulling back, she repeated the words in sign.

Little Stevie McCauley was deaf and had wandered off on his own. With swelling tears in his big blue eyes, the boy apologised in sign and told his nanna how much he loved her. After this performance, whispers of a Gold Logie were rife in the industry.

The flame flickered.

Scenes from an extraordinary life continued. The image of little Freckles appearing as Aladdin in pantomime at the London Palladium seemed to hover and shudder like it was stuck. Was this the turning point of no return? The fans outside the stage door screaming and grabbing at him as he made his way to a waiting limousine. Thank goodness for security. Cory knew Barry had seen to this. Good old Bazza. He'd also made sure every news station in the UK was present to witness the scene.

'Are you okay, sweetie?' A-list actress, Natalie Hinderman, placed a hand on Freckles' shoulder between shoots. They were on a sailing boat in the Whitsundays.

Freckles nodded. He was eight years old. Still as cute as a button but taller now.

Peering over the side of the boat, he saw his parents sitting on the deck of a luxury yacht. Dressed like typical wealthy tourists, they were drinking cocktails and having a nice time. At first, Cory thought it unusual that his mother was there. She'd grown tired after the first couple of years and usually stayed home. But of course, this *was* the Whitsundays and her son's first major movie role. Cory realised this wasn't a retrospect thought of the twenty-two-year-old him. It was from the mind of the eight year old who was beginning to resent his greedy parents.

Scenes from more movies followed. Pity-filled faces of more A-list stars came and went as if lining up to say goodbye. A minor scene with Robert De Niro in his first Hollywood movie flickered just as the Aladdin pantomime one had. Was this another turning point? Cory knew it was. It was the time when the Freckles brand hit the world.

Ten-year-old Cory wasn't allowed to sit in the meetings with his father and the movie executives. Instead, he'd wait outside the office until prompted to enter, do the little spiel that Barry had written, then leave without saying another word. If asked questions, he was primed to smile that smile, blush that blush, and smack them silly with that giggle.

Normally the memories of Barry's anger, the tantrums, the bullying, and the physical abuse would cause Cory's chest to constrict tightly like a block of ice. But not anymore.

Like the Olympic torch, the lowering of the flame was about to grab the attention of a nation. With the reel of film nearing its end, and Freckles' final performance pending, who said he could no longer bring his audience to tears?

Looking back on himself now in that stupid cowboy outfit and toy gun, Cory realised how pathetic the smile must have become to the Australian public. He was no longer cute, more awkward. The movie was a remake of the 1958 Australian classic, *Smiley Gets a Gun*. After the premier, the eleven year old had an inkling that things weren't going well. There were no appearances on the *Roy MacDonald Show* or *Entertainment Tonight*. Barry only confirmed his fears by mentally beating him with a barrage of newspaper headlines:

'Is the Golden Child Tarnished?'
'Pre-teen and already burnt out?'
'From cute to pathetic!'

The scenes of fourteen-year-old Cory on stage fronting a boy band didn't linger for long. They passed as quickly as the music career that never was.

At nineteen, images of the court cases flittered by like landscape views from a speeding train. The threats mainly. His father's anger. The glamorous mummy slowly morphing into the haggard trailer trash when everything she owned was stripped away. These were followed by images of the drinking days, the heroin, the sleaze surrounding a wealthy young man who was out of control.

But then his little brother, Wesley, interrupted his thoughts. The sibling he hardly knew because he'd spent most of his life working. Did he feel sorry for Wesley? Of course, he did. But it was way too late for regrets now.

The flame flickered for the last time. The trees rustled on a gentle breeze as if whispering their final pleas. 'Don't do it!'

The hand holding the lighter hesitated momentarily as if the killer was having second thoughts.

Cory closed his eyes.

When the flame finally touched the passenger seat, the petrol-sodden fabric ignited, and the killer barely had time to withdraw before the ferocious flames engulfed the car's interior. The surrounding shadows elongated and danced with the rising intensity, and black toxic smoke bellowed upwards into the starless night.

Within minutes, the flames reached the petrol tank, and the tiny vehicle exploded. A fierce fireball rose into the air, carrying with it the last remnants of Freckles, the little boy who just wanted to be loved.

2

There'd been no Schoolies excitement for Wesley Cummings when he'd finished Year 12 two years earlier. Maybe that's why now, walking among the groups of laughing, mischievous graduates in Surfers Paradise, he realised he'd unconsciously developed a sense of resentment towards this time of the year. Of course, it didn't help that he now lived on the golden strip. At least when he was in the Tweed, he didn't have to come near the place.

After the pressures of sitting their HSC exams, the annual Schoolies festival held in Surfers Paradise was a time for the high school graduates to let their hair down, goof around for a week and party—kind of like Australia's answer to the US spring break. No adults, no parents, no teachers. Wesley was aware that things could get wild.

Halfway up the mall, there was a large group of kids blocking the way. Jumping up and down, they were chanting a mantra that must have been their high school motto. Even though it was early in the morning, these guys were obviously starting the day how they meant to continue. Although large, the group seemed to be quite exclusive and made up of the clichéd jocks and bimbo types. The guys were tall and muscular. The girls, mostly blonde, wore pink hoodies and fake eyelashes. Wesley had to push through them to get by. As he did, he accidently knocked a Justin Bieber look-alike off balance.

'Hey!' The guy swung around and pushed Wesley backwards.

'Sorry,' Wesley said.

Two other guys joined Bieber. *Were mullets back in?*

'What the hell ya doin, Toolie?' one of the other guys growled down at Wesley.

'Nothin, just heading home.'

'We've been warned about you lot. Older kids here to cause trouble,' Bieber said.

'I'm not a Toolie, I—'

'How old are you then?' the third guy piped in, as if not wanting to be left out.

The rest of the group formed a circle around Wesley.

'I'm just heading home from the beach. I live in Surfers.'

'Fucking Toolie. That's what you are,' one girl spat.

Wesley tried to push past them, but the group blocked his way. 'I don't want any trouble, guys.'

'I don't want any trouble, guys,' Bieber mimicked, moving in closer.

One of the girls began to chant, 'Toolie, Toolie, Toolie.'

The group joined in. 'Toolie, Toolie, Toolie.'

'Let's show this little fat fucker what we do with Toolies,' Bieber cried above the chant. He leaped forward and grabbed Wesley in a headlock.

'Okay, break it up!'

The chant turned into wolf whistles and hoots as two police officers waded into the crowd.

Bieber quickly let go but got in a jab to Wesley's kidneys as he did so.

'What's going on here?' The female, and shortest of the two cops, demanded. Her name tag said Constable Karen Smith.

One of the girls stepped forward. 'It's this Toolie. Causing trouble already.'

'Is that true?' demanded Smith.

'No,' Wesley said, massaging his side. 'I was just heading home from the beach.'

'Are you a Schoolie or a Toolie?'

'Neither. I live in Surfers.'

'Are you okay? Seem to have a problem there with your side.'

When Wesley glanced at Bieber, the lad looked away. 'I'm fine. Just want to get home.'

'Okay, get yourself away,' the police officer said. 'I'd recommend you stay out of sight for the next couple of weeks.'

'What?' Bieber stepped forward. 'You can't let him go. My uncle's a copper and he said you guys are clamping down on the Toolies this year.'

'Do you even know what a Toolie is, son?' asked Smith.

'Yeah, they're older kids who probably never graduated or are just here to cause trouble.'

Wesley had to get away. Not because he was angry, embarrassed or frightened or anything like that. He needed to get away because he wasn't sure how much longer he could keep the smirk off his face. Pushing through the group there were jeers and boos as he continued on his way.

With his head down, the smirk finally broke and morphed into a grin. Venturing out on his own was a big achievement but doing it just as the Schoolies event was about to kick off made it all the more important, exciting, dangerous! Would he dare go out again? Of course, he would.

When he reached the Milton Plaza, the lift took him swiftly up to the penthouse suite on the 57th floor. As always, the apartment was quiet at this time of the day. With the windows open, the sea breeze seeped into the room. His brother, Cory, never rose until lunch time, but he didn't go to bed until around two in the morning. In the three weeks since Wesley had moved in, he'd found this routine quite strange but soon adapted to it. It sure beat living in a caravan on the Tweed with his alcoholic mother and her abusive boyfriend.

The Bieber look-alike's description of a Toolie resonated in his mind. The fact that Wesley didn't get the chance to experience Schoolies was definitely an issue he'd ignored until now. Was he going to be labelled a Toolie over the next couple of weeks just for stepping outside his door? Should he lock himself away until the festival was over?

No, he'd done enough of that. He'd already decided that, if possible, he'd try to blend in the best he could.

3

CASSIE EVANS climbed from a taxi outside the Surfers Paradise Island Resort and really did try to be as enthusiastic as her two friends, Jenna and Ellie.

'I can't believe we're actually here,' Jenna yelled, throwing her arms around her friends as the driver retrieved their bags.

Ellie did a little shimmy, shake and squeal routine.

'God have mercy on my soul,' Cassie said under her breath as Jenna joined in on the dance. And when the girls reached out to her to join them in a group hug, she pulled away.

After standing in a long line of Jenna and Ellie clones for what seemed like hours, they eventually checked in and went up to their room.

'I can't believe we're sharing a room in Surfers Paradise.' Since getting into the taxi at Hope Island, just about every sentence Jenna Reynolds had uttered began with, 'I can't believe … ' And it was already annoying the shit out of Cassie.

Two of the three girls skipped around the apartment, opening cupboards, checking empty drawers, exclaiming out loud with absolute delight how the kitchen had an electric jug and a drawer with three knives and three forks, a bathroom with a shower and body gel, and a toilet with a sanitised seal. It seemed every little detail of the basic studio apartment that was, in reality, far too small for the three teenage girls, elicited the kind of excited reaction you'd associate with an Ellen DeGeneres audience after finding out they'd each receive a George Foreman grill for free.

'Oh my god, oh my god. This is soooo comfortable!' Ellie exclaimed as she stretched out on one of the beds. 'Shotgun this one.'

There was one single bed and one double. Neither Cassie nor Jenna put forward an argument when Ellie claimed the single. Although Cassie didn't relish the thought of having to sleep with Jenna, it was a much better proposal than sleeping with 'Smellie Ellie', the queen farter.

'Let's just dump our bags and go out,' Jenna said.

'Good idea,' Cassie agreed. Although each of the girls was familiar with Surfers Paradise, they couldn't wait to explore the transformed, party central streets.

Of course, just dumping the bags and heading out was never going to happen. For Cassie it was as simple as doing exactly that, but not for Jenna and Ellie. A change of clothing was required because at least thirty other girls had seen them in the queue.

Cassie sighed and sat on the end of the double bed, watching her friends as they decided which outfits to wear, and which shade of lipstick. She knew from experience that this was going to take time. *Should she nick out without them ...? No, not yet.* Luckily for Cassie, she didn't need to apply fresh make-up. In fact, she hardly wore any. Unlike her two blonde friends, she preferred to live a more natural life.

As the two girls leaned into the wall mirror, Cassie got glimpses of herself. Because of her Asian complexion, the family eyes seemed even bluer than those of her half-brother. She hated those eyes and quickly looked away 'Come on, you guys,' she complained. 'We're just going to check the place out.'

'Almost ready,' Jenna said, puckering her lips and applying more lippy.

Following another costume change by Ellie, after deciding the pink mini skirt was too much, the girls finally headed out.

Surfers Paradise was awash with teenagers. Cassie quickly sorted them into four groups. There were the posers, like Jenna and

Ellie, but of both sexes. Eighteen year olds, who walked around nonchalantly as if they were thirty. Then there were the jocks—the sports orientated individuals, lean and spotty. These guys were loud and seemed to jump up and down a lot. Then there were the kids. This group, although eighteen, acted as if they were fourteen. Partying for them comprised of endless practical jokes, hooting and climbing street poles. The fourth group was the geeks. They were awkward, quiet, had unruly hair, and wore faded T-shirts that you never saw in the shops. This group kept themselves to themselves, only venturing out between online gaming or to replenish their stock of Twisties and Pepsi. Fortunately, the Gold Coast City Council catered for all groups and the annual event was a huge success for generations of Schoolies.

Cassie wondered which group she fell under. She certainly wasn't a poser, or a jock, or a geek. Was she just a kid? No, she was Cassie—could-have-been-a-superstar-if-her-father-had-had-his-way—Evans. And she was happy. Maybe.

Jenna and Ellie walked together with their arms entwined. Cassie was having none of that. She walked slowly by their side. The pair giggled and staggered as if intoxicated. Although the Schoolies festival was strictly alcohol free, that didn't stop the kids from sneaking in as much contraband as possible. Both Jenna and Ellie carried throw away water bottles, offering themselves as role models while exhibiting the importance of keeping hydrated in the Queensland humidity. But of the course the water was poured out earlier and replaced with gin and lemonade. Cassie's bottle, however, contained water.

Cavill Avenue was packed. There were stages set up for live performances, market stalls selling hippy clothing, beach gear and iced drinks. There were buskers and street performers struggling to perform among the heaving masses. It was hot and sticky, loud, and the air was a little tense as if something was about to happen.

And then it did.

A large hand, that seemed to come from nowhere, suddenly came down hard and clamped onto Cassie's shoulder. 'Excuse me, miss. I need to know what's in the bottle.'

She turned to see the face of a square-chinned police officer peering down at her.

With anxious glances and lowered chins, Ellie and Jenna continued through the crowd, leaving Cassie alone with the cop.

'Did you hear me?' The cop snatched the bottle from Cassie's hand. He unscrewed the top and took a sniff. 'Is there any alcohol in here?'

Cassie shook her head. A panicked side glance confirmed her friends had abandoned her.

The cop screwed on the top and handed the bottle back to Cassie. 'Ok, miss. Thank you for your cooperation.' Then he was gone.

And so had Cassie's so-called friends.

Continuing to wade through the crowd, she soon forgot about Jenna and Ellie. Her thoughts were on the real reason she had come to Surfers in the guise of a Schoolie. The more time she could spend away from those two, the more chance she had of instigating her plan. She was nervous but excited—two emotions that, until now, had eluded Cassie Evans.

4

The situation with Jenna and Ellie could have been uncomfortable or even nasty if Cassie was as insecure and as shallow as they were. The truth was, she didn't care about what they did now that she was there. After losing them in the crowd the evening before, she went back to her room, watched some TV and turned in early. The giggling twosome returned around 2.00 am, stinking of booze and pot.

Cassie rose with the sunrise. Leaving the girls snoring, she was on a mission, following a hunch. If her suspicions paid off on the very first morning, she'd have the rest of the week to put her plan into action.

The streets of Surfers Paradise looked vastly different without the hordes of moronic schoolkids. Council workers went about their business cleaning up. The odd surfer was making his or her way to the beach. The throbbing sound of a road sweeper vibrated through the ground. The high-pitched beep of a delivery truck echoed through the tall buildings, and the whiz and trundle of the not-so-silent electric tram whirred by. The day was already heating up, but remnants of the cooler nighttime temperature were being carried in from the ocean as if chased towards the west by the rising sun.

Cassie didn't have an actual address. All she knew was that her half-brothers, whom she'd never met, lived in Surfers Paradise. Of course, she didn't expect to see Cory. According to the *Sixty Minutes* expose that aired a month earlier, he'd been holed up in his penthouse for the last couple of years, never venturing out, living off pizza and playing video games all day and night. Cassie wondered if she'd even recognise him. No, it was Wesley she was hoping to see. The hunch she'd developed after learning he'd moved into his brother's apartment was that to avoid the Schoolie masses, he'd be out early in the mornings.

Although *Sixty Minutes* didn't identify the building specifically, possibly in fear of being sued by the hotel group, Cassie recognised it as the Milton Plaza on Orchid Avenue. The tallest of the two towers was the hotel. The second was the exclusive residencies. One of two top floor penthouses were where she expected Cory to reside.

An industrious entrepreneur was serving coffee from a converted VW Kombi across the street from the Milton entrance. Cassie ordered a flat white, sat down on the kerb and waited. To her surprise, she didn't have to wait long. A plump chap wearing a dark singlet, boardshorts and thongs stepped out of the Milton foyer with his head down. After a glance in each direction, he marched towards Cavill Avenue. Cassie recognised him at once from the photographs her father had hidden in his phone. It was Wesley Cummings, her half-brother. Jumping to her feet, she followed. From behind, she couldn't see too much of him, only that his hair was dark and unruly. Slung over his back was a small Billabong backpack. The dark clothing made his skin look awfully pale. He was chubbier than she'd expected. A distinctive roll of fat around his kidneys wobbled as he walked, and Cassie guessed exercise wasn't high on his list of priorities. For a moment, she felt a sudden wave of panic. *What should she do next?* Although she'd planned this meeting for some months, she'd visualised it as being on the beach or around a pool in some exotic resort.

Wesley turned left into Cavill Avenue, cut across the mall and entered the Paradise Centre.

A skip in Cassie's step was required for her to keep up.

Apart from the newsagents and Coles, the rest of the stores in the shopping centre were closed. Wesley stopped briefly at the entrance to the supermarket and used the hand sanitiser. Then he picked up one of the plastic baskets and entered the store.

Cassie planted herself on a wooden bench and waited. From this vantage point, she could see inside the store and watch Wesley as he wandered around the aisles. He didn't seem to be in a hurry. Instead of going to specific shelves where the goods he required were, he wandered aimlessly along them all. When he was halfway around the shop, his basket was still empty.

Cassie's tummy suddenly rumbled. She realised she hadn't eaten since leaving home the day before. Should she approach Wesley when he came out of Coles? Looking around, she wondered if this was the right place to do it. And if so, what would she say to him?

She watched him go through the self-serve checkout. He only appeared to purchase one item—a bottle of milk. When he finally emerged from the store, Cassie suddenly felt riveted to her seat. The moment she'd be planning all this time was finally here, but she couldn't move. It was as if an inner thermostat had overheated, clicked off and shut down her system. All she could do was watch as the lad, two years older than her but very much a lad, marched back the way he had come. But to do this he would need to pass right by Cassie.

When he was just a couple of metres away, he looked up from the floor and their eyes met.

Cassie tried to look away but couldn't. It was the eyes. The eyes of her father. Her eyes.

Wesley slowed his pace then stopped walking and just stared. It was the first time Cassie had seen his features close-up. The photographs she'd seen weren't that clear.

Wesley frowned.

Cassie offered a slight smile.

As if regaining his senses, Wesley suddenly broke eye contact, checked his surroundings then marched past her.

Without thinking, Cassie jumped to her feet, ran after him and grabbed him by the arm. 'Wait.'

Wesley turned slowly.

Cassie could feel him trembling in her grip. 'You're Wesley, right? Wesley Cummings?'

Nervously glancing from side to side as if plotting his escape, he didn't answer.

Cassie moved in closer. 'I'm Cassie. Cassie Evans.'

'I know who you are.'

'You do?'

'Yes, and the answer is still no.'

'What do you mean?'

Still with the rapid side glances, Wesley pulled his arm free, leaned in and lowered his voice. 'She's not getting any more money!'

'Who?'

'You know who.' Still unable to re-establish eye contact, he was frowning now.

'I don't know what you're talking about.'

'Your mother. She's had enough.' He pushed past her and marched towards the exit.

This wasn't quite the reaction Cassie was hoping for, she thought as she ran after him.

5

The last thing Wesley Cummings was expecting to do was bump into his half-sister. He'd known of her from the court case. Even though he hadn't attended the daily hearings, the sordid details of the family had become common knowledge to the Australian public because of the nightly news bulletins during that time. But even though he'd never seen a photo of her, he knew right away that the girl sitting outside Coles staring back at him with *his* eyes, although slightly oriental, was his sister. He didn't know her name. Apart from the Evans eyes, the only other give away was that she looked like her mother, Josie, whom he'd first seen regularly on TV, arm in arm with his father, entering and leaving Southport Courthouse. It was the recent exchanges with her mother that evoked the anger. Josie Evans was a gold digger. When his brother had sued his father, won the case and taken him for everything he had, Barry Evans was left with nothing—or so it was reported. But Barry, ever the wily businessman, perhaps expecting the inevitable, had registered his prestige car dealership in his wife's name. But this hadn't stopped the fiery little Filipino from approaching his brother and demanding he repay her husband for the years of hard work that that went into making him a star.

The girl was strong and wasn't about to let go. Had she come to take over where Josie left off? He broke away from her grip, but she ran around him and blocked his exit from the Paradise Centre.

'I'm not interested in any of that,' the girl said. 'I just wanted to meet you.'

'So, you've met me.' Wesley tried to move around her, but she stood firm.

'Look, I can't change what happened between you and my parents.' Her eyes were fixed and penetrating. 'I came here to meet you in the hope that I could get to know you.'

When Wesley had found out only a year ago that he had a half-sister, he understood why his parents had broken up and gone their separate ways. At first the divorce hadn't affected him in the least because his father, along with his older brother, was away from home most of the time anyway, so it was always just him and his mum, Patty. Life was good, living in a nice house on Currumbin Beach, and the lifestyle continued even after the divorce. It wasn't until Patty was sued by her eldest son that everything changed drastically for the awkward, unassuming boy.

'Why would you want to do that?' Wesley asked.

'Because you're my brother.'

Although he was trying hard to remain nonchalant, Wesley was intrigued.

'I just wanted to meet you, that's all. I'm Cassie.' She released her grip on his arm and held out her hand for him to shake.

Wesley reluctantly shook it. 'Wesley.'

'It's great to finally meet you,' Cassie said.

'So, you're here for Schoolies, no doubt,' Wesley said.

The girl blushed and nodded.

'Wanna get a coffee?'

The silent nod sustained.

Wesley turned, headed out of the Paradise Centre and onto the Cavill Avenue Mall.

Skipping to keep up, Cassie followed him. 'So, what's it like living in Surfers?'

'Good, apart from this time of the year.'

'Schoolies.'

'Yep. It's hard to remain conspicuous when you've got thousands of stupid kids pointing you out and calling you a Toolie.'

'Conspicuous?'

'Out of sight,' Wesley quickly added as he turned into a coffee shop at the beach end of the mall.

There was a group of kids, Schoolies, occupying two of the outside tables. It was impossible to distinguish between them being early risers or remnants from the party the night before. Wesley suspected the latter. The boys were high school-little lunch-loud, and the girls were giggly and whiney. Wesley couldn't stand it so immediately turned and exited the establishment.

'What's wrong?' Cassie asked.

'You! That's what's wrong,' Wesley said, marching back up the mall. 'Fucking Schoolies.'

With the girl still skipping every other step to keep up, Wesley turned into Orchid Avenue and headed for the Milton.

When they entered the foyer, the girl asked, 'Are we going up to your apartment?'

Wesley nodded. You okay with that?'

'Sure.' She seemed suddenly excited.

'You'll need to be quiet though,' Wesley said as he held the key card over the lift consul and pressed button 57. 'My brother … *our* brother will be sleeping.'

'Cory?'

Wesley didn't answer.

There was little movement in the lift as it whizzed them up to the 57th floor then opened into the penthouse suite.

'Wow!' Cassie said as she looked out over the 180-degree view of the sunshine strip and the ocean.

'Pretty impressive, huh?' Wesley said removing his backpack on the kitchen counter, retrieving the bottle of milk from his bag and placing it in the fridge.

'You're not wrong.'

'What would you like to drink?'

'Got juice?'

'Sure. Orange?'

The view and the breeze from the decent sized balcony were intoxicating. This was where Wesley liked to sit and think. In the two weeks since he'd moved into the apartment, Cassie was his first guest.

'So why did you really come here?' Wesley asked, taking a seat in the shade.

'Like I said, I wanted to meet you guys.'

'Cory?'

She shrugged and blushed a little.

'He won't like that. I'll need to speak to him first.'

The familiar, factory default tone of an Apple iPhone rang out and Wesley's pocket lit up. Ignoring it, he sipped his drink. There was a silent moment between when the ringing stopped and the missed call tone dinged.

'It'll just be my mum. She rings a lot. She'll text me now.'

Sure enough, a few minutes later, the phone dinged again. This time Wesley checked the screen. 'Shit!'

'Is everything okay?'

'No, it's not Mum. It's the police.' He called back the number, turned his back on Cassie and strolled back into the apartment. He appeared again a few minutes later. 'I'll need to go downstairs. One of the cars has been broken into.'

Cassie followed Wesley back into the kitchen.

'You stay here. It shouldn't take too long.' An anxious gait escorted him into the lift.

6

BARRY EVANS outlined the image of his daughter's face with his finger. Cassie was around nine years old, posing on the beach in Kuta, Bali. The silver-framed picture stood proud of place on his office desk. There was one other picture, freshly framed, of Cassie in her high school graduation gown, beaming between two proud parents, Barry and Josie. But it was the younger Cassie that Barry missed—the child he was forced to keep secret during those years when he'd lived a double life. A lingering sigh carried with it the familiar feeling of regret. There was a question he'd been asking himself a lot lately—would he have done things differently if he had the chance again? As always, he shook his head with enough velocity to shake him out of his pointless stupor. Taking a deep breath, he quickly wiped the moisture from his eyes with the back of his hand.

And now she was eighteen and, if that wasn't enough of a reason to cause ongoing stress for a doting father, his baby girl was at the Schoolies festival. The fact that he vividly remembered his own antics at *his* Schoolies week back in the early nineties, didn't help. In fact, it was the memory of the good times that worried him. Would his daughter be subject to the wild times he had experienced?

He scanned his surroundings. Although the glass walls of his office meant his every move was on display, it also meant he saw everything that happened in the showroom. Monday mornings were usually quiet. Jeff Baker, his senior salesman, was sitting at his desk, drinking a coffee and reading the *Gold Coast Bulletin*. Toby Johnson, the younger and newer employee, was at his desk scrolling through his iPhone. Trudy, the receptionist, was removing the weekend flowers from the vases around the room in readiness for the fresh delivery. Old Jim, the semi-retired mechanic who came in two days a week, was running a shammy over the 1972 red, Ferrari Dino.

Barry was grateful for their distractions, not noticing his moment of weakness. However, he couldn't help feeling a little irritated by the younger salesman who was either checking his Facebook or his bets from the weekend. Rising from his desk, he straightened his jacket and marched out of his office.

Jeff looked up, folded the newspaper shut, threw it to one side and tapped his computer keyboard.

Toby continued to scroll on his phone.

'Have you finished the paperwork for the SL?' Barry asked Toby, approaching his desk.

'All done, boss,' Toby said without looking up.

'So why is Jim cleaning the Dino and not the Merc?'

'He's already done it. First thing this morning.'

Barry felt like snatching the phone from his hands and smashing it on the polished concrete floor. 'When are the buyers coming?'

Toby dragged his eyes from the iPhone screen and looked at his watch. 'Should be here anytime now.' His eyes returned to his phone.

'Put the fucking phone down, lad. I'm talking to you!' Barry yelled, causing the other three people in the room to halt what they were doing and look his way.

Startled, Toby almost dropped the phone as he placed it on his desk.

'Did you sell them the gold warranty like I asked?'

'Up sold them to platinum, boss.'

Cocky little shit. Got all the answers. Although Barry saw the handsome, confident young man as a junior yet to prove himself, the truth was he was outselling Jeff by about four cars to one. The disdain was a personal thing on Barry's behalf. He glanced out of the front window to see the sixty-year-old, silver Mercedes glistening on the forecourt. 'Have you checked it over?'

'Huh?'

'Have you double checked everything before the buyer arrives?'

'Jim has, boss.'

Every time the young man addressed him as 'boss', a mental wince jolted Barry's cerebral cortex and he realised what the problem was. He desperately wanted the lad to fuck up so he could get rid of him, but Toby Johnson was excelling. 'Okay, well, I want you to check it again.'

'Yes, boss.' He jumped industriously to his feet and marched out of the showroom.

Barry strolled over to Jeff.

'Giving the young bloke a bit of a hard time, mate,' Jeff said.

'There's just something about him I don't like.' Barry was more comfortable with Jeff. They were around the same age and shared the odd beer now and again after work.

'He's doing a bloody good job. Sold the Jag over the weekend.'

'The XJS?'

'Yep. That piece of shit you took as part exchange for the Healy.'

'Was it roadworthy?'

'Barely. But Jim got it running.'

'What'd he get for it?'

'Forty k.'

'You're kidding me.'

'Nope. Probably ease up on him a bit, eh … boss,' Jeff grinned.

But Barry's attention was elsewhere. A familiar sound had distracted him. The roar of a Harley Davidson. When he glanced over the forecourt, he realised there were three of them. 'Damn,' he cussed under his breath.

'Shall I call the police?' Jeff said rising to his feet.

'No … it'll be okay. The bastard's getting nothing else from me.'

Mick Brennan was the biggest of the three bikies that just about blocked the entrance to the showroom with their machines. As if heralding their arrival, all three revved their engines, sending a thunderous vibration through the building. The silence when the V8 motors finally fell silent was welcome, but the presence of the three Neanderthals that climbed from their bikes in perfect sync, wasn't. As they strutted through the large glass entrance doors, they removed their helmets and held them in their right hands as if they were about to use them as weapons.

With menacing eyes, Brennan glared at Barry as he approached.

Barry turned and ambled casually towards his office.

The thugs followed.

Brennan entered the office and what had only moments prior been a haven of quiet, floral scented peacefulness, was now tainted with the aromas of petrol, cigarette smoke and male sweat.

Remaining calm as only Barry Evans could, he sat down at his desk.

Brennan closed the door behind him while his two henchmen took up guard outside the office.

'What is it you want now, Mick? More money?'

'What you owe me.' The tattoos on his face and neck complemented the appearance of perpetual dirt and Barry wondered if this guy ever showered.

'And what do you think it is that I owe you?'

'You owe me for taking that bitch off your hands.'

Barry threw his head back and laughed. 'You seriously think I should pay you for shacking up with my ex-wife?'

'Why else do you think I'd be tolerating her?' Although his voice was exactly how you'd expect—more of a growl—Barry suspected there was intelligence in that meaty head, one that controlled every move of the Chinderah Wasps bikie club.

Regardless, Barry kept his shields up high and continued with a patronising chuckle. 'We've been through this before, bud. You're wasting your time. There ain't no money left. Cory made sure of that when he sued me and Patty.'

'Everyone knows you stashed it away before the courts could take it.'

'It's a myth, mate. An urban legend derived by the media.'

'You're a lying bastard!'

'Look … ' Barry rose to his feet and circled his desk until he was standing face to face with the bigger man. 'I get it … you saw a chance with Patty, the estranged mother of Freckles and ex-wife of the notorious Barry Evans who, as the media would have you believe, swindled his mega rich son out of millions of dollars. Well, I'm sorry to disappoint you my old mate, but none of it's true. Cory left me broke.'

Now it was Mick's turn to laugh, but there was no humour in the sickly gargle. 'So, how do you explain all this, dickhead?' He waved an arm around.

'Hard work. Had to start again from the ground up.'

'Yeah right. I want two mill.'

'Hah … ' Barry returned to his desk and dropped back into his chair. 'You're just not listening. Cory has all the money now. Perhaps you should go pay him a visit.'

'Perhaps I will.'

'Good. Give him a slap for me, eh?'

'Two million by the weekend. I'll be back Friday arvo.'

'I'm sure you can see yourself out, Mick. Give my love to Patty.'

'You'll be wise not to cross me, Barry Evans.'

Barry jumped to his feet and exhibited anger for the first time. 'You'll be wise not to cross *me*, Mick Brennan. You don't know what you're dealing with, son!'

'You've got until Friday.' Brennan marched out of the office.

Barry watched the three men as they made their way through the showroom and out to their motorcycles.

After putting on their helmets, Brennan nodded to one of his sidekicks, who then strolled over to the immaculate 1964 Mercedes SL 500 and ran his key along one side of the vehicle.

'You'll pay for that ...' Barry whispered to himself.

7

PATTY CUMMINGS sat in her recently acquired BCF camping chair under the awning of her static caravan. In one hand was a tall glass of Bundaberg Rum and Coke, and in the other, the ever-present cigarette. Bundy was her chosen anaesthesia. If there was no Coke in the fridge, she'd drink it neat. If there was no Bundy, she'd drink Mick's bourbon, which would result in him going apeshit and likely sending her to the floor with a nasty backhand. But she didn't care about that. As long as there was enough alcohol in her system, the physical pain would never come close to the pain she kept medicated inside. If there was no whiskey, she'd drink whatever she could find, usually beer. Mikayla, her neighbour, was good to her. She was always happy to share her husband's beer, it seemed—taking pity perhaps—or maybe edging her bets, believing that one day Freckles' mother would be released from this sentence of poverty, to be reinstated with her fortune.

The tiny cigarette butt was hot between Patty's brown-stained fingers. She took one last drag, threw it onto the grass, then lit another one. When her glass was empty, she wobbled to her feet, staggered back into the caravan and fixed herself another one. From the kitchen, she glimpsed herself in the wardrobe mirror through the open bedroom door and shivered. Could that haggard old woman really have once been Patty Evans, the Gold Coast socialite who wore Gucci dresses, Jimmy Choo shoes and expensive jewellery? Now, the pair of pre-loved St Vinnies jeans, two sizes too big, and the faded singlet, made her body appear as if it were in the final stages of atrophy. She quickly looked away and headed back outside.

For most people, the view over the Tweed River would be a consolation for living in a caravan park, but Patty hardly realised it was there. Self-pity and a relentless hatred of her eldest son and her ex-husband, kept at bay by an inebriated state, meant she no longer cared about her surroundings or felt the emotions that made a person feel good or happy to be alive. And to make things worse, her younger son, Wesley, had recently moved out. Lured away to a life of luxury by Cory, that ungrateful little brat, who not only broke his mother's heart but broke her will, taking everything she owned, including the family photographs. But she didn't blame Wesley. Good on him for getting out. Hell, she'd do the same if she could. Although she hated her eldest son with all her heart, if he offered to throw her a lifeline, she'd take it. Pride was another of the emotions diminished by alcohol. The last thing she'd said to her youngest son was to tell Cory she needed help. Wesley simply nodded, then left. Her little boy was gone. The boy she'd protected from the media and given her all for him to have a normal upbringing.

The rip-roar of a Harley Davidson engine, still a couple of streets away, shattered the early evening serenity along with Patty's stupor. The pig was coming home. She wondered if he'd got the money. Prayed he had. Knowing he'd be in a foul mood if he hadn't. There was only one month left for Patty to mount a final appeal against the court ruling that had allowed her eldest son to sue her for literally every penny she had. For this she needed fifty grand. It may as well have been fifty million. She didn't even have fifty dollars to her name.

The sound of Mick's Harley grew louder but changed to more of a rumble and she realised he'd turned into the park and was approaching at a slower speed. When he pulled up, climbed from his motorcycle and removed his helmet, Patty knew straight away that he hadn't got the money. The hate-filled scowl directed her way would have petrified her if it weren't for Dr Bundy.

Mick threw his helmet against the caravan side, narrowly missing Patty, and stormed into the caravan. She heard him open the fridge door, followed by the clink of a beer bottle, then the *shwerp* of a twisting bottle top.

He came back out and slumped down into his BCF Delux model throne.

'So, I take it you got nothing from Barry?'

'Not yet. But I will,' Mick said before taking a long swig of beer.

'I told you, you wouldn't.'

'What do you know?'

'He's cunning. How is it he's not living in a caravan? He was sued too, and for a lot more than I was.'

'Oh, he's cunning alright. But the fox always falls prey to the hunt. I'll have the 50k by the end of the week.'

'Hah … ' Patty's alcohol dulled bravado was fool worthy. 'And what about Cory?'

'What about him?' Mick took another swig of beer.

Apart from anger, Patty sensed a sudden change in Mick's demeanour when she mentioned her son's name. 'Did you go see him?'

'What, are you a fucking cop?' Mick finished his beer, threw the bottle in the empties bucket and went to get another one.

When he returned, Patty was lighting another cigarette. 'Well, did you?'

'What?' Mick's voice rose to the level that caused the neighbours to close their windows and turn up the volume on their TVs.

'Go and see Cory? That's where the money is.'

'That's been taken care of.'

'Yeah right. Like you took care of Barry.'

'Just watch your mouth, woman.'

Ignoring the threatening glare of the man who had proved there truly wasn't a God after delving her life into even greater depths of misery, Patty pushed on. She needed that money. She needed to win the appeal. It was her only way out of this hell, and if that meant exploiting the talents of The Wasps bikie gang boss to win back her millions, then so be it. This was the only reason Mick Brennan was sharing her bed. A mutual understanding, she had no doubt. 'So, what happened? Did they get to see him?'

Mick finished his second beer. The bottle clinked loudly as it bounced off the first bottle in the bottom of the empties bucket. 'I've got to go out.' Retrieving his helmet from the floor, he returned to his bike, kicked it over and pulled away.

'If you can't sort this out, Mick Brennan. I'll have to do it myself,' Patty said beneath her breath. She finished her drink, took a huge drag of her cigarette, then began the increasingly difficult trek back to the fridge.

8

ANNETTE SLATER (Netty) had her doubts about the Gold Coast City Council's plan to introduce a morning fitness routine on the beach during Schoolies. When they approached her with the idea, she'd shared her concerns about making it exclusive to the kids, free of charge. Although an admirable gesture, she'd argued it would be a waste of time, stating that an early morning bootcamp would be the last thing on the minds of kids hungover from the night before. Strolling along Cavill Avenue, making her way back from the beach after the first workout—a sixty-minute, high-intensity session—she was happy to admit she'd been wrong. Ecstatic, in fact. She had just instructed the largest class in her life—over a hundred participants. They were all great kids, and not the drunken stereotypes one would expect. It restored her faith in the millennials.

The fact that she was still a little sweaty when she entered the Milton foyer didn't matter. Netty looked good regardless. Thankfully, the concierge on duty that morning was an old friend of hers. Joey Baxter was a part-time personal trainer before entering the hospitality industry. He had worked with private clients at many of the gyms Netty had also worked at when she was still building her fitness empire. Now that she had her own gym in Ashmore, the private, one-on-one mobile sessions were for the rich and famous.

'Hey, Netty. How's it going?' Joey asked, looking up from the tall concierge desk, the smart charcoal grey suit accentuating his tall, lean physique.

'Wow, don't you look smart,' Netty said. 'Have you seen him yet?'

'Nope. Just the brother.'

'But he has to have left the building in three months, surely.'

'Yeah, must have just not been on my shift, or slipped by unnoticed. Easily done.'

'Hmm … ' Netty wasn't so sure. She'd gotten to know Cory Evans quite well during the six months she'd been training him. For him to just stop and break ties with her seemed odd. 'Can I go up?'

Joey pursed his lips and glanced from side to side.

'I'm his personal trainer, and I'm worried about him.'

'Worried about him?' Joey lowered his voice and sniggered. 'Pigging out on Tim Tams, you reckon?'

'Something like that.'

Joey opened a drawer in the concierge desk and retrieved a white plastic swipe card. 'I'll probably get the sack if anyone finds out I gave you this.' He quickly handed her the card.

'Don't worry, I'll say I used my own key that Cory gave me. See you soon.' Netty headed towards the lifts. She had a key of her own, but it hadn't worked the last time she was there. It had been deactivated according to Micky Chen, the other concierge who'd been on duty that day.

As the lift shot up to the 57th floor, Netty was trying to work out why Cory had stopped seeing her. He'd been doing so well with his training. Not just mentally, but physically too. She remembered how he'd told her he could gain or lose weight in the drop of a hat. The one-hour sessions, three days a week that she'd spent with him over a six-month period, had transformed him from a short, overweight man back to a trim, good-looking young bloke. And although both versions were a million miles away from the Freckles persona—that adorable little kid she'd grown up watching on TV—there had been a mutual benefit from their time together. They'd become friends and were about to go into business together—or so she thought. She'd already put up her half of the investment securing the lease on the building in Surfers, as well as a non-refundable deposit on the expensive equipment. Registrations, licences—everything was in place. Now she just needed Cory to come to the party with his half. If he didn't, she'd likely go bankrupt. But that wasn't an option.

The lift slowed, came to a halt, then dinged. The door slid open. Netty stepped into the private foyer of Cory's penthouse apartment. 'Hello, Cory?' She called out. 'Wesley?' She had never met the brother, but like most Australians, she'd become familiar with the Evans/Cummings family from the televised court case. Although Cory's younger sibling hadn't appeared in court, details of his existence were common knowledge. 'Is anyone here?' Silence.

As if guided by an inadvertent career gene, she made her way through the expansive apartment and to the private gym. The large area with mirrored walls on three sides, a floor to ceiling window with a view of the ocean on the fourth, and exclusive equipment and weights placed strategically around the room, was immaculate like it was cleaned often, but not used in a while. Fond memories of making them both post-workout protein shakes crossed her mind as she strolled back past the open kitchen. Beyond the open plan living area was the bedroom wing. She wasn't sure how many bedrooms there were. Apart from using the bathroom on a couple of previous occasions, which was the first door on the right, she had never been in this part of the building. 'Hello, is anyone home?' Still no reply.

Not really realising what she was doing was illegal, Netty was about to venture into the bedroom wing when she heard the lift ding. Someone had travelled up to the apartment. She quickly turned and rushed back to the kitchen just as Maria, the housekeeper, entered from the foyer.

'Miss Slater!' Maria said, with the usual genuine, friendly smile.

'Maria, it's so good to see you,' Netty said, hoping the blushes wouldn't betray her.

'You're back?' Maria's Brazilian accent was strong.

'Yes,' Netty said. 'We're in training again.'

'Oh, that's wonderful news. He needs it.'

'Do you know if he's home ...? I was supposed to meet him here.'

'Oh yes, he is always home.'

'In his room?'

Maria nodded as she placed a bag on the kitchen counter.

'How is he?'

'I don't know. I haven't seen him for months. Since the last time you were here.'

'Really?'

More nodding as she pulled out a roll of bin bags from beneath the sink and snapped one off.

'Don't you find that odd?'

'No. He never comes out of his room. Not when I'm here anyway. And I never go in there. Out of bounds.'

'So, you think he's in there?'

'Of course. He'll be playing video games or watching movies or whatever it is he does. I hear the TV sometimes when I am cleaning the other rooms.'

'What about Wesley?'

'Yes. He is here most of the time.'

'What's he like?' Genuine curiosity fuelled Netty's question.

'Quiet, doesn't say much.'

'Is he anything like Cory?'

'No. He's not cute like his brother.'

Netty checked her watch. 'Okay. I'm going to knock on Cory's bedroom door. We're supposed to have a session.'

Maria shrugged as she pulled out the full bag from the bin and went about her work.

'Hello Cory,' Netty called out as she crept along the corridor of the bedroom wing. 'It's Netty. Netty Slater … Wesley … anyone home?' She hadn't known which bedroom was Cory's, so she'd asked Maria. It was the room at the end of the corridor. Of course it was. When she reached it, she placed her ear up against the door. There was no sound from within, so she gently knocked. 'Hello, Cory. Are you there? It's Netty.' Still, there was no sound from the room. Checking her watch again, it was 9.30 am. He was likely sleeping in. She knocked again, this time a little harder.

9

As far as Wesley knew, the three-year-old Porsche Cayenne had never been driven.

Constable Brian Taylor remarked how showroom immaculate it was. 'Do you realise it was unlocked?' He asked, with an air of contempt.

'No, I didn't' Wesley replied. 'It's not my car. It belongs to my brother.'

The tall policeman rifled through the glove box and arm rest compartment. When he finished, he opened the back of the SUV. 'Do you know if your brother stored anything in here? Golf clubs, anything like that?'

Wesley shook his head and shrugged. Although he knew nothing was ever stored in the car, he didn't let on.

After an inspection of the spare wheel, Constable Taylor declared that the exclusive Porsche branded tools and the driver's manual were missing—items that could easily be sold on eBay.

Wesley didn't anticipate leaving Cassie alone in the apartment as long as had.

The note was brief and to the point. *Got to go. Meet me in Gino's tomorrow at 8.* Wesley was glad when he realised Cassie had left, but a little worried at the same time. *How long had she stayed for? Had she snooped around the apartment? Of course she had. Did she go into his bedroom? Had she gone into Cory's room?*

The next morning, Orchid Avenue was a bustle once more with street cleaners, council workers and volunteers as they worked to clean up the street from the previous night's teenage shenanigans. The odd group of Schoolies laughed and joked as they made their way to the beach, but none of them paid any attention to the chubby Toolie who walked among them with his head down.

Cassie was waiting for him when he entered Gino's at the end of Orchid Avenue. There were two large flat whites in take-away cups sitting on the table before her.

She smiled and stood up when she noticed him entering the coffee shop. 'Hey, how's it going?'

When she hugged him, Wesley smelled fresh shampoo on her damp hair. 'I'm good.'

'I'm sorry I had to bail yesterday,' Cassie said as they took their seats. 'Had things to do.'

'That's okay. This for me?' Wesley pointed to the second coffee. Cassie nodded.

There was a pause as the two sipped their hot drinks.

Then Cassie said, 'Did you tell Cory about me?'

Wesley shook his head nonchalantly. 'No … I haven't seen him.'

'But you live in the same apartment.'

'I've hardly seen him since I moved in.'

'Really? What does he do? Where does he go?'

Wesley replied with a shrug and a shake, followed by another sip of coffee.

'Are you sure he's even home?' Cassie asked.

'Nope, could be in the Bahamas for all I know.'

'Don't you care?'

'Of course.'

Wesley was relieved when Cassie didn't continue with the questioning because he was on the verge of walking out. *Had she been in Cory's room?* He guessed she had. She was Barry Evans' daughter after all. Then something dawned on him he hadn't thought of before. Could Cassie be here on behalf of their father? Had he sent her here to snoop around? *Shit, why hadn't he thought of this before he'd taken her up to the apartment and left her alone there?* What the heck, he released the captive question. 'Did you go into Cory's room?'

Her face screwed up like she'd just bit into a lemon. 'No … why would I?'

'I don't know. You tell me.'

'I waited for about fifteen minutes. You didn't return, so I headed back to my hotel.' Her brow tightened and her voice quivered.

Wesley recognised signs of the family anger that he too possessed but kept locked away in the far paddock. He didn't know this girl, but what he did know was that she was an Evans, and an Evans could not be trusted. He should know. 'I got to go.' His chair slid back as he stood.

'Fine,' Cassie spat, scowling. She crossed her arms and looked away.

'This was a mistake. You're just like the rest of them. Using me to get to my brother.'

'That's not true.'

'Isn't it?' He fixed her with his most intimidating stare. Cory Evans wasn't the only actor in the family. 'Don't contact me again.' He was about to leave, but before he reached the door, he turned back. 'And you can tell Barry to go and get fucked!'

Walking with his head down, Wesley had no recollection of the time it took him to return to the Milton, but when he entered the foyer, something jolted him to the present. Constable Brian Taylor, who had checked the car the day before and taken his details, was standing at the concierge desk. But it wasn't him that stole Wesley's attention—it was the person standing next to him. Cory's personal trainer. Wesley lowered his head and headed for the lifts.

10

'Excuse me, Mister Cummings. May I have a word?'

Wesley turned to see Jack, the middle-aged English concierge, standing behind him.

'Sure. What's up?'

'If you'd like to just step over here, please, sir.' He gestured towards the concierge desk where the policeman and the fitness trainer were standing.

Reluctantly, Wesley followed the immaculate little man across the foyer.

'Good morning, again.' Constable Brian Taylor stood with his hands on his utility belt like Batman. 'Do you know this person, sir?' He gestured towards the fitness trainer.

A simple 'No' accompanied the nonchalant Wesley shrug.

'She claims to be your brother's fitness trainer.'

The shrug again, but this time with a lazy shake of the head. 'I wasn't aware he had a fitness trainer. He certainly hasn't for … for at least three months.'

'That's right. That's what I've been saying,' the young woman said. 'I haven't seen him since August.'

'We've reason to believe this person unlawfully entered your apartment this morning.' Constable Taylor was all business, no emotion.

'What?' Wesley glanced at the concierge accusingly.

'I caught her slipping this back onto the counter.' He held up a pass key card. 'It was programmed to enter your apartment this morning.'

Wesley's eyes moved back to the young woman. She was standing with her arms folded. Her expression displayed a mixture of anger and fear. Wesley was trying not to say too much. This was another test for him. So far, so good. 'Is this true?' He asked with minimal eye contact.

'I needed to see Cory. It was important.'

'So important that you got the young concierge, who was coming to the end of a night shift, to program a key for you so you could enter the apartment unlawfully?' Constable Taylor said.

'Ex-concierge,' Jack threw in, a reassuring glance towards Wesley, confirming the young man would be severely dealt with.

'No … yes … but … but I just needed to see Cory. It was really important.'

'And did you? See Mister Evans, I mean?' Taylor asked.

Netty shook her head and looked away.

'Would you mind if we came up to the apartment?' The constable didn't address Wesley as 'sir' or by name. 'I'd like to check on your brother and make sure nothing's been taken from the apartment,' Taylor added.

The shrug again. 'Sure.'

The constable and the fitness trainer followed Wesley to the lifts.

'How was your brother before you left this morning?' Taylor asked, as they piled into the waiting lift.

'Oh, I didn't see him. He's a late riser.'

The policeman checked his watch. 'Will he be up now?'

The shrug and headshake. 'Doubt it. Usually gets up around lunchtime.'

The lift slowed, dinged, and the doors slid open.

With Wesley leading the way, and the policeman following closely, the threesome stepped into the foyer. There they were met with the sound of idling suction. When they turned into the living area, Maria was vacuuming the large rug in the open living room. Wearing EarPods, and unaware she was no longer alone, the middle-aged housekeeper almost hit the ceiling when Wesley tapped her on the shoulder.

The vacuum instantly stopped. Maria pulled out one of the EarPods. 'Mister Wesley, oh my goodness. I didn't see you there.' She frowned when she noticed the fitness trainer and the copper. 'Netty?' Her gaze flicked between the threesome. 'What's going on?'

'Do you know this person, mam?' Taylor asked.

'Yes. It's Netty, Mister Cory's trainer.'

Taylor frowned and looked questioningly at Wesley.

'See, I told you,' Netty said.

'Were you here when Miss Slater was here earlier?'

Maria nodded.

'Does she come here regularly?'

'Uhm, no, not anymore. Used to.'

'When was the last time you saw her?'

'A couple of months maybe, a bit more perhaps.'

'Is Mister Evans at home?' His eyes cleverly directed the question at both Wesley and the housekeeper.

'Yes, he's sleeping.'

'When was the last time you saw him?'

'I'm here in the mornings, three days a week. Mister Evans doesn't rise until after I've left.'

'Do you clean his room?'

'No never. Nobody is allowed in there.'

Wesley nodded in agreement.

'When was the last time you saw him?'

'The last time Netty was here.'

Taylor was transposing the conversation into his notebook. After a scurry of pencil on paper, he looked up and directed his attention to Wesley. 'Would you wake up your brother, please?'

'I don't think that's a good idea,' Wesley said.

'I knocked earlier,' Netty said, 'but there was no reply. I don't even think he's in there.'

'How about I take a look?' the constable said and without waiting for a reply, he added, 'Which way is his room?'

Reluctantly, Wesley led the way to the bedroom wing and to the master suite. 'Cory,' he called out in a hushed tone while knocking on the door. There was no reply. He knocked again and raised his voice. 'Cory, wake up.'

After a couple more attempts, the constable stepped forward. 'Can you open the door, please?'

'It's probably locked.'

'Try please.'

Wesley pressed down on the handle and the door opened.

'Mister Evans, Queensland Police. Are you in there?' Taylor called out.

There was no reply.

Taylor gestured with his eyes for Wesley to lead them through the door.

The room was light. Opaque sunlight streamed in through a wall of net curtains that hung across the open balcony door. The place was a complete mess. The bed was unmade, and there were clothes and underwear strewn about the floor along with empty pizza boxes and bottles of half empty Coke. And even though there was a gentle sea breeze drifting into the room, there was a distinctive smell that could only be described as nasty.

'Mister Evans, are you here?' Taylor repeated, scanning the room.

After checking the bathroom, which was even more disgusting than the bedroom, it was obvious there was no one there.

'When was the last time you saw your brother?' Taylor asked.

The shrug again that Wesley knew annoyed the shit out of people, but he did regardless. 'A couple of days maybe.'

'Would he go away without telling you?'

'I guess. He's a grown man. Can do as he pleases.'

'Has he done this before?'

The shrug.

'Something's not right here,' Netty said. 'I've been trying to contact him for months. He was my friend. He wouldn't just suddenly ignore my calls.'

Constable Taylor looked at the empty pizza boxes. 'Doesn't look like fitness was a priority just lately. But you're right, something is wrong … so let's put it right and get you down the station and charged with unlawful entry of a property, eh?'

11

The water from the beach shower was a couple of degrees cooler than the ocean. Letting it pour through my hair and down my back, it washed away the salt and sand. This was the first time I'd ventured out into the surf, since the cooler months, without my wetsuit. Pulling out the waistband of my shorts from behind allowed the clean water to run through the crack of my arse and down my legs. When my skin felt a little less like sandpaper, I rinsed off my board, then stepped aside allowing a fellow surfer to do the same.

As always, Trish at the kiosk beneath Kirra Surf Club refused payment for a large coffee. 'You saved us all, Scotty Stephens. The least I can do is make sure you never pay for a coffee again.' Although a year had passed since I brought *X*, the vicious serial killer who murdered eight young woman, to justice, the people of the Gold Coast hadn't forgotten me. I was still recognised wherever I went, patted on the back, and gifted everything from coffee to beer, to restaurant meals, to Domino's pizza. The gratitude and generosity of the local community and the holidaymakers from as far as Western Australia and even New Zealand, constantly amazed me. Of course, the little Scotty inside of me, that voice of reason, still tried to convince me I was a fraud who didn't deserve all the accolades. But the truth was, I *did* crack the case and put an end to a reign of terror by Australia's most notorious serial killer, while also exposing the ring of corruption by the ex-Gold Coast mayor and the ex-police commissioner.

Sitting on the low wall across from the kiosk, half listening to the group of Good Old Boys who congregated at the same spot this time every morning to put right the wrongs of the world, I wondered if it was that little nagging voice that had talked me into quitting the police force when I was at the peak of my career. Even after solving the Tallebudgera mystery on my first case as a private detective and putting a psychopath—who had killed two people—behind bars, it did little to quell the doubts. The voice of Little Scotty was stronger some days than others, usually when I was feeling down. For some reason, today was one of those downer days. Glancing over at the water bowl that Trish kept topped up for passing dogs, didn't help. Memories of my little mate, Romeo, could bring me to the brink of tears instantly. The image of the little Staffordshire terrier pup with his head in that very bowl, lapping up the water and sending it splashing all over the place created a tightness in my chest. I quickly took a mouthful of hot coffee and nodded as one of the Good Old Boys expressed his opinion about the fabled train line as to whether it would ever be extended from Varsity Lakes to the Gold Coast Airport.

But it was none of this that had put me into the current state of funk. Although I now had some money in the bank after shamelessly exploiting my fifteen minutes of fame, and I ran my own private detective agency, my personal situation was still the same—single bloke, living in a bachelor pad with his best mate, drinking, surfing, watching the footy. I was approaching my mid-forties for God's sake, so shouldn't I have been married with kids by now? Settled into a nice house in suburbia with an SUV and a golf handicap? The hardest thing was that my best mate, Elvis, mirrored my situation. The same age as me, we'd been best buds since kindergarten. Recently, he'd traded in his Lexus for a Porsche. The boys had joked about his mid-life crisis. *Shit!* Something suddenly dawned on me. Was that was happening to me? Was I having *my* mid-life crisis? Was this the reason for me quitting a promising career as a detective inspector and starting my own business, which was basically me sitting in a little office in Coolangatta not knowing where the next pay cheque was coming from?

A new debate between the Good Old Boys was getting a little heated. Unknowingly, my passive nods had made me a part of the conversation.

'What do you think, Scotty? Should Trump be shot?' Dingo asked. I didn't know his real name. Short, white haired, tanned and stocky, he wore a pair of orange Speedos every day when he braved the early morning waves for a swim.

'Uhm … no … yeah … well … I … maybe,' was my only contribution.

'See. And he'd know!' Dingo exclaimed triumphantly.

The others nodded as if my opinion, whatever that was, instantly changed their views.

I checked my watch. It was seven thirty. Elvis would be leaving for work about now. Recently, I'd started staying in the surf longer. It was good to get home to an empty house. *Was I avoiding my best mate?* The bachelor life had become a little stale of late. Our other good mate, Tetley; that cheeky little Pommy was still in the UK. Johno, our Kiwi buddy, was married, and Elvis, after his latest relationship with a girl called Sandy failed, was moping around the house like a dazed koala. Whatever happened to the carefree days when the four of us would sit out in the man shed until all hours, drinking, watching the footy and talking shit? With another swig of coffee, I reminded myself that it was me who craved the change. Apart from Johno, the others loved the lifestyle and wanted it to continue forever. As it often did, my mother's voice whispered, *'Be careful what you wish for, Scotty.'*

'I've got to go, boys,' I said after finishing my coffee and standing.

'No worries, Scotty,' the group said in unison.

'Off to save the world, mate?' Dingo asked cheerfully.

'Something like that.' *Off to save myself, at least.* Picking up my board, I headed back towards Ruby Street.

12

I hadn't worked a proper case since the Tallebudgera killings some months ago, but I'd been busy with the more lucrative pastime of appearances and speaking events. This was something that a year ago I wouldn't have dreamed of doing. The thought of standing in front of an audience at a fundraiser or corporate event was ridiculous. The old Scotty would have branded such practices as selling out or milking the system. And perhaps that's what I'd been doing, but I didn't care. The mature, middle-aged version of myself, who was taking stock and worrying about his future, was a different person to the partying, surfing unmotivated detective constable of the past.

Having bugger all to do all day though, sitting in my office, waiting for the phone to ring, or the sound of the street door opening at the bottom of the stairs, was bloody boring as all hell. My main pastime was sitting in the alcove looking down on life in Coolangatta.

The day was somewhere between the typical Queensland, 'Beautiful one day, perfect the next!' A slow stream of traffic followed a number 700 bus along Griffith Street towards Tweed Heads. As far as I could see, all the roadside car parks were taken. On the southern end of the coast here, most of the people going about their business were locals. The tourists were easy to spot. Families mostly. Kids carrying boogie boards and buckets and spades. Dad in boardshorts, a large Bunnings, brimmed, straw hat, sunnies, and zinc covering his nose and lips. Mum, wearing that bikini she wouldn't get away with for much longer. I'd always been a people watcher. This probably came with the territory of an ex-police detective and current PI. Recently, I'd developed a game where I'd home in on a person in the street below and create a life scenario. The Jamaican lady rushing down the street, cussing under her breath, 'Oh no, I's left dhe kettle on.' The middle-aged man stopping to look in the window of the real estate agents. 'Today's the day. I'll take the penthouse, please.'

A lady crossing the street caught my eye, and the game began. She was short and round, middle-aged, late fifties, early sixties perhaps. Her olive skin and slightly greying, dark hair told me she was Latino, Brazilian perhaps. The beige uniform was the kind worn by a domestic of some kind. Her name was Maria Gonzales. She was a housemaid at The Pink Hotel. The haste in her step told me she was on her way to the Coolangatta Magistrates Court to support her son, Miguel, who was appearing for the second time this year on charges of disturbing the peace. She'd hoped to get away from work earlier but was held up after cleaning the rooms of a group of Schoolies who had chosen to stay down this end of the coast rather than Surfers. 'Bastardos sujos!—dirty little bastards!' she uttered beneath her breath in Portuguese.

I was jolted back to reality when I realised the lady I'd named as Maria had stopped outside the door to my office, taken a deep breath, then entered. The bell that hung above the door to the street was old school, yes, but effective. When I heard the *clump, clump, clump* of footsteps on the linoleum covered stairs, I rose from the alcove, skipped to my desk and opened my laptop.

There was a knock at the door and I could see Maria's outline through the opaque glass. Very Philip Marlowe. 'Come in,' I called out. The image shimmered, and I realised Maria was adjusting her uniform. The door opened slowly and in she stepped.

'Hello, may I come in?' she asked, blushing. There was an accent, but I guessed she'd lived in Australia for quite some time.

'Sure, come on in love.'

'Ah, Mister Stephens,' she said, ambling towards my desk with her hand held out.

Standing, I shook her hand. 'Scotty … Mister Stephens was me dad.'

'Scotty, my name is Maria Constanta.'

Bloody hell, how good was I?

'I need to talk to somebody about a missing person.'

'Right, take a seat.' I gestured to the empty chair on her side of the desk. 'Can I get you a tea or a coffee?'

'No. I am fine. Thank you.'

'So, you say someone has gone missing?' I wondered if it was Miguel. *What's he bloody done now?*

'Yes, my employer.'

Although I had the laptop there, my old police training prevailed. Reaching into the top drawer of my desk, I retrieved my notebook and pen. 'Okay, let's start from the beginning. Your employer is?'

'Cory Evans.'

Cory Evans, Cory Evans, where did I know that name from?

'*Thee* Cory Evans.'

Thee Cory Evans, that helped a bit. Her employee was famous. Footy perhaps?

'Freckles!'

My gasp was involuntary. 'Freckles?'

Maria nodded.

'Freckles?' Picture the Milkybar Kid but with enormous blue eyes, golden hair and … freckles, and you'll see the image that occupied my mind at that moment. 'Freckles?'

'Yes, and I'm worried that someone has hurt him.'

'What?' The idea of someone hurting little Freckles was beyond my comprehension. Everybody loved that bloody kid. Me included. 'What makes you say that?' My hand was shaking as I attempted to take notes.

'He's gone. He never leaves the apartment. And if he did, he wouldn't go anywhere without telling me.'

'When was this?'

'Yesterday. His room was empty, but I'm not sure how long he's been gone. He rarely comes out of his room when I am there.'

'Have you notified the police?'

'Yes, it was the police that discovered his room was empty.'

There was a slight sense of relief when I learned the police were on the case. 'Oh good. So they're looking for him,' I said without looking up from my notebook.

'No, they're not interested.'

'What?' The thought of that little chap out there somewhere on his own, possibly abducted, horrified me. 'But he's a kid. They'll have to take action.'

'Mister Stephens. Scotty. He's twenty-two years old!'

'What? No … he's only … about ten or … isn't he?'

'He's twenty-two.'

Images of the cherub with melted Tim Tam around his mouth, little Casey Turner from *Neighbours*, deaf Stevie from *Home and Away*, Freckles' Saturday morning kids' show, the movies, the appearances in just about every Australian drama made between 2003 and 2010—there was even a bloody Freckles cartoon show—filled my mind.

Then I vaguely remembered the older kid—not so cute anymore, awkward. It was as if my mind had blocked out those recollections, concentrating instead on the fond, familiar memories that we Aussies all cherished and loved. The image of an awkward, chubby bloke fronting a boy band in an attempt that could only be described as poorly-choreographed-karaoke flashed through my mind, but I quickly pushed it away and returned to the cheeky little chocolate-covered kid. 'Is he really twenty-two?'

Maria nodded.

It made sense when I thought about it. The kid had been around forever, thanks to the reruns, but the realisation that Freckles had grown up and was no longer cute, hurt somehow. Almost like the world would never be the same again. 'Okay, Maria, let's go over the events leading up to when you realised Freckles … Cory was missing.'

<h1 style="text-align:center">13</h1>

'And where are *you* off to then, little bloke?' the homeless man asked, parking the shopping trolley against the bus stop.

'I'm going to see me mum,' replied six-year-old Casey Turner.

'Ah, right, and where might she be?' The skinny, unshaven man wearing a knitted Collingwood footy hat, a baggy T-shirt, tracky pants, and odd thongs, joined him on the bench.

'In heaven!' The brilliance of the tiny actor was evident in the myriad of expressions that passed across his chubby little face while uttering those two words. Until this time, audiences all around the country had fallen in love with the cheeky little lad after advertising companies had clambered to use him in their commercials. But now, in his first appearance on the popular soap opera, *Neighbours*, he got to show his natural acting skills, vulnerability, humour, intelligence, and compassion, all silently displayed on the face that was a cute as a button.

'So how are you gonna get to heaven, mate?' The homeless man asked.

'Mount Kosi … Kosi … osiko.'

'Mount Kosciuszko?'

'Yep.' The boy nodded industriously.

'And why's that?'

'Paster Tony said that heaven is in the sky.'

'Right. I see, so seeing as Mount Kosciuszko is the highest mountain in Australia, you figured you can get to heaven from there?'

'Yep.'

'And how you gonna get there, bloke? The Snowies are a fair old way.'

'On the bus.'

'Might get hungry.'

'Hmm …' the boy nodded as if he hadn't thought of this.

'How about I take you home, and you plan your trip for another day?'

'Okay.' The lad jumped to his feet.

The homeless man stood, retrieved his trolley and the two new friends headed off down the street.

It was the acting debut that would melt the hearts of the Australian public as easily as a chocolate-covered biscuit in a toddler's hand. Casey Turner, the orphan, would only stay with the long running soap opera for four months, turning up a month later as Stevie McCauley, the deaf nephew of Alf Stewart in the rival show, *Home and Away*. It was also around this time when the nickname 'Freckles' was coined—for obvious reasons.

Not that I was an expert on the career of Cory Evans, you understand? I was harvesting all this information from his Wikipedia page. Clicking on hyperlinked words and phrases such as Mitre 10 commercial, *Neighbours, Home and Away*, would take me directly to YouTube, where I could watch short snippets.

It's funny, but in hindsight, I did remember the nasty stuff that came later in the star's life. The rise to the highest level of fame, only to come crashing down again, all because he was no longer cute. My subconscious must have blocked out the movie flops that came later, the failed music career and the nastiness of the televised court cases when the kid sued his parents. Instead, I'd chosen only to remember the forever six year old who, for a moment in time, had captured everything that was good in this world and delivered it to the hearts of a nation.

This was how I'd spent the rest of the day. Sitting at my desk, trolling through my laptop, searching for everything to do with Freckles and Cory Evans. Seeing the old ads again brought back some good memories of a time in my life before I'd moved up into the detective ranks. Constable Scotty Stephens. In truth though, my life back then was exactly the same as it was now. Work, surf, party. The only difference now was that there was a lot less partying.

I checked my watch. It was 5.00 pm. Time to go home. While driving from Cooly to Kirra, I'd be checking the waves. If they were up, I'd go home, change into my boardies, grab my board, and go out for another surf. The second of the day.

'Bugger!' I cussed as I trundled around Kirra Point in the Dub (my old Volkswagen Beetle). The surf was flat.

Wandering out to the man shed was mandatory whenever one of us returned home. As expected, Elvis was sitting at the bar drinking a stubby. I'd noticed a difference in him over the last couple of months. He'd become quieter, more serious, reflective. This was a far cry from the mischievous Greek kid who had sported the best Elvis Presley quiff this side of Memphis. He'd been my wingman for as long as I could remember. We could have both been footy pros, but that didn't work out. Instead, here we were approaching our mid-forties, single and sharing the same house for over twenty years.

'You alright, bud?' I asked, joining him at the bar.

'Hey mate, how's it going?'

I didn't feel like drinking, but I grabbed a beer from the fridge anyway and perched myself on a stool. 'How was your day?'

Elvis shrugged. 'Ah, you know. Same old.'

I guess the daily life of an accountant wasn't that exciting. I knew what'd cheer him up. 'Guess what?'

He immediately straightened up on his stool. 'What?'

Those two little words were like a tennis ball to a puppy. Elvis knew that whenever I began a sentence with them, there was something important to follow. I sipped my beer.

'Come on, tell me.' He instantly submerged from his miserable midlife stupor to that inquisitive, excitable lad I knew and loved. 'Come on, ya bugger, what's happened?'

Taking another sip of my beer, I was enjoying the moment like slowly revving a V8 at the lights. 'One word.'

Elvis' head nodded and wobbled at the same time. His bulging eyes were fixed on mine as if he were about to learn the fate of the world.

'Freckles!'

'Freckles?'

My nod was more of the nonchalant kind. Adding another swig of beer kept the tension going.

'No ...!' He lifted his hands to the sides of his head. 'You're going to be working with Freckles? Can I meet him? Can you bring him round? We can take him to the park. We can—'

'He's twenty-two years old, mate.'

'No, he's not. He's only ... six, seven?' Like me, Elvis seemed to have blocked out those latter years. 'So, so, so ... so what's ... what's he doing? What's happened? Is he okay? Does he need your help? Will he need a place to stay? He can sleep in my bed. I'll kip on the sofa. Does he need an accountant? Will he—'

'Steady on, mate. Bloody hell.'

'For fuck's sake, Scotty. What's happening with Freckles?'

I was hoping this would cheer my mate up, not give him a coronary. Now I was regretting saying anything at all. But I should never have said what I said next. 'He's gone missing.'

Elvis jumped to his feet. 'What?'

'Yep, seems like he may have been missing for some time.'

'Are you kidding me? That little lad's out there somewhere, alone maybe?'

'He's twenty-two.'

'What are you doing sitting here? You should be out looking for him.' He either didn't hear me or was ignoring my indifference. Slamming down his beer, he retrieved his car keys from his pocket. 'Let's go, we'll take my car.'

'Go where?'

'To look for him, of course. I'll never sleep again knowing that kid isn't safe.'

'He's not a kid, and he's probably not alone.'

'I can't believe you're taking this so calmly, Scott. It's Freckles!'

'Take it easy, mate. Sit down. Finish your beer.'

Elvis was all shook up.

'I haven't even said I'll take the case yet.'

'Why?'

'I need to look into it more, and there's a tiny problem …'

'Problem? What's the problem? Why does there have to be a problem? There shouldn't be—'

'As far as I can see, it's not a paying gig.'

'But he's worth millions, surely.'

'Yeah, but his housekeeper isn't. It was her who came to see me today.'

'Barry then?' He was referring to Cory's father.

I shook my head. 'Doubt it. Probably hates the little shit.'

'You don't think …?' His eyes scanned the floor as if he were searching for answers down there. 'You don't think Barry's done away with him, do you?'

'Nah, my guess is he's just gone away while Schoolies is on.'

'What does he know about Schoolies? He's six!'

'Elvis, HE'S TWENTY-TWO!'

'You've got to take on the case. Find him. Find him now, Scotty. He could be anywhere. Someone could have grabbed him and—' He lifted a fist to his mouth to gag an impending sob.

This was really affecting him badly. I wondered if it was a sign of things to come when the Australian public found out about Cory's disappearance.

'I'll pay you. Your going rate, expenses, everything.' He took a long swig of his beer, calmly placed the stubby on the bar, looked at me through earnest eyes, and said, 'Bring Freckles home, Scotty ... bring him home!'

14

DETECTIVE INSPECTOR JENNY RADFORD looked good in a half-length wetsuit, but when she peeled it down to her waist, she looked more than just good. If it weren't for the red bikini top she wore, I'd be getting a heavenly view as she stood under the beach shower.

'What are you staring out?' she asked, running her hands through her hair.

'Nothing. Just having a perv.'

She playfully punched me, rinsed off then we grabbed our boards and headed up Goodwin Terrace towards her apartment. Surfing off Burleigh Heads was a rare occurrence for me these days, basically because the parking around Burleigh was impossible. Fortunately, Jenny's car was in the shop being fixed, so I parked the Dub in her underground garage space.

We walked down the ramp to the basement, propped our boards up against the wall behind the Dub, then Jenny peeled off the wetsuit all the way. The quick dry boardshorts she wore underneath were almost dry already.

'Fancy a coffee?' she asked as we made our way back out onto the street.

'Sure.'

With the sweeping bay of the glorious Gold Coast to our right, we made our way back down the hill towards town, me in only my boardshorts, both of us with bare feet. Simplicity and perfection of the Gold Coast lifestyle personified.

Burleigh Pavilion and the indoor swimming pool was the first beachside building. On the streetside was a coffee shop kiosk.

'My shout,' I said, producing a credit card from the back pocket of my shorts.

Jenny didn't argue. 'No worries, I'll have the usual.'

The usual was a tradie pie and a flat white to go. I had the same. This was our recapturing-our-youth breakfast treat. Evoking a time when life was even more perfect, when we didn't need to worry about heartburn or cholesterol. A time when you'd ride to the beach on your bike and leave it propped up against the fence while you surfed without fear of it being nicked. A time when Burleigh Heads still resembled a country town yet to be discovered by the tourists, many of whom wouldn't venture south of Broadbeach.

'There ya go,' I said, placing a paper bag and two takeaway drinks on the Ibis-shit-stained picnic table.

Jenny ripped open the bag, squeezed a ketchup sachet over one of the pies, then bit into the crispy pastry. 'Hmm, you really know how to treat a girl, Scotty Stephens.'

With a mouthful of pie, I nodded in agreement.

We ate in silence, looking out across the bay to Surfers Paradise in the distance. Then, sipping our coffees, we watched some kids playing on the children's playground.

'So, have you got another case yet?' Jenny asked, breaking the serenity of the moment.

'Maybe.'

'Yeah?' Her attention peaked. 'Tell me.'

I was curious to see if I'd get the same reaction I'd received from Elvis. 'Freckles!'

'Freckles?'

I nodded proudly.

'*That* annoying little bastard. What's he done now?'

I almost choked on a mouthful of pie.

'Slapped around another sex worker? Been caught slipping roofies in underage girls' drinks again?'

'What …? No … I'm talking about Freckles.' Jenny was obviously getting the little bloke mixed up with someone else.

'Yeah. Cory Evans.'

'You know him?'

'Of course. He's got form.'

'Are you havin a lend of me?'

'No. He's no longer that loveable little kid everyone remembers.'

'You don't like Freckles?' The question felt alien leaving my lips. How could anyone not like Freckles?

'Hate the little fucker.' With a matter-of-fact shrug, she sipped her coffee.

'But why?' I was almost pleading. 'Because he sued his parents?'

'No, not at all. I can fully understand that. Barry Evans was a nasty piece of work, deserved everything he got ripping off and exploiting a little kid. And Patty? Well, I can't talk too much about Patty at the moment.'

'Why?'

We often talked about work. Being an ex-fellow detective myself and working with her on the X case, Jenny knew she could trust me, so didn't have a problem quietly sharing the odd bit of police information with me. She lowered her voice. 'You remember the bikie case I was working on last year?'

'Yeah, while I was out in Tallebudgera?'

'That's the one. Well, it's flared up again. The prick got away with it.'

'Brennan?'

Jenny nodded. 'Nash got him off on a technicality. Said we obtained evidence unlawfully.'

Although I wasn't familiar with the fine details of the bikie case, from my days in the police force I was familiar with The

Wasps bikie gang from Chinderah and their leader, the infamous Mick Brennan. I'd also crossed swords with the high-profile defence lawyer, Craig Nash, during the *X* case. 'What's this got to do with Freckles?'

'Nothing, as far as I know. It's his mum, Patty.'

The rise of an eyebrow was a prompt for her to continue.

She hesitated, which was normal, took another sip of coffee, then leaned forward. 'She's shacked up with Brennan.'

'You're kidding.' Then I remembered how attractive Patty Cummings (née Evans) had been the last time I'd seen her on TV. It was during the televised court case when her son ended up suing her for something like three million dollars.

As if reading my thoughts, Jenny added, 'She's no longer the glammer queen everyone remembers. Alcoholic, broke and living in a trailer down the Tweed.'

'Really?'

'Yep.'

'So, what would Brennan see in her?'

At first I read the shrug as saying, *Your guess is as good as mine*, but then Jenny presented a cultivated hypothesis, 'Patty still has a chance to appeal the court ruling. My guess is Brennan has spotted an opportunity and spoken to Nash. If Nash agrees to take on Patty's case, she could win it and not only get her money back but also win substantial damages by counter suing.'

'That makes sense. Brennan would know a cash cow when he saw one. What about Barry? What do we know about him?'

'He supposedly lost everything too, but he soon bounced back. It was obvious he'd stashed away most of the money overseas, but we didn't have any proof. He was a slippery little sucker. Still is.'

'What's he doing now?'

'He owns a car dealership in Southport. Very prestige. Probably started as a front, a way to launder a bit of money, but apparently it's quite the growing concern now. But hold on a minute, you haven't told me why you're interested in Freckles yet. Are you going to be working for him?'

'No … well … not really.' I ran a hand through my hair. The warming sun had dried it nicely. 'Thing is, he's gone missing.'

'Missing?'

'Yeah. That's what I wanted to talk to you about.'

'Oh, so you didn't just come around for a surf then, or to catch up?'

I was used to being castigated by this adorable little pocket rocket; it was all part of the banter. 'No. Just need some information.'

'No wonder you're still single.'

'You're single too!'

'Touché. What do you need?'

'Cory's cleaner, Maria Constanta, reported Cory as a missing person to the police, but she's worried they're not taking it seriously.'

Jenny shrugged. 'Why would they?'

'Uh, cause he's missing?'

'He's an adult now. A very wealthy one I might add. How long has he been gone?'

'She's not sure.'

'He's probably in Bali or Las Vegas. What would you be doing if you were in his position?'

'I don't know, probably be in Bali or Las Vegas.'

'Exactly.'

'I reckon there's more to it, Jen, so I'm going to look into it.'

'Great, it'll give you something to do.'

Was the sarcastic tone just more banter or was I being patronised?

Good job I loved her.

15

My work hours these days were flexible. Jenny had a rostered day off, so I'd spent the previous day chilling in Burleigh. But now it was time to get back to work.

The surf was non-existent the next morning, so it gave me an excuse to get into the office early. I'd decided to take on the Cory Evans case, even though I wasn't being paid—I wouldn't be taking Elvis up on his offer. And Jenny was right. Even though the twenty-two-year-old man may have simply taken off on his own for a while, it would give me something to do. Anything was better than moping around the office. So, I was keen to set up the whiteboard. I'd been mentally forming a list of names since Maria's visit.

A recent photograph of Cory's that I'd downloaded from the internet took centre stage. You could still see Freckles if you stood back a little and squinted, but in reality, he was far from being that cherub-like being he once was. There were pox marks on his cheeks and chin. Those big blue eyes took on more of a froggy look now. His hair was still golden, but it no longer looked real. He was chubby and there were no signs of that mischievous grin. While on one hand it was breaking my heart to remember him how he used to be, on the other I felt sorry for him. He was a product of a throwaway society, loved by everyone, but only while he fitted the mould. His story in many ways was like those of Michael Jackson, Macaulay Culkin and Gary Coleman. I was hoping nothing had happened to him. Visions of the lad sitting atop a mountain in Tibet, meditating or relaxing at a spa in the Maldives offered some comfort, but my detective instincts were telling me otherwise.

If Cory had come to harm, was it at the hands of someone he knew? Normally, during an investigation, other players would be revealed, but for now, I could only go on what I knew, so I needed to form a list of suspects.

At the top of the list was Cory's father, Barry Evans. I debated against using one of the haggard, oh-woe-is-me photographs taken of him outside Southport Courthouse during the court case, or one of the middle-aged flash-git shots of him beaming with confident arrogance. I chose the latter. Not having met him yet, my assumption that this was the closest to his personality was fuelled by the numerous articles I'd read about how he'd manipulated his son's career, as well as the YouTube interviews I'd viewed. I'd know if my assumption was correct or not once I got to meet him.

The next on the list was Patty Cummings (née Evans), Cory's mum. As with Barry, I had a decision to make regarding which type of photograph of her to display. The young, blonde socialite dripping with jewellery, or the more recent shots of her. Once again, I chose the latter. Unlike her ex-husband, her situation was different in that she never bounced back after losing everything.

The next on the list was Cory's younger brother, Wesley. There was little more than the odd sentence about him anywhere on the internet, but I managed to get a rare photograph. And it was recent—only a couple of days old. Apparently, he'd been in an altercation with a group of Schoolies and a reporter from the *Gold Coast Bulletin* just happened to be close enough to take a snap with her phone of Wesley being pushed around by a couple of lads bigger than him. Once I'd zoomed in and trimmed the image to a head and shoulders shot, the quality wasn't great, but it was enough for me to familiarise his appearance. In the absence of information, I'd need to speak to Wesley. The fact that he lived with his brother meant it was likely he was the last person to see Cory. Studying the image and noting the differences between the two brothers, I wondered if Wesley's less than average looks had been a blessing for him or a curse.

I was surprised to learn from Barry's Wikipedia page that he had a daughter from his second marriage. Cassie Evans was eighteen years old. As with Wesley, there was bugger all information about her on the net, so I'd need to do some research on her before deciding if she was a suspect or not. I managed to freeze frame a shot of her from one of Barry's TV car ads. The unsmiling shot suggested she didn't want to be there, but Daddy would have insisted no doubt. The image was pixelated when I blew it up, but it was adequate for now.

As with Cassie, I wasn't sure if Barry's second wife, Filipino Josie Evans (née Dexter, née Johnson, née Ramos) was a suspect, but she was a member of the cast. The picture was a wedding shot, Barry beaming as usual, but Josie not looking so happy for some reason.

The next name was Maria. Although she was a lovely lady and I doubted she was involved, I still felt the need to include her on the list. A small picture scanned from her driver's licence was the only accompaniment to her name.

There was one more person to add to the list. Maria had mentioned Cory's personal trainer, but the only name she had for her was Netty. A Google search: 'Surfers Paradise Personal Trainer, Netty' revealed a lot more information than I had expected. Annette Slater was more than just another buff young person with a Cert IV in Fitness. Through her regular podcasts and appearances on *Channel 7*, the brand 'Net Fitness', along with her own style of personal training, saw this motivated entrepreneur as an emerging Gold Coast personality. Was she a suspect? Probably not, but it was her that had raised the alarm when she turned up for a gym session at Cory's home and found his room empty. That was all the info I had on her for now. And although there was plenty of history on the net and endless images, I didn't feel the need to add a photograph. For now she was a peripheral player.

There was enough room to add to the list if required. Jenny had mentioned that Patty had gotten herself involved with Mick Brennan of The Wasps bikie gang, but she'd also insisted he was out-of-bounds due to a sensitive ongoing investigation. 'Stay away from Mick Brennan, mate. I don't want him getting spooked,' Jenny had said.

The marker pen hesitated over the surface of the whiteboard for a moment until I scribbled down the name Brennan. Just the mention of this individual in relation to this case meant that something nasty may have happened to Cory after all.

The last run-in I'd had with the bikie gang leader was at the Coolangatta Hotel when he'd decided to single-handedly go into battle with the bouncers while I was having a quiet Sunday arvo drink with Elvis. When it was apparent that he was getting the better of the four door men, I reluctantly stepped in. 'Detective Constable Stephens, you need to calm down, mate,' I yelled, stepping in between the group and feeling like the footy ball thrown into a scrum.

Brennan's attention, momentarily distracted by my intervention, shifted to me. Ignoring my threats of an arrest, he grinned, rolled back his right fist and was just about to let fly— which would probably have seen me catapulted out of the pub, across the road and into the Coolangatta surf—when the bouncers pounced and overpowered him.

For the next thirty minutes, I'd stood over the heaving, cussing mass of muscle waiting for a paddy wagon to arrive.

'I'll fucking get you for this, you scrawny little bastard,' Brennan spat, as we bundled him into the back of the vehicle. This was prior to the X case, so I was still unknown then, but I often wondered if Brennan would remember me if our paths ever crossed.

'Fucking hell, mate, who do you think you are? Batman?' Elvis demanded when I rejoined him back at our table.

'Part of the job, I'm afraid.'

'But you're off duty!'

My grin was wily. 'Never off duty, son.'

'But do you know who that was?'

I did but shrugged it off.

'That's Mick-fucking-Brennan.'

'Yeah, I know. So?'

'So?'

A guitarist was setting up on the stage. In an attempt to change the subject, I nudged Elvis as a couple of sorts fresh from the beach passed by. Elvis was easily distracted. By the time two bikini-clad girls had passed by, he'd moved on.

So, the whiteboard was complete. I had a map, and now all I had to do was follow the directions. It felt good to be busy again. I was ready to do some serious detective work.

16

A young woman wearing Armani gym wear met me at the top of the stairs. She had the perfect figure, the perfect tan, perfect teeth, perfect hair. She made me feel out of shape and old. Her name was Stella. We were standing in a trendy office. One wall was a floor to ceiling window looking down over the street, another was made from reconstituted bricks with a huge flat screen showing snippets of Netty Slater conducting various workout routines. Along the third wall hung Net Fit branded gym wear for sale, shelves of vitamins and supplements, protein powders, drink bottles, towels, and equipment. The remaining wall was completely glass and looked over a small, pristine gymnasium where Netty was assisting an overweight man to touch his toes. Stella sat at a plain desk and there was a leather Chesterfield sofa.

'If you'd like to take a seat, please Mister Stephens, Netty will be with you shortly.' She handed me a clipboard and a pen and asked me to fill out a medical history form, which only took a couple of minutes. I was purposely early for our appointment. After handing back the completed form and a signed disclaimer, I had time to collect my thoughts.

It felt good to be working on a case again. Out and about, talking to people, searching for clues. But was this actually a case? Basically, all I had to go on was that a young bloke was reported missing by his housekeeper. An able bodied and very wealthy adult. He could have been anywhere, could have gone any place in the world. One good thing about remaining on good terms with the police force, especially Jenny, was that I got to use their resources on the odd occasion. Jenny had someone checking the airport records, buses and trains for a recent traveller, under the name of Cory Evans, leaving the state or country. I'd know the results later that day. If the name was flagged, we'd know exactly where he went. But of course, that would be too easy. If his name didn't come up, as I suspected, it could mean he was within the country somewhere. He could have hired a car, or he could have been travelling under a false name. Australia is a vast place where it's easy to disappear. The final scenario was that using his wealth, he'd been able to obtain false documents and travelled overseas using a counterfeit passport. Or he could have just been over on Straddie Island in a bloody tent or cruising the Whitsundays.

So far, there were no signs of a crime being committed. No suspects. Was I wasting my time? After deciding to give it a couple of days, I'd talk to as many of the people on my list as possible, and see what came up. Aided by my old detective instincts, which hadn't let me down so far, hopefully I'd have a better idea of how to proceed after that time.

Netty pushed open a frameless glass door in the transparent wall and lead her latest victim from the gym. With a spring in her step, she marched over to the merchandise and picked up a new folded towel from the pile. When she handed it to the sweaty young man, she side glanced Stella and issued a quick nod. Stella wrote down the purchase on a pad. 'The showers are just to the left, Todd,' Netty said, pointing to the entrance door at the top of the stairs. 'When you've finished, come back and see Stella and she'll explain your supplement routine.' She handed him the towel, shook his hand and added, 'I'll see you the same time next week.'

'Thanks, Netty,' the young man said, lowering his head in that familiar way we've come to associate with the socially awkward techies.

'Scotty!' Netty suddenly yelled as if she'd known me all her life. I was getting used to this kind of treatment.

Beaming, she skipped over and held out her hand for me to shake. 'Netty, Netty Slater.'

For some reason, I felt the need to reply with the same gusto. I think I may have even attempted a little Sean Connery. 'Stephens, Scotty Stephens.' Tetley, my old Pommy mate's voice whispered in my head. 'You fuckin twat!'

'It's great to meet you. Come on through.' She grabbed the clipboard from Stella's desk then led me into the gym.

Pilates equipment, pulleys and hand weights gave the impression of a very trendy torture chamber. In the corner of the room was a desk with two chairs. Beside this was an apparatus that looked kind of like a sophisticated pair of electronic scales. If you'd like to slip off your shoes, stand on here and grab hold of the handles, we'll measure your BMI.

'My what?'

'Your Body Mass Index. It will give us an overall picture of your health.'

'Oh right. Cool.' I did as I was told.

'So ... Scotty Stephens, eh?' Netty said as the machine did its thing. 'What brings you here?'

'Time to get fit.'

'Doesn't look like you need the belly blaster.' She gestured with her eyes to a reasonably flat stomach.

The machine went *ping* ... well, more of a *grrrr plep*, and spat out a sheet of paper.

Netty asked me to step down and put my shoes back on, while she settled at the desk and studied the sheet. 'Hmm,' she said when I took my place in the other chair. 'Why are you really here, Scotty? Is it about Cory?'

Damn, my notoriety had buggered me up again. Knowing that I was a private detective and realising from my chart that I wasn't here for the belly-blaster routine, Netty had put two and two together. It was pointless trying to lie. 'As a matter of fact I am.'

'Good, I've been so worried. We need to find him.'

'Why? Isn't he just a client?'

'He was, but I got to know him really well during the time we trained together. Come on, you're not going to get away without a bit of pain.' She led me to the nearest torture rack and showed me how to use it. In a lying position, I reached for the pulleys and stretched my back, which actually felt quite good.

'What's he like? Cory.'

Netty shrugged. 'He's great. A bit fucked in the head as you'd expect but working through his issues.'

'Issues?'

'No, look, he's fine. Just got problems with low self-esteem, anxiety, all the things that we except as normal nowadays.'

'So, you say you got to know him?' My biceps and back were beginning to burn.

'Yeah, as well as anyone could, I guess. He changed daily.'

'In what way?'

'Moody one day, manic the next, quiet and brooding on another.'

'Was he ever aggressive or …?'

'Uhm, not aggressive, bit temperamental maybe but nothing extreme.'

I was silently cussing that I didn't have my notepad. 'Do you think he would just up sticks and bugger off?'

'No, not on his own.'

'What makes you say that?'

We moved onto another piece of equipment that resembled a leg press.

'As far as I know, he doesn't have any friends and rarely goes out. I couldn't imagine him out in the world on his own. I think in the two months I knew him he never even went out of the apartment.'

'What about Wesley?'

'Don't know him. He moved in after Cory stopped training.'

'Do you think he had anything to do with Cory not training anymore?'

'Maybe, but I doubt it. We were two months into a three-month routine. I was amazed at the transformation in just the first few weeks. He really worked hard, concentrated on his diet and excelled.'

'So, what happened?'

'I think he got bored. At first it was something new, something for him to focus on, you know? But then the motivation seemed to waiver. He cancelled a couple of sessions, and when we did work out, the passion was gone. He even gained a little weight again.'

'Then he cancelled permanently?'

'Yep, out of the blue.'

The hot shower was welcome after the workout. The five-star facilities seemed like a hundred stars compared to what I was used to at Ruby Street. I was grateful to Netty and Stella for not bothering with the marketing routine—sign up now and get a discount, buy one of these towels and a lifetime supply of fat burning powdered mushrooms.

The information I'd harvested so far was helpful. Along with the snippets supplied by Maria, the housekeeper, I was forming an image of Cory Evans. The importance of separating the reality from the factual world of Freckles would be a big factor. I still wasn't sure whether or not there was a case, but my gut feeling was telling me there was. The next obvious thing to do was to talk to the person closest to him. For that I'd need to return to Surfers Paradise early the next morning.

17

Cavill Avenue was awash with litter and debris, resembling what I could only describe as the aftermath of a riot. High-vis clad council workers busily went about their duties, cleaning up the area like automated workers from a dystopian society. There were a few fresh-faced kids making their way to the beach, the sensible ones that probably hadn't had such a good time the night before and weren't sleeping it off until lunchtime.

I'd driven up in the Dub as parking wasn't a problem at that time of the morning. After finding a spot close to Surfers Paradise Surf Club. I didn't really know where I was going, but the Milton seemed like the right place to head. There was a coffee shop across the street from the iconic hotel beneath the nightclub I remembered back in the day as Shooters. Approaching the small, open-fronted venue, I couldn't believe my luck. There were only two patrons, Wesley Cummings and a young girl who I recognised from the one family shot I had, as Cassie Evans. This was more than I could have expected.

I was trying to not describe the people I needed to speak with as suspects, because as far as I knew, there'd been no crime committed, so 'people of interest' was probably a more apt description. Now was another of those occasions when I regretted my celebrity. There was no way of blending in. Ideally, I could have sat down behind them and listened, but Wesley's blushed cheeks and lowering head told me he'd clocked me as soon as I'd entered the joint.

Cassie turned to check out the reason for her half-brother's sudden change of demeanour. When she saw me, her face lit up with recognition.

'Hey guys, how's it going?' I was out in the open. Engagement was the only option.

'Good,' Cassie replied.

Wesley didn't speak.

'Mind if I join you?' Without waiting for a reply, I plonked myself down next to Cassie. 'You guys enjoying Schoolies?'

'I am,' Cassie said. 'Not so much for the Toolie though.' She nodded in Wesley's direction and grinned.

'Oh right. Not the best place to be if you're not included, eh, mate?'

A slight shudder and a shuffle on his stool was his only reaction.

'So, I was hoping to catch up with Cory.' For the reaction this brought, I may have just delivered devastating news or asked them to accompany me to the station for questioning. The blooms on Wesley cheeks spread across the rest of his face and deepened to a crimson red. Cassie's complexion was the exact opposite, sinking into an ashen grey. 'You guys okay?'

Cassie nodded vigorously as if shaking away the chill.

Wesley glanced at me and offered a kind of shimmy, shake and shrug.

'I was supposed to be meeting him, but he's not answering his phone.' The little lie was thrown out there to gauge their reactions. As a copper, a police detective and now a private detective, I'd honed my skills of what I called 'reaction analysis'. Both youngsters frowned, which told me they knew I was lying.

Wesley glanced at me. Our eyes met. His expression said, *Can you fuck off please?*

'Do you know where he is?'

Heads shook in silence.

Wesley's gaze moved to the shop window, and I wondered if he was contemplating escape.

'We're good mates, you see, and I haven't seen him for a while.'

'How do you know, Cory?' Cassie asked. She was slapped with a sudden scowl from her brother that said, *Do not engage!*

'Oh, he helped me when I was going through some shit during the *X* case. There was a time there when it seemed like the Australian public was going to lynch me. I was king-shit one day, then jack-shit the next.' My improvisation was feasible, but once again, I sensed Wesley was about to stand up and yell, 'You lying bastard.' It's like I was reading sign language, but instead of using his hands, the only tool of communication he had was his mutable expressions. I continued regardless. 'With him experiencing a similar situation, he knew what I was going through and reached out.'

Now it was Cassie's turn to engage in silent communication with her brother. Her gaze towards him asked, 'Is this true?'

A dismissive scowl followed by that same shimmy shake told her it wasn't.

'Do you reckon you could call him for me, Wes?' My familiarity was warm and friendly. 'Or perhaps we could go up to the apartment?'

The familiar reaction was becoming more than a little annoying, so I jumped in before it was executed. 'What's that, mate?'

'No. He's not home.' At last, the creature spoke.

'Right. Do you know where he'd be?'

'Meditating … thinking … relaxing.'

'And where would he be doing that?' My quick-fire questions were an attempt to increase the momentum.

'He goes to a retreat.' Wesley's words were bolstered with his awkward body language.

'On the coast?'

'Hinterland.'

'Do you know which one?' I didn't really need to ask this. Although there were two or three health retreats in the Gold Coast Hinterland, there was really only one that was used by celebrities or wealthy businesspeople who needed time out from the world. 'The Door of Eden?'

The shrug.

'When was last time you saw him?'

The shrug again. 'A couple of days ago.'

'He didn't tell you where he was going?'

No shrug this time, just a shake of the head.

'What about you, Cas?'

'I've never met him.' Her searching eyes were asking her brother if this answer was okay.

'Really? How come?' I already knew the answer. Her parents had purposely kept the girl away from her siblings.

She didn't reply, instead taking a sip of orange juice through a straw.

'Listen, guys. I'm worried about your brother. I think he may have come to harm.' I was still fishing for those telltale reactions.

'What makes you say that?' Wesley's responce carried with it the first signs of emotion.

'I have reason to believe he may have been abducted.' Outlandish I know, but my gut feeling was telling me something wasn't right about the situation.

'That's crazy,' Wesley said. 'Cory's not that cute little kid anymore. He's a grown man.' Was there a hint of scorn in his tone? My bloody oath there was.

'His personal trainer said he'd never go off like this.'

'What does she know?'

'Seems to know him quite well.'

Wesley leaned forward on his stool and lowered his voice. 'Perhaps she's the reason he's gone walkabout.' Finally, being able to engage in a conversation was a breakthrough.

'Why would you say that?'

'Ask her. Did she tell you about the money she was demanding from him?'

'Netty?'

Decisive nod. No shrug. No shake.

'Demanding money from Cory?'

'Yes.' This came out as an impatient hiss, betraying a temper that lay within.

'For what?' After finally turning over the engine, I needed to keep it revving.

'She wanted to open a new, bigger gym and she'd talked Cory into becoming her partner. She just wanted his money though.'

Hmm. I wonder why Netty hadn't mentioned this. I'd need to speak to her again.

'So, you're not worried about him?'

'No. He's fine. Like I said, he'll be meditating somewhere.'

'What about you, Cassie? You worried about your brother?'

Glancing at Wesley as if requesting permission to speak, she shook her head.

'Got to be curious, but.'

'Not really.' Her attempt at being nonchalant wasn't working.

'Famous brother that you've never met. And now he's gone missing.'

'He hasn't gone missing!' Wesley interjected.

'I hope you're right, mate.' Now it was my turn to lean forward and lower my voice. 'I've been asked to find him. And that's what I'm going to do.'

18

The drive out through Tallebudgera Valley brought back memories of my time staying in Mary's Mansion. Not really a mansion, of course, but a tiny loggers' cabin, built by Callum Murphy in the eighteen hundreds and dedicated to his wife Mary. The little place that was home for a couple of weeks during the Kathy Brown case wasn't visible from the road, but the enormous Fenton horse stud next door was. I briefly considered swinging in there to see how everyone was, but decided against it. Maybe on the way back.

The Door of Eden was situated almost as far as you could drive in the valley. The road up to that point was still single lane bitumen, but beyond that it narrowed until it eventually ended at the beginning of the historical Cream Track, a heritage-listed hiking trail from Tallebudgera to Springbrook.

The retreat was surrounded by a ten-foot high, perfectly manicured privet hedge. Behind a solid dark green gate, the interior was hidden from the road and impossible to access without reporting via an intercom at the entrance. The idling Dub shuddered as I rolled down the driver's window, stuck out an arm and pressed a button on the keyboard. A familiar voice came straight back through a small speaker.

'Hello.'

'Hi. Is that you, Jazz?'

'Scotty?'

'Yep, the one and only.'

The gate slowly slid to one side. For as many times as my reluctant fame caused me hassles, it also issued its perks. When the *X* case was over, and I was recovering from a serious knife wound, the stress had also taken its toll on me mentally, leaving me a little drained. My partner on the case, Bradley Foster, had sensed this and, without my knowing, booked me a two-week stay at the retreat. At first, I was apprehensive and when I realised I couldn't watch the footy, I was dead set against it. But both Bradley and Jenny insisted. And I'm glad they did. Two weeks of eating good wholesome food, gentle exercise, mostly yoga, meditation, and lots of walks through the beautiful rainforest were exactly what I needed. There were decisions to be made at that point of my life—my career, my family, my lifestyle, all of which were departmentalised by the time I left this wonderful haven.

That was a year ago. I was surprised Jasmine recognised my voice. She'd been one of my healing coaches. The memory of her soft voice assuring me everything would be okay, and that the universe had a place for me, still resonated, and often assisted me to drift off to a deep, peaceful sleep.

Once through the gate, a private concrete road led through a huge, freshly mowed meadow towards a dense wall of Eucalyptus trees, with hardwoods and palms in the distance. Driving slowly into the forest, I lifted my sunglasses onto my head, adjusting to the light that instantly changed from bright sunshine to speckled shade filtering down through the canopy above. The road inclined and curved. At the top of a ridge, the view was both familiar and very welcome. Situated in a small, secluded valley of its own, thick rainforest surrounded the retreat on four sides. The accommodation was a series of private cabins scattered around the edges of a clearing. A large hexagonal structure made from logs was the main building. I remembered this well—the community hall. Just the sight of the place induced a state of relaxation.

Looking down the side of the northern facing ridge, I was actually contemplating booking in again.

There were no cars allowed beyond this point. The road ended at a gravel car park. The handful of vehicles there were your highend SUVs: a Porsche, a Jaguar, and a Lamborghini. Hard to believe that the old Dub was no longer out of place in such illustrious company.

The familiar *whir* of an approaching golf buggy seemed out of place with the sounds of the forest—the whipbird calling out in the distance and his mate instantly responding with the *crack* at the end of his *whip*.

The dark green buggy appeared from a track between the trees, and the infectious smile of Jasmine Carter welcomed me. 'Hey Scotty,' she called out as soon as she saw me standing next to the Dub. There was a little forward jerk before the buggy came to a halt, then she jumped out and threw her arms around me. The white shorts and white polo shirt were as pristine as I remembered them. 'How are you, ya bugger?'

'I'm good. Thanks, Jazz.'

'It's great to see you.' She pulled back and held me at arm's length. 'You're looking awesome!'

'Thanks.'

'Come here. Give us another hug.' Her welcome was sincere. 'So, what brings you here?' she asked, finally letting go of me. But before I could answer, 'Need to get away again? There is a cabin free, but you should have called.'

'No, no, nothing like that. I've been meaning to come around and see you, but—'

'When you were staying just down the road, you mean?'

Bugger, the notoriety again. The Kathy Brown case had been all over the news. I was hoping the hint of anger in Jasmine's tone was in jest, but I wasn't sure. 'Yeah … well … you know how –'

'Breathe and relax, breathe and relax, remember?' She playfully punched me on the arm. 'I'm just kidding. I know how busy you are.'

My embarrassed grin made her giggle.

'So, what can we do for you?'

'I'm here to see Cory Evans.'

'Cory Evans?' The puzzled frown looked out of place on her jolly face.

'Yeah, he's staying here, isn't he?'

'No. Cory's not here.'

'Really. That's funny. His brother told me he was.' Aware of the client confidentially clause, I was hoping my attempt at keeping the conversation casual, even though Wesley had said nothing of the kind, would break through the wall of privacy. I needn't have worried.

She shook her head. 'I shouldn't really be telling you this, Scotty Stephens, but no, he's not here I'm afraid. We haven't seen him for about six months.'

'Would he use any of the other retreats?'

'No. He loves it here. Comes at least twice a year.'

'So, he's about due for another visit?'

'Yeah, I guess.'

Hmm. Interesting. After a quick chit-chat, I bid Jazz farewell with the promise of booking into the retreat again very soon.

19

It was only the second day of the case, but there was still no proof a crime had been committed. Although I hoped Cory was safe and well somewhere, perhaps boinking surf chicks down at Byron Bay, snorkelling the Great Barrier Reef, or trekking through Kakadu, the detective side of me relished the idea he was in strife and that it was only me who could save him. I seriously wished him no harm, though, but if I was to continue working the case, I'd need a breakthrough soon. Relish doesn't pay the bills. In fact, I still wasn't sure who'd be putting up the bounty. Surely his loved ones would want to see him back safe and unharmed. The only problem was that I wasn't sure if he *had* any loved ones. Wesley was the only proper family member I'd met so far.

It would be easy to say that Wesley wasn't hard to read—awkward, shy, lacking in the social skills that most of us take for granted. But the only information I had about him was that when their parents split, Wesley went to live with his mother, Patty. The older brother, as we know, was an international superstar for a brief time while the younger boy lived a reasonably normal life. But when Patty Cummings' life was wrecked by her eldest son suing her for everything she owned, Wesley's life must have changed too. Moving from a big house on the beach in Currumbin to a caravan park in the Tweed would have an effect on him, surely. Did he harbour resentment towards his older brother? Or did the invite to live with him in his Surfers Paradise penthouse put things right between them? After only knowing his brother for three months, I would have expected more concern.

I needed to know as much about the family as possible. One person came to mind as I drove back towards the coast. 'Hey, Bradley. How are you, mate?' My iPhone looked totally out of place suspended by a magnet from the crude dashboard of the vintage VW Beetle.

'Scott, it's good to hear from you.' The familiar voice of Bradley Foster, the young assistant assigned to me during the *X* case, but who proved to be a worthy partner, always made me feel good inside—easily on a par with Jasmine Carter.

'I'm good, mate.'

'What do you need?'

The insinuation that I only called him when I needed something made me feel more than a little guilty. Probably because it was true. 'Do you remember Cory Evans?'

'Freckles?' The feminine aspect of his voice that he mostly fought to suppress jumped out like an excited schoolgirl. He was obviously a fan.

'I need some information about his family.'

'Barry, Patty. Wesley and Cassie.' Bloody hell, forget the fan abbreviation, fanatic seemed more appropriate.

'Yeah, mate.' I was trying to play down the situation. 'Apart from the two youngsters, there's plenty of stuff in the media about the parents, but as we both know, that's news copy, and not necessarily factual. I need to know about the stuff that's not in the public domain.'

'Right.'

In my mind's eye, I could see him neatly transposing my words to his notebook.

'Will do.'

'Can we meet up when you've got it?'

'Sure.'

'Tonight?'

'Bloody hell, Scott, I do have a job, you know.'

'I know, Detective Constable. What are you working on at the moment?'

'Well I'm, uhm … I uhm … Where do you want to meet?'

'Can you come down to Kirra?'

'Oh yeah, right. I'll drive all the way down the other end of the Gold Coast too if you like.'

'Good on ya, mate. I'll see you at ours later.' Yes, I felt guilty after hanging up, but my hunch was that the young, motivated detective would rise to the challenge. And the fact that he was a Freckles fan would supply the motivation.

During the drive back through the valley, I completely forgot about calling in at the Fenton place to say g'day to Tilly and the gang. I didn't remember until the Dub was nudging into the afternoon traffic at Burleigh. 'Bugger,' I cussed. I'd missed a rare moment of killing two birds with one stone while being out in Tallebudgera.

The traffic was slow to the Gold Coast Highway. Talk about hitting every bloody red light. The fact that I was driving to the other end of the Gold Coast again, the second time in a day, meant the quiet time gave me space to think and plan. Although we'd engaged, albeit it briefly, that morning, Wesley was still at the top of my list of people, not suspects, to talk to. The reason for this is that he was the only person who had spent recent time with his brother, so only he knew his brother's recent frame of mind. It looked like the only time to get close to him was early in the morning before the hordes of Schoolies emerged from their crypts. So that was the plan. Return to Surfers in the morning but try to get Wesley alone if possible. The concierge had said he leaves early most mornings, so my guess was that while Cassie was in town for the Schoolies festival, he'd be meeting her in the coffee shop. Did he always arrive first or after Cassie? My hunch was that he'd be there first, so if I arrived early enough, he might be there alone, waiting. Tomorrow would tell.

But the day was still young. There was one person I'd been apprehensively looking forward to meeting. And I was heading out to his place now.

20

Southport was a few minutes north of Surfers Paradise—and the obvious next point of call. The trip wouldn't have been necessary if I'd found Cory lying on a massage table, reinvigorated by a diet of organic fruit and herbal tea, while undergoing a strict regime of yoga and mindfulness relaxation. But it wasn't to be.

When the site of the old Gold Coast Hospital passed me on the left, I got a view of the sign I was looking for:

BIG BARRY'S LUXURY CARS

The small concrete forecourt was crammed with earlier model prestige cars, mostly black Mercedes and BMWs. There was a Range Rover, a classic Porsche, and a red Ferrari that stuck out like a cherry in a bowl of blackberries. The building looked like it was once a 1950s self-serve petrol station.

Big Barry wasn't big at all. He was shorter than me, in fact, but he was trim and looked reasonably fit. I was surprised when he appeared from the building to greet me. While climbing from the car, I took a moment to analyse the approaching figure. His hair was too black for his age, teeth way too white. His smile reminded me of former Gold Coast Mayor Julian Monroe's—the surgically enhanced kind as natural as margarine. He was smartly dressed in a blue paisley sports jacket, white shirt, beige chinos, and black brogues. When he threw an arm around me and shook my hand, his grip was almost as overwhelming as his aftershave.

'Scotty Stephens. I knew it was only a matter of time.'

'You did?'

'Of course.' He pulled away and ran a hand over the roof of the Dub. 'There she is.' Then, turning to me, he said, 'I can do you a great deal.'

During the drive over, I'd debated how to approach the infamous Barry Evans for questioning. From what I'd read, he was a shrewd businessman, a hard negotiator and a man who suffered fools lightly. But here he was, talking to me as if he'd known me forever. Of course, it was all a part of the car salesman routine, I realised that, but it had never dawned on me to approach him as a customer. Hey … it worked for me. I was happy to go along with it if it meant getting my foot in the door. 'So, what do you reckon she's worth, Barry?'

There was no sign of surprise that I knew who he was. The fact that there was a two-storey head and shoulders shot on the roof of the building may have contributed. Either that or he just assumed everyone knew of the infamous Barry Evans.

'Oh, mate. These can go for as much as 5k these days.'

'Five thousand? Wow?' *You lying barrrrsted*. I happened to know it was worth ten times that.

'What is she? 67? 68?'

'67.'

His authoritarian nod was accompanied by a well-practised, bring-you-down-to-earth frown. 'Not as desirable as the earlier models, but still appreciating.'

'Really? I didn't realise.'

'Yeah, you've come to the right place, mate. Time to get you into something a bit more befitting, eh? There's a nice Lambo around the back.' He reached into his pocket and pulled out his phone. 'Can we get a selfie?'

'Sure.'

He took several shots of us standing by the Dub.

I was happy to go along with the dance. The ballad of the dodgy car salesman, who thought he'd not only snagged another sucker, but a famous one whose picture would lift his social media status no end, and the private detective who played dumb and went along with the routine of being fleeced. I sat in almost every car on the lot, admiring, wowing, laughing at all of Barry's perfectly rehearsed and overused little quips. By the time we entered the showroom, he was my bestest mate of all time, who I could trust no matter what.

'Coffee, Scotty?'

'Yeah, that'll be great.' We'd just entered his office, two walls of which were floor to ceiling glass and looked out over the showroom. Barry lifted an arm and made the universal drink gesture to a young guy out in the showroom, but my attention was elsewhere. The only solid wall in the room was covered with a biographical collage of photographs depicting the illustrious career of his son, Freckles.

'Wow! Freckles.'

Barry beamed with pride as he dropped into the BMW chair at his desk. 'Yep, that's my boy.' There was no sign of resentment, but I also guessed this was a part of the act of being positive and cheerful when baiting a potential customer.

'What's he up to nowadays?'

Barry shrugged and smiled. 'Oh, he's always out and about doing something.'

'Yeah, what? Acting? Singing?'

'Everything. You name it.' Barry was obviously used to being asked about his son—in fact the gallery wall in his office instigated it.

'Do you get to see him much?'

'Yeah. Regardless of what you might read in the papers, we're still very close.'

Yeah? And my classic VW Beetle's only worth 5k. 'When was the last time you would have seen him then?' My aim had been to keep the conversation casual, but I overstepped the mark.

A coldness entered his eyes, extinguishing the warmth of his smile. He must have suddenly remembered I was a private detective. 'Have you seen Cory?'

'Me? No. I'd love to meet him though. Seen all his movies.'

Barry was regarding me with those cool, calculating eyes, when a young guy, wearing a suit that looked at least two sizes too small for him, entered the office carrying two cups of coffee. He received no thanks or even a second glance from his boss. Barry's gaze was still firmly fixed on me.

'Are you here to buy a new car, Scott, or talk about my son?'

'Both.' I picked up the mug that was placed in front of me. 'Who's not going to ask you about him after seeing that?' I nodded towards the picture gallery then took a sip of coffee.

Barry continued to regard me with narrowed eyes.

'I have to be honest though ... ' Another sip of coffee. 'I can't decide between the Merc or the Beamer.'

'I still reckon the Lambo. More your style, I think.'

'Yeah?'

He nodded. 'Yeah. But you're not here for that, are you?'

It would have been a waste of time trying to continue with the charade. I was busted. 'I've got reason to believe your son may be missing. Come to harm even.'

'Really?'

Was this genuine concern or another product of the polished act? 'Yeah, he hasn't been seen for quite some time.'

'It's probably nothing. He likes to go off alone sometimes. Gather his thoughts you know?'

'So, you really do see him now and again?'

There was a hesitation in his reply, a change of tact perhaps from speaking to a gullible customer, to a detective. 'Not as often as I would like.'

'When was the last time?'

'What's this all about? Am I under suspicion?' The volume of his voice rose in anger.

'No, no, nothing like that.'

'Are you sure about that?' He stood and leaned forward on his desk.

'Take it easy, mate. No one's pointing the finger.'

'No matter whatever you or any other bastard says, I still love that boy with all my heart!'

Yeah? And my classic VW Beetle's only worth 5k.

'Get the fuck out of my office.'

'What?'

'You heard me.' He rounded the desk, fists clenched.

'Take it easy, Barry, eh,' I said, standing.

He went to grab my shoulder. I slapped away his hand. Unbelievably, he threw a punch. It caught me by surprise, but I just managed to pull my head back, his fist narrowly missing my cheek. My counter punch was an automated self-preservative jab, catching him full on the nose.

'Ah, you fucking bastard!' he yelled, cupping his nose with both hands, blood oozing between his fingers. 'I'll sue you for this you piece of shit.'

'Self-defence, mate. I'll be taking with me a copy of that,' I said calmy, gesturing with my eyes to the CCTV in the corner of the room.

'Get the hell out.' It was more of a feverish growl.

21

I was looking forward to seeing Bradley again. It had been a while. I was a bit cheeky, not only asking for his help, but expecting him to deliver it the same day, but I'd make it up to him.

The drive back from Southport wasn't too bad. I was home before Elvis, so after a shower and a shave, I was in the man cave having a quiet coldie when he arrived home from work. As soon as I heard the front door slam and saw him come moping across the backyard, I could tell he needed cheering up. 'Hey buddy.' I was standing behind the bar, twisting off the top of a fresh beer from the fridge.

'Hey mate.' He took the bottle and skulled half the contents.

'Hard day?' I suddenly felt like the stay at home wifey who'd been eagerly waiting her husband's return.

'The bloody worst, mate. I'm so over it.' He plonked himself down on a barstool, loosened his tie, and undid the top button of his shirt.

Drinking this early in the week wasn't usual practice anymore, but I was worried about my best mate. The fun, the humour, the banter, all seemed to be lacking of late. 'Are you alright, Elv?'

He shrugged and took another swig of beer. 'Might need to borrow your car on Thursday.'

Now it was my turn to shrug. 'Sure.'

'I've dinged the Porsche. Gavo'll need it for a couple of days.' Elvis' office was only in Coolangatta, probably a kilometre—tops—from our house in Ruby Street. It was an easy walk, but one he would never contemplate.

'No worries. What happened?'

'Some idiot cut me off on Griffith Street.' He finished his beer, jumped down from his stool, rounded the bar, and got another one from the fridge.

'You seem to have been a bit down just lately, mate.'

'Have I? Can't say I've noticed. Been too miserable.'

'What's up, buddy?' I placed a hand on his shoulder.

'You know what the worst thing is, Scotty?'

I shook my head.

'When people keep asking, what's up?' He swanned past me and back into the house.

This wasn't just a mood. It had gone on too long for that. I was worried that he was suffering from depression. Was it the stress of work? Or had something happened to affect his business? Or maybe, like me, he was just over the bachelor life.

I followed a few minutes later, but he'd retreated to his bedroom. I was about to tap on his door when there was a knock at the front door. Opening it, the fresh smiling face of Detective Constable Bradley Foster greeted me.

The way he breezed in reminded me of our first meeting. It was in this very spot. I'd been inexplicably promoted to Detective Inspector and placed in charge of Australia's biggest murder investigation, the X case. Bradley was assigned as my assistant with the brief to clean me up. I guess my worn Best and Less suits were no longer suitable for a high-profile detective. He'd marched into the house carrying a swag of expensive suits over his shoulder, along with a sports bag carrying all the necessary accessories. Bless him. He had proved to be a much-needed vehicle of calm in a time of madness. We'd remained friends ever since.

'Bradders.' He hated being called that, but I used the greeting playfully as we hugged at the door.

'Scott.'

'How d'ya go?' I asked, leading him out to the man shed.

'Good. No, better than good. In the time you've given me, I'd say bloody amazing!'

Bradley wasn't a beer drinker. He liked a glass of red Chardonnay. Unfortunately, we weren't wine drinkers, but I purposely kept a Caskaway in the fridge just for him. He hadn't been around for a while though, and I wasn't sure how long the opened cask had been in there. Luckily, from his barstool, he didn't have a view of the under-bench fridge behind the bar. If he'd known it was a cask and not a bottle, he would have kicked up a stink. If he'd suspected it may have been out of date, he wouldn't have drunk it, and if he'd seen me blow out the dead spider from the dusty wine glass, he probably would have fainted.

'There you go, mate.' I said, placing the half full glass on the bar in front of him. 'Just how you like it.'

'Thank you! Cheers.' He held up the glass and I touched it with my stubby. His lips may have puckered and twisted when he tasted it, but he was far too polite to complain.

'So, what have you got for me?' I asked, climbing onto the stool next to him.

'Oh, it's juicy. The Kardashians have got nothing on the Evans.'

'Really?' I wasn't sure who the Kardashians were. I think they were friends of Elvis'. I'd often heard him mention the name.

'Where to begin, where to begin?' Bradley said, retrieving a manila folder from a briefcase that I hadn't noticed until now. 'How about we start with the star of the show?' Without waiting for an answer, he opened the folder and read from the first sheet. 'Cory William Evans, aged twenty-two. I know you're already familiar with the details of his professional career, so I wanted to dig deeper.'

'And what did you find?'

'Not a lot. Pretty much every aspect of his life was documented, all of which you can easily find online. Which I'm assuming you already—?'

'Yep. From the Tim Tam ads to Hollywood. I know all that—'

'I know you do. So, since suing his parents, his net worth is estimated at around thirty million dollars. And that's where the buck stops. But not quite. Although there's been very little activity in the last couple of years, there have been a couple of warrants.'

'Warrants?'

'Some minor infringements: drunken disorderly behaviour, the time when he was thrown out of Asylum Nightclub, an altercation with a taxi driver, etc. There was also a couple of incidents involving sex workers.'

'What kind of incidents?'

Bradley scrolled his finger down the sheet. 'Uhm … ah, here. There were two complaints of aggressive behaviour, each on a different occasion, both of which resulted in girls being roughed up.'

'He beat up a couple of hookers?'

'Seems so.'

'But how come the media never got a hold of this?'

'He paid off the girls, but I think the media had also moved on at this time. He was no longer news. There was a new big shot in town they were clambering over themselves to get to instead.'

'Who?'

'You, silly.' He slapped me playfully on the shoulder.

'Oh, right.' I swigged my beer, feeling my face redden.

He turned over the sheet, laid it face down on the bar, then lifted another. 'And that brings us to the patriarch of the family.'

'Big Barry,' I said with a smile.

'Yes, Big Barry indeed. Once again, everything's common knowledge, so there's not a lot to tell. It's obvious, though, that although he claims his son sued him for every penny he owned, he's never been poor.'

'Yeah, I get that impression too. How did he pop back two years later with a prestige car yard if he was broke?'

'Well …' Bradley said, as if about to reveal a piece of juicy info. 'Apparently, his wife, Josey, is worth a bob or two. Barry is her fourth husband, and let's just say she married well and outlived all her former husbands.'

'Yeah, I'd read that.'

'So, I suspect he'd been filtering his fortune into her bank account leading up to the case.'

'Or in a Swiss account.'

'Or both.'

'Hmm … but I know all this, Bradley.'

'Yes, but here's the juicy bit.' He paused for dramatic effect. 'A year ago, Cory hired a private investigator to look into his father's affairs.'

'Wow. And you think he got something on him?'

'Maybe. If so, it would certainly give Barry a motive.'

'Who was the investigator?'

Another quick scan of the sheet. 'A … Frank Scanlan.'

'Scanlan?'

Bradley nodded. 'Do you know him?'

'I do.' And I did. Frank Scanlan was an ex-bent copper. It was well known he'd had rackets going on all over the Coast, from taking bribes to being associated with a couple of bikie gangs. When he finally got caught, he was sacked from the police force, but somehow evaded charges and a prison sentence. Not long after that, he emerged as a private detective.

'There are no records of Scanlan's findings or dealings with Cory or Barry, but it's interesting, eh?'

'It certainly is.'

'And next, we have Patty Cummings, née Evans.' He lifted the third sheet. 'Once again, we already know Patty's story. Estranged wife of Barry. She too lost everything after the court case—the beachfront house, etc, etc.'

'I've heard she's shacked up with Mick Brennan. What's that all about?'

He didn't look up from the sheet. 'Not sure, but did you know Patty was trying to launch a new appeal against the case?'

'I know she's already lost a couple of appeals. Can she go again?'

'Apparently she can if additional evidence comes to light. But it would be an expensive exercise.'

'And she's broke … hmm … I'm wondering if that's why Brennan is hanging around.'

'Could be. If he thinks there's a chance Patty could claim back Cory's fortune. He could be helping her.'

'Makes sense.'

Bradley added the sheet to the face down pile on the bar, then took out the next one. 'Wesley Cummings.'

'I've tried speaking with him, but so far *pff,* it's like trying to get mutton from a vegan.'

Bradley grinned.

'What? You've got something on Wesley?'

'Yep.' His grin expanded to a beaming smile.

'Well?'

'Did you know that two months ago, Cory transferred his entire fortune to Wesley's bank account?'

'What?'

'Every penny!'

'You're kidding me. Why would he do that?'

'When did you say was the last time anyone saw Cory?'

'I don't know about Wesley yet, but everyone else, two or three months ago.'

'That's right. About the same time the money was transferred. Do you find that odd?'

'Very.'

'Apart from that, there's little documentation about him. He'd lived with his mother after the split but was forced to move into a caravan park with her after the case. Then out of the blue, he went to live with his brother.' He added the sheet to the pile but didn't pick up the remaining one. 'Now we come to Cassie Evans. We have nothing on her. Only just eighteen. Went to school at Saint Hilda's School for girls. Still lives at home with her parents in Hope Island.'

'So, who's the final sheet for?' I asked, pointing to the folder.

'This is interesting, and I just came across it by chance.' He picked up the sheet. 'Anette Slater.'

'Netty?'

'The very same. Apparently, she had an unsigned agreement with Cory Evans.'

'An agreement?'

'Yes. Cory was about to sign a multi-million dollar deal that would see them go into partnership together. There was to be a huge new gym on the coast, but more importantly, the brand would become a franchise.'

'Right.' Funny. She hadn't mentioned this when we'd met, but it explained why she'd illegally gained entry to Cory's apartment. 'What happened?'

'It appears as if Cory had second thoughts and pulled out. The only problem was, though, for poor Netty, she'd already borrowed, and invested, a large amount from the bank.' With an accomplished expression, Bradley picked up the sheets from the bar and placed them back into the manila folder.

'You are awesome, Bradley. Thank you so much, mate.' The information he'd dug up would be helpful. For the first time since meeting with Maria, the domestic, it felt like I had a case.

'You're welcome.' He slid over the glass of wine. 'Now remove this cheap, out-of-date shit and give me a beer.'

22

The next morning, I was an hour earlier than the previous day, hoping I could catch Wesley alone before Cassie arrived. But I was a little too early, it seemed. The coffee shop wasn't quite open yet. A girl with pink hair, an arm of tattoos and wearing highly polished Doc Martens, was setting up tables and chairs out the front. This was okay. Good, in fact. It meant I'd be able to catch Wesley leaving the Milton and spend more time with him.

The usual army of council workers was cleaning up the mess from the mass street party the night before and counting down the days to when their duties would return to a more normal pace, no doubt.

The Milton foyer was busy for that time of the morning. There was a family taking an early checkout. Early beach walkers crossed paths, some on their way out, some on their way back. A group of surfers wearing half wetsuits and carrying thruster boards beneath their arms, joked and laughed as they hurried towards the exit.

Thankfully, the concierge from the day before, the older guy, was nowhere to be seen. Maybe he only worked the day shift. Instead, a young blond guy with matching blond eyebrows and a deep tan manned the concierge desk. Wearing my baseball cap and sunnies, no one had recognised me yet. I was making my way towards the concierge when something caught the corner of my eye—a hulk of a figure marching from the lifts. Ducking into a foyer sofa, I picked up a tourism magazine and pretended to read. The reason for my need to hide was because the monster approaching was none other than Mick Brennan, the leader of The Wasps bikie gang.

Holding the magazine just below my eyeline so I could monitor the situation, I watched Brennan as he headed for the exit. He seemed to be in a hurry. Without stopping, he skimmed something across the foyer that hit the concierge and made him jump. It was a key card. Then, the beady eyes deep set in a neanderthal-shaped skull flicked towards me. I purposely didn't flinch or lift the magazine. That would have alerted him that he was being watched. Luckily, the sunnies concealed my eyes. I noticed a slight change in his expression, though, a scowl. *Did he recognise me?*

He marched past, through the automatic glass doors and out to the street. From there, I watched him climb onto a Harley Davidson parked on the pavement to the left of the entrance that I hadn't noticed when I'd entered. Brennan kicked over the engine, and it roared into life. The sound ripped through the high-rise buildings as loud as the V8 machines that had hurtled through the streets of Surfers during the NASCAR 500 only a couple of weeks earlier. After strapping on a helmet that resembled a World War II Nazi stormtrooper's, and twisting the throttle, he was away.

What the hell was Brennan doing here? Was he here to see Cory? Or is it just a coincidence? Had he been up to the apartment? If so, had he harmed Wesley? My mind was racing with questions. I needed to find out if Wesley was okay.

When the concierge looked up from his note pad, I could tell right away that he'd recognised me. 'Ah yes, sir. What can I do for you?'

'I'm here to see Wesley Cummings.'

'Right, does he know you're coming?'

'Yeah. We're meeting for coffee, but I can't get him on his phone.' I didn't have his number. 'I'm a bit worried about him, to tell you the truth.'

'Oh right. I'll give him a call.' He picked up the handset from the in-house phone, punched in a number, then listened. There was no reply. 'Probably in the shower or something. He's usually an early riser.'

'No worries. Can you let me up there?'

'No, I'm afraid I can't. It's against the hotel rules.'

'But you let the other guy up.' It was a hunch.

The name tag on his lapel read 'Tom'. His cheeks reddened. 'The other guy?'

'Yeah, you know. The big bikie fellow.'

'No, I, I, I … I didn't …'

'It's alright, mate. I understand. He threatened you, right?'

He lowered his head.

'Mean piece of work, that one. Now let's not make the situation worse than it already is. If Mister Cummings has come to harm, we need to help him.'

'Right.' He opened the top drawer and fumbled inside until he produced the card key.

'Good lad.' Reaching over the countertop, I picked up a pen and scribbled my mobile number on the pad. 'Now you stay here, Tom, and let me know if old mate comes back, or if anything else happens that I should know about, yeah?'

'Okay, Mister Stephens.'

'Just as a matter of interest,' I said, lowering my voice. 'Have you seen Cory Evans, lately?'

Tom shook his head.

'But you would see him entering and leaving, surely.'

'No, never. He would always use the service entrance at the back of the building.'

'Is that right?'

'Yes. Most of the celebrities do. That's why we have the nicest service area in town.' He grinned.

'What about Wesley?'
'What about him?'
'Does he use the front or the back?'
'Oh, the front, always.'
'Why's that?'
'He's not a celebrity.'

23

The lifts to the smaller residential tower were farther along the corridor, past the much busier ones to the taller hotel building. With the elevator to myself, I was surprised when one of the two doors, the one facing, opened directly into Cory's apartment.

'Hello?' I called out gingerly, stepping into the marble clad foyer. 'Hello!'

There was a sudden movement to my left, a rush of air. Instinctively raising my fists in defence, I turned and ducked, narrowly missing the arc of a baseball bat at full swing. 'Wesley, it's me. Scotty Stephens.'

He came at me again, so this time I lunged forward to meet him and restrict the blow.

'What are you doing, mate?' I asked, close enough to kiss him.

'I'm sorry, I'm sorry. I thought … I thought he was …'

'You thought he'd come back.'

He nodded erratically, blinking through watering eyes.

'Mick Brennan?'

He pulled away and looked at me as if I'd just read his fortune.

'I saw him downstairs. We need to talk.'

He led me along a short corridor and into an expansive kitchen.

'So, what does Mick Brennan want with you, mate?' I asked, as Wesley placed the bat on the counter.

'Money.' His voice trembled.

'Money for Patty?'

That incredulous look once more. 'How would you know that?'

'I'm a detective. Remember?'

He nodded, looking momentarily unsure of his surroundings.

'Listen, I'm here to help, mate.'

'Are you?'

'Yes. I am. Truly. I'm guessing you've got no one on your side at the moment.' He was just a kid, awkward and shy. And here he was all alone, living in the metropolis, afraid to go outside for fear of being branded a Toolie, or worse still, attacked. He was estranged from his family and now abandoned by his brother.

He inhaled through his nose, then exhaled loudly through his mouth. 'You're not wrong.'

'Mick Brennan is one mean bastard. He wouldn't be involved if he didn't think it was going to be worth his while.'

'He wants to bleed me dry—Cory, I mean. He wants to bleed Cory dry.'

'And he's using Patty to get to you. Him.'

Wesley's expression had warmed, and I hoped he was coming around to the idea that I was on his side.

'Why don't you tell me what's going on, mate?' I asked, gesturing with an arm to the bar stools.

He nodded thoughtfully, then made his way to a stool while I opened the fridge, like I owned the place, and pulled out two bottles of Sprite. 'There ya go, buddy.' Handing him one, and sitting on the stool beside him. 'Let's start from the beginning, eh?'

'Cory saved my life.'

From my years of experience of being a police detective, I'd learned how to listen. In situations like this, silence was the best option. Just let them speak while throwing in the odd simple question, the understanding nod in the right place, a rise of the brow, and a shake of the head when required.

'He rescued me from a life of hell.' Wesley took a nervous swig of Sprite. 'She didn't care about me anymore. I was in her way. And when that monster appeared on the scene. I had to get away.'

'Brennan?'

'Yes. Thank God for Cory. He found out. Got me out of there.'

'Sounds like you've got a lot to be thankful to your brother for.'

After another swig of Sprite, he nodded lowly.

'So where is he?'

He answered with that familiar shrug, and I worried he was retreating to his shell. I needed to bring him back. 'You must really love him.'

The nod again, this time with more enthusiasm. 'I do, yes.'

'So surely you want to know what's happened to him?'

'I already know what's happened to him.'

'You do?'

He was using the drink as a pacifier to soothe his nerves. The next gulp half emptied the bottle, and he burped loudly. 'He's just gone away for a while. He does that.'

'You said he was at the Door of Eden. I checked. He isn't.'

'It was a guess. He'd spoken of the place. Said he goes there when life gets too hard.'

'So, you don't know where he is?'

'No.' He was nervous, like a schoolboy who was trying to explain why he hadn't done his homework.

I changed tact. 'Do you know of anyone who would want to harm your brother?'

'Hah, all of them.' He sat up straight on his stool and suddenly became animated. 'Barry, Patty, the biker, Netty. They all think he owes them.' He checked his watch. 'I need to go. Got to meet someone.'

'Cassie?'

That look of amazement again, this time though laced with a little suspicion. 'Oh, that's right, you saw us in the café.'

'She seems like a nice girl.'

'Yes. She is.'

'Bet it was weird meeting her for the first time.'

'You bet.' He finished his drink and stood.

'Just one more thing, mate,' I said, also rising from my stool. 'What if he isn't travelling? What if he's come to harm?'

I expected him to brush off the question with a nonchalant reassurance that his brother was okay, but he didn't. He hesitated.

'Surely you'd be concerned and would want to do the right thing. Especially after what he did for you.'

I'd hit a nerve, but I wasn't sure if he was contemplating the possibility that his brother was a victim of foul play or if he was suddenly aware he may be under suspicion of appearing not to care.

'Of course.'

'Then let me find him. Make sure he's alright.'

He became excited, as if he'd made an important decision. 'Okay. Let me hire you.'

'Uhh … okay.' I wasn't expecting that.

'You look for him and uhm … let me know when you find him.'

'Sounds like a plan.' A very stupid plan. Was this a genuine plea for me to find his brother or an on-the-spot decision to get me out of the way?

'I'll pay your going rate, plus expenses.'

'Sweet.' We shook hands.

'Now I really have to go.' The desperation in his voice reminded me of Van Helsing working quickly before the setting sun. Wesley's situation was the opposite. His tormentors rose with the late morning sun. He needed to be out and back to safety before then.

There were still more questions for Wesley, such as how come his brother transferred his fortune into his bank account just before he disappeared? And what was *his* relationship with his parents like nowadays? But I had access now. After exchanging phone numbers, we travelled down in the lift together, walked out onto the street, and even strolled side by side along Orchid Avenue.

Cassie was waiting in the coffee shop, sitting at a high bench, looking out through open concertina windows. Her raised eyebrows displayed surprise when she saw us approaching.

'G'day, Cass. How's it going?' I said from outside.

Wesley continued into the shop.

'I'm good, thanks.'

'Big night last night?'

'Oh yeah.'

Wesley went straight to the counter and placed an order, giving me a free moment with his half-sister. 'Cass, can we meet up for lunch sometime or …?'

'I suppose.'

'Today?'

'Can't today. It *is* Schoolies week, you know.'

'Yeah, right, sorry. Reaching into my pocket, I withdrew my wallet and pulled out a business card. 'Call me when you're free.'

'Sure,' she said, taking the card.

'You have a good day, eh?'

'I will. Thanks.'

24

I was burning fuel like a bugger, driving up and down the coast, but at least I had someone to foot the bill now. The drive south gave me time to gather my thoughts. Wesley's body language was hard to read. He appeared to be in awe of his brother and certainly owed him a lot, being rescued from a life that was forced upon him. But then, on the other hand, it was Cory's actions that had put him there. When Patty was sued, lost everything and was forced out of her comfortable home, Wesley lost everything too. Did he harbour resentment because of this?

Patty was the obvious person to speak to next, hence the drive from Surfers to Chinderah—a little town just over the border in New South Wales. Thankfully, I'd be passing through Kirra, so I had enough time to duck in home for a quick sandwich. Expecting the house to be empty, I was surprised to find Elvis lying on the sofa.

'Hey, mate. What's going on?'

'Hey, bud. Not much.' He was wearing one of the smart suits he wore for work.

'Are you okay?'

A Wesley-style shrug was his reply.

Retreating to the kitchen, I made two cheese salad sandwiches, then returned with them on a tray with two mugs of tea.

'Thanks mate,' Elvis said, sitting up.

We ate in silence. Once again, this was odd. Elvis was never usually quiet.

'So how come you're not at work?' I asked, after finishing my sandwich and sipping my tea.

'Not much to do. Not very busy.'

'Do you wanna go out later? Surf club?'

'Sure.'

There was a need to speak with my mate, find out what was wrong with him, but now wasn't the time. Greasing him up with a few beers later would hopefully do the trick. When I returned from the kitchen after taking away the plates, he was back in the lying position, looking up at the ceiling. Something was up with Elvis.

'I'll see you later, mate.'

'Yeah, see you later.'

Chinderah was only a few minutes' drive from Kirra. The caravan park was on the right-hand side of the M1, so after taking the Kingscliff exit and following the road to the left and under the overpass, I soon found myself in the quaint little riverside town. The caravan park, which wasn't so quaint, was situated right next to the motorway.

Bradley had supplied me with Patty's address. Driving through the park at six kilometres per hour, I observed mostly old caravans with faded awnings, as well as some smart mobile homes dressed to look like small houses with manicured lawns out front, bougainvillea and palm trees. Patty's van was at the far end of the park. It was a solid old thing, maybe six berth at a pinch. There was an awning, but it was open on three sides like a canvas pergola. Beneath this was a couple of large camp chairs and a table. Patty sat in one of the chairs, watching me approach through a cloud of cigarette smoke.

'Patty Cummings?' I asked after parking the Dub and climbing out of the car. Of course I already knew who she was, and although she looked nothing like the glamourous, wealthy Patty of old, I recognised her from the more recent shots taken outside Southport Courthouse.

'You can fuck off!'

Charming. 'Can I have a word?'

'Are you paying?'

'Maybe.' Thankfully, she didn't seem to recognise me. I guessed she'd assumed I was a journalist.

She took a large drag of her cigarette, then blew the smoke into the air. 'I've got nothing else to say. You bastards only twist my words, anyway.'

'I'm not from the press.' I took off my sunglasses. 'I'm Scotty Stephens.' Like everybody knew who I was. 'TWAT!' Tetley hissed in my ear once more.

'Who?'

'I'm a private detective.'

Patty shuffled in her chair uncomfortably, stubbed out the half-smoked cigarette in an old yellow XXXX ashtray that was piled high with butts, then went to light another. 'I've got nothing to say. You can talk to my lawyer.'

'Lawyer?'

'Craig Nash!'

So Nashy *was* involved? Craig Nash was the celebrity defence lawyer who had defended the Monroe twins during the *X* case. High profile indeed and very expensive. I continued with the approach I'd decided on earlier. 'Your son is missing. I've got reason to believe he may have come to harm.'

She stopped short of lighting a fresh cigarette, the lighter flame millimetres from the end. Her hands were shaking like the old boy who sat in the pub all day nursing a schooner and watching the races. 'Wesley?'

'No. Cory.' Without asking, I sat down in the other chair.

'Cory?' She continued lighting the cigarette. 'He's no son of mine.'

'When was the last time you saw him?'

'At the court case.'

'Do you hate him?'

'Damn right I hate him. The little fat bastard. Took everything.'

'Hmm, doesn't seem fair.'

'It's not fair. It was Barry who ripped him off, not me. I was his mother, for God's sake.'

Was her use of the past tense a way of expressing her feelings towards a son she had disowned, or a son that was no longer with us? 'You are still his mum.'

'No.' She took a drag of the cigarette, then stubbed it out. This appeared to be a nervous tick.

'What does Barry think of it all?'

'Wouldn't know.' She leaned over the table and slid out another cigarette from the pack. 'Don't care.'

'But at least you've got the appeal coming up, eh?' I was talking as if we were friends.

'How do you know all this?'

'I'm a detective, remember?'

'I remember you was kicked out of the police force.'

Ah, so she did recognise me. Not such a twat after all, Tetley. 'No, not kicked out. Left voluntarily.'

'Couldn't handle the pressure, eh?' She lit another cigarette.

'Something like that. So, when's the appeal?'

'There is no appeal,' she snapped.

'Right. Too expensive?'

'Mate, can you fuck off?'

'Sorry. I don't mean to pry.'

'Yes, you do. That's why you're here.'

There was a deep rumble in the distance, but it wasn't thunder.

Patty narrowed her eyes and leaned in. 'You don't want to be here when he gets home.'

She was right. I didn't fancy a confrontation with Mick Brennan. Rising from the chair, I pulled out a business card from my pocket. 'Can I leave you this?' I said, placing it on the table.

Patty picked it up and skimmed it onto the road.

The rumble was getting closer. By the time I got into the car, started the engine and pulled away, the hulk on wheels was coming down the roadway. When we passed, and although we both wore sunglasses, he stared into my eyes. *Did he recognise me? Did he remember me from the foyer of the Milton that morning?* I needed to tread carefully. Jenny had already warned me to stay away from him. Of course, that would never happen. If he had something to do with Cory's disappearance, which I was beginning to suspect he had, our paths would inevitably cross.

A possible scenario was forming in my mind as I drove back to Kirra. If Patty won the appeal, it meant she'd be open to counter sue and possibly take back her fortune and a decent compensation payout. And with Nashy on her side, that was definitely a possibility. But Nashy didn't come cheap, neither did a high-profile court case. For these things, she needed money. Enter Mick Brennan, extortionary extraordinaire. He could easily get his hands on that kind of money. The Wasps owned most of the tattoo parlours in the Northern Rivers area, along with bars and brothels—not to mention the alleged drug dealings and money laundering capers—but my guess was that he'd worked out a plan to get his hands on Cory's fortune while getting Cory to pay for it by squeezing him for the money required for the appeal. Had this caused Cory to run? Was he in hiding? Or was he being held against his will by The Wasps bikie gang? Or had Mick Brennan killed him? I was getting way ahead of myself. Why was Brennan at the Milton that morning? Had his attention moved to Wesley? Had he found out that Wesley now had control of the money? These scenarios made sense, but they were nothing more than fanciful conjecture. One thing was for sure, though, before heading home, I'd be swinging into the office and adding Mick Brennan to the list of suspects.

25

It was after 5.00 pm when I arrived back at Ruby Street. Elvis had changed into a casual polo shirt and shorts. He seemed chirpier than earlier. Excited even.

'Still on for that drink? I'm thinking of a stroll down to Greenmount Surf Club for a change. What do you think?' he asked, handing me a cold stubby.

'Yeah, no worries. I'll just get changed.' I was heading to my room when my phone rang. It was Jenny. 'Hey, Jen.'

'Hey. Are you home?'

'Yeah, just got back.'

'Stay there. I'm five minutes away.' She hung up.

'Everything alright?' Elvis asked, reading my puzzled expression.

'I think so. It was just Jenny. She's on her way here.' But it wasn't alright. The rushed urgency in Jenny's tone told me something was up. Had she found out I'd been dangerously close to Brennan?

Elvis' expression reverted to the sad puppy dog face. 'I suppose she can come with us.'

I guess he'd been looking forward to some time with just the two of us.

'Sounds like she was on her way somewhere. Probably just popping in to pick something up.' Heading off to my room, I changed into a T-shirt and shorts. When I returned, Jenny was standing in the hallway with an arm on Elvis' shoulder.

'Shit. Is everything okay?' I was gripped by a sudden fear that something may have happened to one of Elvis' loved ones.

'Yes, fine,' Jenny said.

Elvis wiped an arm across his eyes and sniffled. *Was he crying?*

'What's happening, mate?'

He pushed past me and hitched his thumb towards Jenny as if to say, ''Ask her'.

'We've got to go.'

'Where?'

'Come on. I'll explain in the car.' She headed out the front door.

I wanted to check on Elvis first, see if he was okay, but there was no time. Jenny was already in the car and starting the engine. 'See you in a bit, Elv. I'll be right back. It's early so we can still go for that drink.' There was no reply.

'What did you say to Elvis?' I asked, climbing into the car.

'Nothing, just that I needed you for a while. Next thing I know, he starts blubbering. Is he okay?'

'Something's going on. I'll find out when we get back. So, what's so important and where are we going?' I asked as we pulled away from the kerb in her late model MINI.

'We got a call from Northern Rivers Police this afternoon, said they'd found a burned-out car with Queensland plates in Bangalow National Park.'

I already knew where this was going. Jenny also knew I'd clicked right away, but she continued anyway.

'It's registered to Cory Evans.'

'Really?'

'Yep. And uhm … there was a body inside.'

Shit. That I didn't see coming. 'Is it Cory?'

'Too early to ascertain an identity. The body's in a bad state. So bad, in fact, they didn't even realise it was there at first.'

'Will there be enough to extract DNA?'

'All I know so far is what I've just told you. Apart from, they think it was a suicide.'

'Suicide?'

'Yeah, there was no sign of a collision. Looks like he just drove into the forest, and …'

'Bloody hell. Freckles.'

We headed south along the M1 through northern New South Wales, then took the Byron Bay exit, but swung west towards the hinterland instead of east to the popular seaside town. Bangalow was a little village nestled in the McPherson Ranges.

Jenny had the directions in her phone via Google Maps, but when we turned into a narrow laneway covered by a thick forest canopy, she lost the signal. The lane was long and winding and for a moment we considered turning back until we came across a police patrol car waiting for us in a small circular car park. Next to it was a paddy wagon and a blue, unmarked Toyota.

A young police constable tipped his hat when Jenny showed him her badge. 'A bit of a hike, I'm afraid through there, but they're waiting for you.'

'Thank you.'

Luckily, he didn't ask to see my badge, which he probably should have done. But I didn't stick around to point out his rookie error. I was on the tail of Jenny, struggling to keep up with her.

The track was only wide enough for a compact car to pass through. I noticed fresh tyre marks in a patch of mud. There were no other tracks, so it was obvious that vehicles didn't use it.

The young cop wasn't kidding when he said it was a bit of a hike. Must have been a couple of kilometres, but we knew we were getting close when the fresh smell of the forest became tainted with the aroma of burning rubber. Another thirty metres and we entered a clearing, in the centre of which was the burned-out shell of what would once have been a late model MINI, identical to Jenny's. Two plain clothes detectives, one male, one female, approached us, while two constables were hanging a barrier of crime scene tape around the car.

'Hi. Detective Constable Kelly Blake,' the female detective said, holding out a hand to Jenny.

'DI Jenny Radford.'

'This is my boss, DI Geoff Richards.'

Jenny shook hands with them both. 'This is—'

'Scotty Stephens,' Geoff said. 'Didn't know you were back on the police force, mate?'

'He's with me,' Jenny interjected. 'Let's just say he's helping us with our inquiries.'

'Right. Interesting.'

It was obvious he was a prat, but I shook his hand anyway. I needed to keep them on side because although Jenny outranked them both, she was out of her jurisdiction, so they could have insisted I leave.

Kelly was more friendly. 'Hi.' We shook hands and when our eyes met, there was a lingering. *Or did I imagine that?*

I realised I hadn't when Jenny shot me a sharp glance. 'Okay, so what have we got?' she asked Kelly.

Perhaps in a moment of misogynistic FOMO, Geoff took over. '2022 Mini Cooper.' We followed as he led the way to the car. 'The plates were cactus, melted, but we managed to get the VIN. When we realised who the car belonged to, we called you guys. Not sure why we had to do that, but there you go.'

Kelly rolled her eyes towards us as an apology.

'And the occupant?'

'Uhm … dead. Obviously.'

Although his sarcasm was pissing us both off, we remained professional.

'Any way of identification, I mean?' Jenny asked.

'See what you reckon.' He pulled open the driver's door.

Jenny lifted a hand to her mouth and gasped. Kelly looked away. I fixed my eyes on the flaky black piece of charcoal that was slumped in what was once the front seat. Geoff's gaze was fixed firmly on me.

'If he had a licence on him or anything, it was destroyed.' Kelly said. 'Forensics are on the way. Hopefully we can get a DNA sample.'

'Who found him?' I asked. Peering in through the door.

Kelly pulled out a notebook and read out loud. 'A Mister Dev Kahany and his wife Sutra. Avid hikers apparently. Came across it this afternoon.'

I was wandering slowly around the scene, scanning the area near the car. Because the ground was quite moist, there were copper's footprints everywhere. 'Can we open the boot?'

Jenny side glanced Kelly.

Kelly nodded and was about to oblige when Geoff pushed in front of her.

'I'll do it,' he said. 'Wouldn't want to break one of those lovely nails, would we?'

I wanted to smack him. By Jenny's expression, I knew she was thinking the same. Good job for bloody Geoff, we're professionals.

Unfortunately, the boot wouldn't budge. The mechanism under the dashboard was long gone, and we had no tools to force it open. We'd have to be patient and let the forensics do their job.

Jenny handed Kelly her card. 'Let me know as soon as the report comes back.'

'Will do,' Kelly said, taking the card.

'What do you reckon?' I asked as Jenny and I walked back through the forest.

'It's got to be Evans, hasn't it?'

'I guess.'

'Suicide, you think?'

'There'd be easier ways to do it, surely. Hose from the exhaust.'

'Hmm. Let's see what the report brings back.'

The walk back to the car seemed a lot quicker. In no time at all, we were driving out of the forest and back into civilisation.

'Fancy a drink?' Jenny asked, as we zoomed up the M1.

'Yeah, why not?'

26

As soon as Jenny dropped me off at Ruby Street, I remembered my promise to Elvis to come straight back so we could go for a drink. It was 9.45 pm. *'Damn!'* I cussed under my breath, hurrying up the front path.

The house was dark and quiet. He must have gone to bed. Creeping across the living room, something suddenly startled me.

'Where were you?' It was Elvis' voice.

The light switch was close by, so I flicked it on.

Elvis was sitting in an armchair, still dressed in his polo shirt and shorts, as if he'd been waiting for me.

'Sorry, mate. Got called away on some important business.'

'Jenny, of course. Very important, eh?'

'No, it's about the Freckles case.'

There was no reaction, which was very odd. The mere mention of Freckles two days earlier had brought on a wave of excitement.

'What's going on, Elvis?' I asked, dropping into the other armchair.

'I'm thinking of going back to Melbourne.'

'What?'

'The olds are there. The family.'

'But you love it up here. And the business.' It was over twenty-years ago when Elvis moved up from Victoria. His parents had bought the house on Ruby Street while he was studying for his degree at Southern Cross University. After graduating, he'd stayed in Queensland, started his own business, then eventually purchased the house. I'd lived with him ever since, and in all that time, I'd never once heard him talk about going back to Melbourne.

'The business is cactus, mate.'

'Why? What's happened?'

'Lost the Melany account.'

'The developer?' Although I had very little knowledge of his business, I knew the Melany account was huge. When he'd snagged it about fifteen years ago, his business changed from a one-man high-street tax return specialist to a trendy accountancy firm. Melany was arguably one of the biggest property developers on the Gold Coast, with their logo plastered over a dozen or more new high-rise projects along the length of the strip.

Elvis nodded. 'Yep, and now all the other accounts are starting to pull out as well.'

'But why?' For all the years of partying, barracking loudly for Essendon Footy Club, and being the general larrikin, Elvis was actually a respected local businessman in his day job.

'I fucked up. Simple as that.'

'How?'

'Made an error with this year's tax return.'

'They're not going to worry about one little error, surely not after all these years.'

'A few million dollars, mate. That's not a little error. And now they're considering taking legal action.'

'Shit!'

'Yep. Big stinky shit!'

During renovations of the old fibro house years ago, Elvis had the wall knocked out between the tiny kitchen and the equally small living room to create an open-plan kitchen diner. The kitchen was only a few steps to the fridge and although we kept most of the alcohol in the industrial, glass doored refrigerator in the man shed, we always kept a few coldies in the kitchen fridge. Within a few seconds, I was up and back with two stubbies. 'Here you go, mate,' I said, twisting off the tops and handing one to Elvis. 'We'll get through this, buddy. We always do.' Over the years, we'd had our share of troubles, as most people do, but we'd always rallied when one of us was down. I suddenly wished our Pommy friend, Tetley, was here. The three of us were tight. We had the kind of bond that could withstand treacherous bouts of banter that would bring most people to tears, while maintaining a supportive and strong friendship that most would envy.

'Not this time, Scotty. If they take me to court, I'll lose everything.'

'No, mate. You're just not seeing the situation for what it really is. It's not like you embezzled them or anything like that, skimming money to an offshore account. It was a genuine mistake. No court is gonna condemn you for human error.'

'You don't understand, they're a multi-billion-dollar company. They'll crush me.'

'Yeah, I know, but what *they* don't realise is that they're dealing with Elvis and Scotty Stephens.'

This should have at least brought on a smile, but there was no reaction. My best mate was hurting, afraid, and it was breaking my heart. 'Sleep on it, mate. I reckon you'll have a clearer head in the morning.'

'I haven't slept for over a month.' He stood and placed the untouched beer on the coffee table.

It was lunchtime the next day when Jenny texted me to say the forensic results were back. I'd spent the morning in the surf. Elvis was still in bed when I'd left just before dawn. He was at work by the time I got back. After arranging to meet Jenny for lunch in Surfers, driving up the coast for the third day running made me feel like I was working back at the Surfers Paradise Police Station, although there seemed to be a lot more traffic on the roads these days.

Jenny was waiting for me at Omeron Café in Chevron Island. We'd decided to stay clear of Surfers central because of the

Schoolies festival, opting instead for the more village-like feel of Chevron only a stone's throw away from the metropolis.

'Hey.' Jenny rose from one of the alfresco tables on the street and we kissed each other's cheeks. 'I've already ordered. Burger and chips.' She knew me well.

As soon as I sat down, a waitress parked two tall lattes in front of us.

'So … ' I said, scraping the top off the frothy coffee with a teaspoon before putting it in my mouth.

'So …' Jenny performed the same manoeuvre. 'Still waiting on the toxicology report, but there were no fingerprints. No fingers actually, and as we know, the corpse was beyond recognition due to the extensive burning. But the forensics have managed to extract a DNA sample.'

'Awesome. So, we'll know for sure if it's Cory or not.'

'Not really. We have his fingerprints on file from the couple of altercations he had last year, but no DNA.'

'Right. So, we'll need to get some.'

'A sample from his apartment, perhaps? Or worst-case scenario, a swab from Wesley or one of the parents. At least that will prove the corpse is or isn't related to them.'

'Yep, I can do that.' Recalling the state of Cory's bedroom when Wesley had shown it to me, including the bathroom, Cory's DNA would be everywhere.

Our food arrived and my attention switched back to Elvis.

'Sounds like he's suffering from depression or anxiety, or both,' Jenny said. Employed in the police force all our working lives, we were both familiar with these forms of mental illness.

'I've got to help him, Jen. He's always been there for me. When my mum was killed, and when the shit hit the fan during the *X* case, etc, etc, there's always been one constant in my life.'

'Elvis!' We spoke in unison.

27

'Hey mate. Are you home?' It was mid-afternoon. I was pretty sure Wesley wouldn't be venturing out into the land of Schoolie zombies emerging from their dark apocalyptic lairs.

'Yes I am.'

'Can I come up and see you please, bud? I've got some important news.'

'The New South Wales Police already called last night. Said they've found Cory's other car.'

'Did they? Right. Well, it's about that.'

'Have they found him?' His voice shook with emotion.

'I can be there in about twenty minutes.'

'Okay, text me when you're in the foyer. I'll come down and fetch you.'

Knowing that parking would be a problem at that time of the day, I'd cruised north along the esplanade searching for a spot. One didn't come up until halfway between Surfers and Main Beach. The walk back was pleasant enough, though. It was late spring and there was already some warmth in the sun.

'Hey Scotty!' A brightly coloured VW Kombi trundled by with a bunch of kids hanging out the windows. Once again, my disguise of a baseball cap and sunnies was proving useless.

The hub of the Schoolies festival was on Cavill Avenue. Stages and market stalls were set up all within a temporary compound. Even though I approached Surfers at the northern end via Elkhorn

Avenue, there were still teenagers everywhere. I pitied the police officers on duty that week. I'd done my fair share of Schoolie shifts when I was in uniform. Breaking up brawls, holding back the hair of young girls as they puked in the gutter, weeding out the Toolies, who were there purely to cause trouble.

As usual, the Milton foyer was a welcomed relief. Entering those glass sliding doors was like passing through a dimensional wormhole from an apocalyptic, utopian world into a haven of peace and serenity.

When I didn't get a reply to my text, I worried Wesley had gone out or just wasn't answering his phone. When I rang him and it went to message bank, I was more than a little peeved.

'Scotty.' The voice was familiar.

Looking up, I saw Wesley standing by the lifts, beckoning me towards him with a hand.

We got into the lift and although the journey up to the penthouse only took a few seconds, it was one of those awkward, silent moments where you felt the need to speak but didn't.

We entered the apartment and headed straight for the kitchen. Wesley went to the fridge while I climbed onto a stool at the bench.

'Drink?'

'Got a Coke?'

He nodded and lifted out two cans of Pepsi, but instead of joining me on the stools, he remained standing behind the bench like a stout barman. 'So … you said you have some news?'

We opened our cans in unison with a loud *shwerpt!*

'I do, mate.'

'Have you found him? Is he okay?' The desperation in his voice seemed out of place compared to his usual matter-of-fact manner.

In preparation for delivering the devastating news, I took a long sip of Pepsi. 'What did the New South Wales Police tell you?'

'Just that Cory's car had been found.'

'Thing is, mate, the car was burned out.'

'What?'

I was regretting my decision to come here alone. But it wasn't like I could have requested a WPC to accompany me. Jenny perhaps. A female presence was always calming at moments like this. I was a PI, not a copper, so I wasn't here to deliver the bad news in an official capacity. My mission was to get a DNA sample.

'And there was a body inside!'

He dropped his Pepsi and lifted his hands to his mouth. The brown liquid fizzed like acid as it spilled across the bench. 'Cory?' His eyes welled with tears.

'We don't know. There's no way of identifying who the person is at the moment.' I purposely didn't point out that the body was burned beyond recognition.

'But. It would have to be him, wouldn't it?' A single, thick tear broke away from the damned deluge and streamed down his cheek. 'Who else would have been driving Cory's car?'

'Well, that's why I'm here, mate. The only way we can find out is to get a DNA sample.'

Wesley's hands were shaking over his mouth.

'I'm really sorry to be the bearer of such bad news.'

'Who would want to hurt Cory?'

I could think of a few people.

'He was the kindest, most thoughtful person you could ever meet.' He was openly crying now.

The detective part of my brain noted his inadvertent use of the past tense. 'There's a chance it may not have been him. Could have been someone who stole the car, or maybe Cory had just sold it, or—'

'No, it's Cory. I just know it is.'

'We won't know for sure unless we can match the DNA sample they have. Would you have anything of Cory's I can take? A hairbrush, his toothbrush or something like that?'

'Sure. Yes. Yes, of course.' As if suddenly realising he'd spilt his drink, he opened the cabinet door beneath the sink, pulled out a roll of kitchen towel and mopped up the liquid.

The vision of Cory's room from the day before entered my mind. Crap everywhere, discarded pizza boxes, soiled clothing. 'Something from his room, perhaps?'

Wesley nodded vigorously, finished his task and threw a heap of soaked paper towel in the bin. 'Yes. No worries. I'll go and get something.'

'Mind if I tag along?' I asked, standing.

Wesley shrugged and headed towards the bedroom wing.

'Holy shit!' I said out load as we entered Cory's room. The space was guest-ready-five-star-hotel-room clean. The king-sized bed was freshly made, with a deep rich doona and a nest of cushions and pillows against the headboard. Gone were the layers of garbage and discarded clothing. There wasn't a single spec on the immaculate carpet. The walls were clean, and the furniture polished. The room smelt of mountain dew with an undercurrent of disinfectant. 'You had the place cleaned?'

'Yes. I wanted it to be nice when Cory got home.'

'You did a bloody good job,' I said, strolling into the room. 'Did Maria do this?'

'No. I got a firm in to do it this morning.'

The bathroom was squeaky clean. Along the marble benchtop was a row of small bottles containing body wash, shampoo and conditioner, as well as a folded hand towel. This really was like a vacant hotel room. 'Is there anything of Cory's left?' I opened the cabinet beneath the sink to see a new shaver still in the packet, a new toothbrush and an unopened tube of toothpaste. There was a can of deodorant, a bottle of David Beckham cologne, nail clippers, and a hairbrush that had never been used.

'Yeah, that's all Cory's. He'd been complaining about how untidy his room was, so I decided to clean it up before he got back.'

My eyes fell on a black comb at the back of the cabinet. It was standing on its edge behind the deodorant and cologne. Lifting it out, I was relieved to see it wasn't new. It was used. There was dust along the bottom of the prongs and fine hairs intertwined. 'Is this Cory's?'

The shrug. 'I guess.'

In my pocket was a plastic resealable bag that I'd brought along for this occasion. 'Brilliant,' I said, scanning the comb closely. The hairs were too small and fine to determine the colour, but hopefully they'd be enough to extract a DNA sample. 'This should be enough.'

Wesley let out a sigh of relief. 'Thank goodness. I thought I'd fucked up there for a minute.'

'Yeah, me too,' I said regarding him. He seemed to be genuinely relieved.

28

Rather than walk all the way back to Main Beach to get the Dub, it was quicker to walk from the Milton to the police headquarters on Ferny Avenue. Entering the building was quite strange. I would have expected a feeling of familiarity after all the years working there as a detective constable, but after just a year of being away from the place, it was as if I'd never worked there. Was the reception area smaller? Had the walls always been that colour? Or had they been painted since I'd left? I didn't remember the place smelling like disinfectant. There was no urge to just breeze in and head up the stairs to where my office used to be. I was a visitor to an unfamiliar place. Thankfully, when I left the police force it was on good terms. There were no enemies left behind—no burnt bridges that would have prevented me from going back. I was relieved to see some familiar faces. Maureen, behind the desk, stern as hell but who always had a soft spot for me. Her smile was most welcoming when I entered the reception.

'Hey Scotty. What brings you around these parts?'

'Hey Mo. I'm here to see—' There was a tap on my shoulder.

Jenny was standing right behind me. I'd texted her while waiting at the pedestrian crossing on Ferny. 'Hey. How'd you go?' There was excited expectation in her tone.

I pulled out the plastic bag from my pocket and held it up.

'Awesome. Mo, can you get this over to forensics right away, please?' She said, taking the bag from my hand. She'd already filled out the necessary forms. 'They're expecting it.'

Mo stapled the bag and the sheets together. 'Sure, ma'am.'

'Come on up,' Jenny said, turning and heading for the stairs.

On the brief journey to the next floor, we passed uniforms and detectives. Some I knew, others I didn't. They all knew me. Most smiled and nodded.

I was pleased to see Jenny had my old office, the best one in the corner. Of course, I'd only occupied it for a few days during the X case, and prior to that, it belonged to DI Des Williams. Unlike these two hard working detectives, I never felt worthy of having it, knowing I hadn't earned it. Whereas Jenny had. It was hard enough just being a woman in the police force, so for her to rise to the top of the ranks and hold the top job was a testament to her skill, her toughness and her determination to succeed.

'Have a seat, mate.' Her use of the term "mate" wasn't delivered like we were friends sharing a beer at the surf club. It was more authoritarian. She was all business. 'Okay. We've launched a joint investigation with the New South Wales Police. If the victim isn't Cory Evans, it shouldn't affect your investigation too much, but if it is ...'

'You'll expect me to back off.'

'Not necessarily.'

'What do you have in mind?'

'We work together.'

This was good news for me. If the burned corpse proved someone other than Cory Evans, I'd be allowed to carry on with the Evans investigation as normal, but if it was him, I'd still be able to continue. This would be an unusual scenario because, in normal circumstances, PIs were usually despised by the police, or not trusted. Thank goodness Jenny was in charge. But I realised she'd be putting her neck on the line to make this happen, so I'd have to make sure I didn't let her down. Her austere expression confirmed that she was thinking just that.

'No worries. I won't let you down, Jen.'

'You'd better not. We'll need to know right away if or when you find out anything at all.'

'Absolutely.'

'We'll be sharing intel.'

'Great.'

'I'll be putting Bradley in charge of the case.'

This news made me smile. I loved Bradley.

The normal time for the results of a DNA test to come through is twenty-four to seventy-two hours. Jenny had insisted we'd only be waiting for the minimum time, but this still meant we wouldn't have anything until the following afternoon.

I didn't want to overstay my welcome, as I could tell Jenny had a lot on her plate by the dark lines under her eyes. After leaving Police HQ, I had one more errand to make, but to do it meant I'd have to run the gauntlet of the zombie herd. Craig Nash's office was in the heart of Surfers. As soon as I stepped across the tramline to the eastern side of Surfers Paradise Boulevard, I was mobbed. Losing count of how many selfies I posed for, handshakes, pats on the back, hugs and kisses from the girls, signing autographs, etc, it took about an hour to get back to Orchid Avenue, which would ordinarily be a two-minute walk.

I'd only been to Nashie's office on one previous occasion. It was during the *X* case when he'd assigned himself as my defence lawyer. Only it turned out he wasn't really defending me at all. He was actually working with the previous mayor to persuade me to cop a plea. That didn't happen, and although charges were never laid against him, I knew he was as bent as a bottle of chips.

The receptionist, although different from the one who greeted me on my previous visit, may well have been a clone of her predecessor. She was blonde, ridiculously perfect and she had an air of being too good for the job she held. Over the last twelve months, I'd identified three kinds of reactions when people met me. There were those who didn't know me—the best kind, those who couldn't hide their surprise, and the third kind who recognised me but played it down or acted as if they couldn't care less. Jacinta was the latter. My Analytic Detective Scanner ran on automatic. I called it my ADS. There was a definite flicker of surprise on the girl's face when I entered the office, followed by a dismissive shudder, as if her inner voice was slapping down the emotion.

'Yes, can I help you?'

'Hi. I'm here to see Craig.'

Jacinta frowned and peered at her computer screen. 'Do you have an appointment?'

'No. We're old mates. I was just passing and wanted to check he hadn't forgotten about our round of golf.' It was well known that Nash was crazy about his golf, often conducting meetings on the Palm Meadows course.

'He is between clients at the moment, but he's asked not to be disturbed.'

'So, he's in the office?'

She nodded.

'Great. I'll go in and surprise him,' I said, heading for his office door.

'I don't think that's a good idea,' Jacinta said, rising from her desk. Luckily, the impractical high-heeled shoes she wore were designed for style, not speed. I was bursting into Nashie's office before she even took a step. 'Craig, me old mate. How are you?'

Australia's highest profile defence lawyer was lying on his back on a leather Chesterfield sofa with his eyes closed. As if suddenly awoken from a deep sleep, he jumped up, startled, with clenched fists. There was a bead of spittle in the corner of his mouth. 'What the hell?'

'I'm so sorry, Mister Nash. He wouldn't listen and came straight in.' It was the classic movie scenario where the hero barges into the villain's office.

'G'day, bloke,' I said, marching towards him with my hands held out as if we were besties.

'Stephens, what the hell are you doing here?' he demanded, standing and ignoring my hand.

'Just in the area. Thought I'd pop in and see you.'

'Liar. You want to know why I'm working for Patty Cummings.' This was why he got the big bucks.

'How do you know that?'

'This is why I get the big bucks.' He was a cocky bugger, but I had to hand it to him, he *was* switched on. 'She called me. Said you'd paid her a visit.'

'I'm looking into the possible disappearance of Cory Evans.'

'Possible?' He rounded his desk and lowered himself into his leather studded chair. 'Is he missing or not?'

'Don't know yet.'

Nash chuckled. 'So, you're harassing people, while little fat Freckles is probably on a yacht in the Bahamas.'

I thought about telling him about the body in the burnt-out car but decided against it. 'You're a criminal defence lawyer. Why would you be interested in Patty Cummings?'

'Because she needs defending, not just against that little prick of a son of hers, but against the system that allowed him to take away everything she owned.'

'There'll be a nice bit of exposure there for you, no doubt.'

'Jacinta, show this person out, will you?'

'You know she can't afford to pay you?'

Ignoring me, Nash opened a leather-bound folder.

'And did you know Mick Brennan's trying to extort the money to pay you from Cory's brother?'

The ADS recorded a definite reaction—a subtle contraction of the brow, a twitch of a pout.

'You certainly wouldn't want to be getting mixed up with the bikies, would you, mate? How would that look?'

'Jacinta.'

Jacinta carefully took my arm and led me out of the office. I didn't resist.

'We both know what Brennan is capable of. I wouldn't want to be *you* for quids,' I called back over my shoulder.

29

The next morning I was keen for a surf, so I headed to the beach wearing my wetsuit and surfboard underarm. But the recent offshore had turned. 'Bugger, bugger, bugger,' I cussed, standing by the surf club. It wasn't even worth getting wet.

Turning with just the hint of a tantrum, I was about to head back home when the sound of mechanical thunder snapped me out of an impending sulk. The engine rumbled loudly three times before extinguishing to silence. Looking up, I saw the unmistakable figure of a bikie kicking out the stand of a customised Harley Davidson. Even though he wore wraparound sunglasses, I could tell he was staring right at me. Loosening the strap of his helmet, he climbed from the bike and marched in my direction. *Shit! Was it Brennan? No, no, not Brennan.* This guy was just as big, but he had a huge, ginger beard. The oil-stained jeans, leather waistcoat over a denim jacket, and the boots were the standard uniform of any bikie, but it was the insignia on the right breast—one, that was also displayed on his back, only bigger—that identified the specific gang. This was one angry Wasp.

I needed to think quickly and defend myself anyway I could. This would have been hard with a lightweight wax encrusted surfboard under one arm, so I placed it down on the grass. The foot soldier sent by his general, no doubt to deliver a single but fatal blow, was coming fast now.

With adrenalin pumping into my system, I clenched my fists and dug my bare feet into the soft ground.

When the terminator was only a few feet away from his mark, the fixed expression of the assassin suddenly broke into a wide smile. 'Fuck me. Scotty Stephens.'

'Huh?' My body was taut and trembling, ready for impact.

'Scotty.' He pulled off his sunglasses. 'It's me.'

'Knackers?'

'Yeah, mate. How are ya?' He threw his arms around me.

'Knackers. I'm good, mate,' I said, pulling away. 'Bloody hell. You had me shitting meself there.'

Throwing back his head, he laughed out loud. 'I know. I'm sorry. You should have seen your face. Ha ha!'

'You bugger!' I was still shaking. Then the realisation that my old schoolmate who, apart from the odd occasion at The Playroom, I hadn't seen since leaving school over twenty -years ago, was now a bikie. 'What's all this?' I asked, gesturing with an arm at his outfit.

'I'm a Wasp.'

'I can see that.' It took me a moment to recall his real name, because I hadn't used it since that unfortunate day in tenth grade. Nigel Kicks (Nige) was a decent league player back in his schooldays—a big front rower. That season the PBC Year 10s went on to win the Southeast Queensland schoolboy championships. There was a team photograph at the end of the game. Thirteen muddy, happy, smiling lads in a half circle with their arms around each other's shoulders as if ready to drop into a scrum. One boy stood in the centre of the pack thrusting the championship trophy up high. It was big Nige Hicks. As he held the large trophy aloft, his shorts had ridden up some. It wasn't until the picture was published in the school magazine that somebody noticed the pudding-sized, pink Brussels sprout protruding from the left leg of his shorts. Word spread through the school like a dose of head lice and that month's magazine became the most popular ever because no one could resist looking at the picture of the Year Ten footy team and the hairy bollock that took centre stage. Nige Hicks was no more. Instead, the lad's status was elevated to new heights when he was christened 'Knackers'—a name that would stick for at least the rest of his school days, and possibly beyond.

He'd been a good mate back in the day, and although he now smelled of engine grease, and petunia oil, I couldn't resist giving him another hug. 'You big smelly fucker.'

He squeezed me tight and for a moment it felt as if he were about to lift me up, swirl me like a baton, then drive me into the ground headfirst like he did to the opposition during his school footy career.

'Buy me a coffee, mister famous detective,' he said, releasing me from his grip.

'Sure.'

We wandered over to the tiny pavilion coffee shop beneath the surf club, and although I had no money on me, my credit was good with Trish, so I ordered two coffees to go.

'Seen you on the news, Scotty. Very impressive,' Knackers said as we waited for our drinks.

'Yeah, well, ya know,' I replied, shrugging off the compliment as always.

'So, what made you become a copper?'

'I don't know. Steady job I guess.'

Trish handed us our coffees in takeaway cups. We strolled across the path to the knee-high wall that retained the sand dunes. The Good Old Boys moved away when they saw Knackers approaching.

'What made you become a bikie?'

Knackers grinned. 'Money for nothing and chicks for free.'

'What happened to the footy? Didn't you sign with The Seagulls?'

'Nah, didn't eventuate. Knee injury. Fucked it up.'

We sipped our coffees, and I wondered if the same thoughts were going through his head as mine. A bikie and a copper, albeit ex-copper, didn't mix well in the usual circumstances. Enemies to the death was more the norm.

'Was you just passing, mate or …?'

'No,' his expression hardened. 'I wanted to come and see you. Brennan doesn't know I'm here.'

'Brennan?'

'Yeah. You're on his radar.'

'What do you mean?'

'In the last couple of days, I've heard your name mentioned on more than one occasion.'

'Why?'

'We both know why.'

'Cory Evans?'

'Yep. I'm just here to warn you, mate. Watch your back. You're getting mixed up in something you don't want to be mixed up in.'

'What do you mean?'

He sipped his coffee and placed it down on top of the wall. 'I've already said too much. Shouldn't even be here.'

'Did Brennan send you?'

Knackers stood and replaced his sunglasses. 'Unfortunately, Scotty, we'll never be mates again. The next time we meet probably won't be under the same circumstances. I'm just giving you the heads up. If you back off now, hopefully we won't meet again.'

'We can be mates. I'm not a copper anymore.' This was a lie. The bikie creed of anarchy and chaos was a million miles from my code of ethics. And we both knew it.

He replaced his helmet.

'What happened to Cory Evans? Do you know?'

'Back off, Scotty. You're getting too close.' He marched back to his motorbike, kicked over the engine, climbed on, then gave a last farewell nod before racing off into the early morning traffic.

30

For the first morning that week, I didn't go to Surfers Paradise. There was no need to see Wesley until the toxicology and the rest of the autopsy results came through. I'd planned on spending at least half of the morning in the surf, then going into the office. That didn't eventuate, so it meant I'd be going into work earlier.

Elvis was still at home when I got back to Ruby Street. He was getting ready to leave for work. 'Hey, mate,' he said cheerfully when I walked through the door. His mood had completely changed from the day before.

'Hey.' I propped up my surfboard in the corner of the hallway.

'Listen, bud. Take no notice of anything I said yesterday. It's all good. Not as bad as it sounds.'

'You were pretty upset.'

'Nah.' He shook off my words with a nonchalant shrug. 'It's nothing I can't handle.'

Placing a hand on his shoulder, I said, 'Are you sure, mate?'

'Yeah. My oath.'

I wasn't buying it. The nervous tick he was trying to play down reminded me of the countless twitchy suspects I'd interviewed over the years. 'How about we have a session in the man shed tonight?'

'Sounds good. We haven't done that for a while.' He was right, we hadn't. When Tetley was here, we'd end up in the shed at least twice a week, every week. Maybe it was because the footy season had finished, and I'd been busy out at Tallebudgera with the last case that it seemed so long ago. Or maybe it was because our lives had changed. We had changed.

'It's a date.'

'Awesome. I'll swing by the bottle shop on my way home from work and stock up.'

'Cool, see you tonight.' Heading to my room, I wanted to believe my old mate was okay, but I knew he wasn't.

On my return to the kitchen after having a shower and changing into the mandatory workwear of linen shirt, shorts and sandals, Elvis had already left. Before making a bowl of cereal, I turned on the TV and switched the channel to *9News*. 'Shit!' I said out loud. The cheeky smiling face of Freckles filled the screen.

'Police have yet to confirm that the body found in the burnt-out car in Northern New South Wales is that of Cory Evans, known and loved by millions as Freckles.' The reporter's voice was offscreen until the image changed to the live commentary of a young woman standing in front of Cory's burnt out car in the Bangalow Forest. 'The Northern Rivers Police have yet to comment, but it's believed Queensland Police have been notified.'

Inevitably, the news would break sooner or later. Once the results were returned that afternoon, it would be big news, and I realised that what I'd originally thought wasn't even a case, could prove to be another high-profile extravaganza.

My plan for the day while we awaited the for DNA results was to summarise the case. Apart from Cassie Evans, and the fact that she'd never even met her half-brother, and of course Mick Brennan, I'd spoken with everyone relevant to the case. So now it was time to ponder and reflect. A good session with the whiteboard was pending.

The tide was high when I strolled around Kirra Point towards Coolangatta. I'd often walk to work; it was usually a very pleasant few minutes' stroll. Looking over my shoulder at the sweep of the bay, the distant silhouette of Surfers Paradise at the northern tip sat stolid like the sprawling metropolis it had become over the last forty years.

'Good morning, Scotty,' a passer-by said. I didn't have a clue who they were, but this happened quite a lot these days.

'Good morning.'

Since losing my dog, Romeo, to the hands of the Tallebudgera killer, the office seemed gloomy and quiet. His bed and toys were still in the corner. I had yet to gain the strength to move them. Each day as I climbed the stairs from the street, I half expected to hear him bark. Jenny and Elvis had suggested I replace him, but that wasn't going to happen.

With a cup of takeaway coffee in one hand and a whiteboard marker in the other, I gathered my thoughts in front of the whiteboard.

In the centre of the board was a picture of Cory, not of Freckles, the cute chubby little chap who we all loved, but the older version, the awkward young man who people still recognised but now pitied rather than applauded. Until I knew better, I'd work under the assumption that the body found in his car was him. Part of me still hoped it wasn't, but my gut feeling was telling me it was.

Although Wesley wasn't the prime suspect, he was emerging as the principal player, seeing as he lived with Cory and was the last to see him.

Placing his picture to the right of his brother's, there was a resemblance between the two, but it was only apparent if you squinted and tilted your head to one side.

So, Wesley Cummings. *What did I have so far?* I wrote the following on the board:

- Moved from caravan park to Surfers Paradise penthouse two months ago
- Last person to see his brother alive

- Took receipt of Cory's fortune
- Did he harbour any bad feelings towards his brother? Or was he forever grateful to him as he suggested for plucking him from a pending life of poverty?

Motive? Nothing apparent at the moment. Jealousy maybe?

What I didn't understand was why Cory would transfer all his assets to his brother's bank account. Was he expecting a challenge from his parents? Patty openly spoke of an appeal. Did Barry also have similar plans? *Hmm.* I'd need to dig deeper.

The next picture, and to the left of Cory, was his father, Barry Evans.

- Authoritarian and shrewd businessman. He controlled his son's career and his life from the very beginning
- Lived a double life for many years, keeping a mistress and a secret daughter from his family
- Was publicly discarded when Cory took over his own affairs
- Lost everything, supposedly, when Cory sued him for loss of earnings, etc
- Humiliated by the media when details of his double life made the news
- May have been planning to launch an appeal

Motive? It was widely believed that Barry had stashed away the largest portion of Cory's fortune in an overseas account. Unlike his ex-wife, he wasn't thrown into poverty when he lost the case. Now successful in the car sales industry, he still had a good life. If he wanted to harm his son, why now? Did Cory find proof that the payout he received was only a fraction of what he'd really earned? *Hmm.* I'd see if I could get Bradley to delve a little deeper into his affairs.

Patty Cummings (née Evans), mother of Cory and Wesley, ex-wife of Barry.

- Like her husband, lost everything when she was sued by Cory. Unlike her husband, Patty was forced to sell her beautiful house on Currumbin Beach and move into a caravan park on the Tweed. Hates her son for what he did to her
- Is mixed up with Mick Brennan, The Wasps bikie gang boss.
- Possibly launching an appeal

Motive? If she was about to launch an appeal, would she want to see her son harmed? Did something happen recently to make her panic? How did she get involved with Mick Brennan, and why?

Mick Brennan. Wasps bikie gang boss, nasty piece of work and living with Patty Cummings.

- May see Cory as a potential cash cow
- Probably living with Patty only because of this
- Visited Cory's apartment. Was he demanding money from Cory?

Motive? If he had killed Cory, why would he be at his apartment if he knew Cory wasn't there? Had his focus moved to Wesley? Did he find out that Wesley now controlled the cash?

Netty Slater, personal trainer and potential business partner.

- Invested her life savings and secured loans for joint business venture
- Was charged for unlawful entry of Cory's home

Motive? Angry that Cory pulled out of the deal at the last minute, leaving her potentially broke. Needed money from Cory to fend off bankruptcy.

Finally, Cassie Evans. Although I had her on the board. I didn't make a list for her or speculate over a motive, purely because I knew very little about her. During our brief meeting, I got the impression she was just a kid who had been curious for some time to meet her half-brothers. She'd never met Cory or even Wesley a few days ago. Motive? Apart from jealousy, which was pretty weak, I couldn't think of one. Unless … *hmm*. What if she got wind that Cory was going to expose her father and take him to court again? Would this be enough of a motive to commit harm to her eldest sibling? Probably not.

My phone rang. 'Hello.'

'Hi, Mister Stephens?' Bugger me. It was Cassie.

'Is that you Cassie?'

'Yes, it is … ' There was a rushed sense of panic in her tone.

'What's up?'

'I was supposed to meet Wesley this morning, but he didn't show up.'

'Right. Could he have slept in?'

'No. We've agreed to meet every morning this week while Schoolies is on. I've tried ringing his mobile, but he isn't answering.'

'Okay.'

'Can I come and see you?' She asked.

'Uhm … yeah, if you think you need to.'

'Great. I have the address on the card you gave me. I'll be in Coolangatta in about half an hour.' She hung up.

I immediately called Wesley's number. It rang out until Wesley's voice said. 'Leave your number. I'll get back to you.'

31

When the door at the bottom of the stairs opened and closed, my heart sunk, and I wondered how long it would be before I stopped grieving. The sound activated the memory of my dog, Romeo, snapping from a deep sleep, hackles flaming, suddenly alert and erect on his bed before racing towards the door, barking and growling. Then, depending on who the visitor was, if foe, he'd continue to bark, proclaiming his territory, until the intruder bowed down and begged for mercy. But if friend, the bark would morph into a yapping, wild-tail-whipped greeting, which would see him launch through the air while emitting a fine stream of urine. Then there was the odd occasion when the trespasser, although unknown to him, would radiate that natural animal-lover authority and he'd fall silent, doggy-blushing, while he was being stroked and asked, 'And what's all this noise about then, boy? Eh? What's all this noise about?' These moments would usually end up with him lying on his back with his legs splayed while his tummy was vigorously rubbed. Some bloody guard dog.

Choking back the emotional strain of those vivid, recent memories, I rotated the whiteboard so the list was facing the wall and waited for my guest to enter. After the *clump, clump, clump* on linoleum, there was a light knock on the door.

'Come in.'

The door opened slowly with the usual squeak and Cassie cautiously entered the room.

'G'day, Cas. How are ya?'

'Good, thanks.'

'Cool. Come on in. Take a seat.' I gestured to the empty chair on that side of my desk.

She crept across the room with her head slightly lowered, as if she were returning from the cinema toilet in the middle of a movie.

'Can I get you anything?'

'A drink of water, perhaps? The taxi ride down here was horrendous.'

Bugger. Apart from my gym bottle, I didn't have any cold water in the fridge. 'How about we go for a walk, get some fresh air?'

'That would be good.'

As usual, Coolangatta esplanade was busy with walkers, joggers, bike riders, and those annoying bastards on electric scooters and skateboards, but it was always a pleasant stroll. When I had things on my mind that required some time for rumination, a walk from Kirra to Snapper Rocks, where I'd sit on the seawall and stare out at sea, before heading back, would be the required tonic.

When we rounded The Strand, crossed at the zebra crossing by the surf club, and cut through the kids playground, Cassie took a drink from the water fountain. I'd offered to buy her a drink from the coffee shop kiosk, but she'd turned me down.

'Better?' I asked as she wiped her mouth with the back of her hand and nodded. 'Sure you don't want a soft drink or a coffee?'

'No, I'm good.'

We strolled side by side south towards Greenmount.

'So, you wanted to see me?'

'Yes, it's probably nothing, though. In fact, I feel a bit silly now, coming all this way.' She made the trip from Surfers Paradise sound like she'd just flown in from Sydney or Melbourne. For some folk, travelling this far south—twenty-minutes' drive, depending on the traffic—would only happen if they had a reason to be there. Heaven forbid they should ever have to venture over the border to Tijuana (aka the Tweed). Thankfully, this attitude was changing, impart to the developers who, after recognising the area as a gem in the rough, were building expensive apartment blocks and lifting the area to the state of desirability that was quickly becoming out of reach for most.

'What's happened?'

'After not being able to reach Wesley on his phone, I went to the Milton and got the concierge to call the apartment. There was still no reply.'

I had to remember that Cassie had only just met her half-brother a few days ago, so in reality, she would know very little about him. Although he was nineteen, he was still a man, so he could come and go as he pleased. But Cassie seemed genuinely concerned. I was surprised, though, that she didn't mention the news that Cory may have been found dead. Perhaps she hadn't heard? 'You could have told me this over the phone.'

'I know, but I wanted to talk to you.'

'Okay.' I lowered my head in the I'm-all-ears manner as we walked.

'I'm worried about Wesley.'

A side glance and a rising brow were the prompts for her to continue.

'I've got to know him quite well over the last couple of days. He uhm … he's quite a complex character.'

'In what way?'

'I get the impression he's hiding something.'

'About Cory, you mean?'

'We haven't spoken about Cory much, can you believe? He changes the subject each time the conversation sways towards our brother.'

'Some resentment, you reckon?'

'Oh yes, definitely.'

'Jealousy?'

She nodded. 'He doesn't like him very much. He snapped at me yesterday when I asked if he'd heard from Cory yet. "Life's not all about my fucking brother, you know!" he yelled in the coffee shop. It was the opposite of his usual sombre mood.'

'Hmm. The impression he's given me so far is that he's eternally grateful to Cory for rescuing him from the caravan park.'

'Yes, I thought that too at first.'

'Putting on a bit of an act, you reckon?'

The nod again.

'Cassie, did you see the news this morning?'

'No. Why?'

I told her about the body being found in Cory's burnt-out car.

She gasped and her face turned white. Her eyes searched mine as if expecting an impending punchline. 'Cory?'

'We won't know until the DNA results come back.'

'Oh my God.' Now her eyes were moving from side to side as if she were speed reading. 'Does Dad know? Why hasn't he called me?'

'I don't know. Maybe he doesn't want to interrupt your Schoolies break.'

'Schoolies? That's a joke. I can't wait until it's over.'

'Would Wesley go to your dad for comfort, or Patty perhaps?' I asked, keeping the conversation on topic.

'God, no. Neither of them. I *can* confirm he definitely hates them both.'

'Where would he go?'

'I would have thought he'd come to me.'

'Hmm … did he seem agitated in any way when you saw him yesterday?'

'He's always agitated. Nervous. It's just the way he is.'

'Did he say anything to you at all about receiving any threats or …?'

'Only from the Schoolies. Apparently, he was set up on at the beginning of the week. They called him a Toolie and bashed him.'

'Anything else?'

She shrugged. 'Basically, our conversation revolved around his hatred for Cory.'

This surprised me. On the couple of occasions we'd spoken, he'd only expressed his gratitude and respect for his brother. I decided to give Wesley another call on his mobile. If he had disappeared, I'd need to let Jenny know right away, but if he'd just slept in, Cassie's concerns would be null and void. The phone rang the allocated number of times before switching to voicemail.

32

I gave Cassie a lift back to Surfers in the Dub. I'd briefly given Jenny the heads up over the phone about Wesley's possible disappearance. She arranged for Bradley to meet me at the Milton. Part of me hoped Wesley was just hiding in his room, but the cynical detective in me suspected something more sinister.

During the trip, Cassie told me about her loathing for the Schoolies festival. On a couple of occasions, she'd actually considered leaving and going home. Apparently, her so-called friends were driving her crazy. The whole hooting, giggling teenager scene just wasn't her vibe.

The late morning traffic in Surfers was horrendous. Parking would be a nightmare. Just before dropping Cassie off at The Island resort, I had an idea. The resort was booked out with kids, which meant in theory, the underground car park should have been just about empty. Cassie's fob key opened the garage door on the Cavill Avenue side of the building. My hunch had proved correct. Rows of empty car spaces greeted us. That universal feeling of pride, that only a bloke can experience, overcame me as I parked close to the lifts. Regardless of what happened for the rest of the day, nothing would top the satisfaction of scoring a great parking spot. Coming first in the world surf championships, fathering a child or winning the lotto wouldn't come close. A blokey thing. I know.

The walking dead were already stirring as I made my way towards the Milton. The mandatory selfies, handshakes and hugs from youngsters exclaiming how great it was to meet me, slowed me down a little, but just as I turned into Orchid Avenue, my phone rang. It was Bradley. Full of apologies, he informed me that something had come up, and he'd be about an hour late. I was just entering the hotel foyer.

Knowing it was hopeless trying to convince the concierge to let me up to Cory's apartment, but hopeful because a young lady, who I hadn't encountered before, attended the desk, I tried anyway. But to no avail. She did call up to the apartment, but there was no reply.

Damn. What would I do for the next hour? Turning away from the concierge desk, I almost bumped into a young woman. 'Oops, sorry.'

'Scott?'

Although I didn't recognise her at first, there was a familiarity in the voice. The gentle transatlantic tone. She wore a daggy pair of tracky pants, a black Bugs Bunny hoody and pink thongs. An NYC baseball cap and the biggest pair of sunglasses I'd ever seen covered most of her head. Under her arm she carried a small, white, curly haired pooch. 'Natalie?'

'Yes. Are you here to see me?'

'No, no, I was just passing. Well, I'm here to see someone else.'

'Is it about Cory?'

Then I remembered that Natalie Hinderman, arguably Australia's biggest Hollywood export, had worked with Freckles on a couple of movies. She must have heard the news and been upset, no doubt. I acted as if I didn't know any of this. 'Do you know, Cory?'

'Of course I do. The little darlin'. Have you got time to come up for a coffee?'

'Sure.'

Lowering her head, she strolled casually towards the residential lifts at the farthest end of the corridor. If she was harbouring any hatred towards me from the *X* case, she wasn't showing it. When we climbed into the lift, she swiped her key card and pressed the top button marked 'P'.

'So how have you been?' she asked as we travelled towards the top floor.

'Good, yourself?' I was feeling a little star struck in the same way I'd felt during the last time we'd met at the beachfront home on Hedges Avenue. Her down-to-earth attitude had relaxed me then, and it was doing the same now. 'Listen, I'm really sorry about what happened to—'

She cut me off in mid-sentence. 'I know.' The lift dinged, and the door slid open into the second penthouse on the top floor. There were two doors in the lift, the one we'd entered opened into Natalie's place. The opposite one into Cory's.

The mirrored car was suddenly flooded with bright daylight. Natalie stepped into an expansive atrium, bent down and put the dog on the marble tiled floor. I'd thought Cory's penthouse was impressive, but this place, *bloody hell!* Natalie had obviously re designed it. The house on Hedges with an infinity pool that started inside the home and lead out to the garden and seemed to become one with the shoreline, was impressive, but this was a palace in the sky.

I guess part of being a good actor was having the ability to change your appearance. Natalie had certainly done that. If she hadn't spoken to me, I would have breezed past her without a second thought.

We made our way into an enormous open-plan kitchen. The view from the floor to ceiling windows cleverly blocking out everything below gave the appearance that we were hovering over the beach, even though it was a couple of hundred metres away.

'Wow!'

'Nice, eh?' She pulled off the cap and removed her sunglasses. Blonde hair with a hint of red cascaded over her shoulders.

'Amazing.'

Without asking, Natalie opened the door of the most enormous fridge I'd ever seen, pulled out a jug of iced tea and poured it into two tall glasses. The little dog, meanwhile, had its head almost buried in a bowl of dried biscuits.

Glancing around the spacious apartment, I realised the layout was similar to Cory's, only bigger and more tastefully decorated. Posters from some of the many movies Natalie had starred in adorned the walls.

With glass in hand, I followed her out to a manicured terrace, which sat in the sky like an oasis of palm trees around a sparkling pool. 'Wow!' Again, I couldn't help myself.

'I don't hold you responsible,' Natalie said, taking a seat at a large glass table, and gesturing for me to take a seat opposite her. 'I just wanted you to know that.' As she sipped her tea, I noticed a tremble in her voice. Understandable.

Nodding gently, I swayed the conversation from memories of the *X* case back to Cory. 'So, you know Cory quite well?'

Her expression warmed and the dimples in her cheeks appeared when she smiled. 'Freckles. Bless him. I loved that kid.'

The use of the past tense went into the mental notebook. 'When was the last time you saw him?'

'A couple of months, maybe.'

'Was he okay?'

She sighed and cocked her head slightly to one side. 'He hasn't been okay for a long time.'

'What do you mean?'

'Poor little bugger. He hasn't had the best life.'

Hmmm. Present tense. Reading between the lines, I assumed when using the past tense; she was referring to Freckles, the adorable little kid, while the present tense was used for Cory, the troubled young man.

'You would have gotten to know him well back in the day.' Now it was my turn to sip, keeping the conversation moving casually.

'I did. I was like his second mum. Well, his only mum. Patty was never around.'

'What about Barry?'

'*Phf.* That dickhead. Cory was never more than a career choice to him.'

'You didn't get on with him?'

'No. Nobody did.'

Ice cubes clunked as we sipped in unison.

'Tell me about Cory.'

'You know what? He was such a smart kid, much more than just an adorable little ball of cuteness. He was actually a brilliant actor. When the *Smiley* movie flopped, it wasn't because of his performance. I saw moments of brilliance in the work he brought. No, it was all down to his appearance. He was growing and entering that awkward phase that the public just didn't like. They wanted Freckles to stay the same, like the little puppy that you never want to grow up.'

'What about Wesley? Do you see him much?'

'Cory brought him over and introduced me to him when he first moved in. He seemed like a nice kid.'

'Have you seen him lately?'

'Not much. I've only seen him once or twice over the last couple of weeks. But he ... he's changed.'

'What do you mean?'

'He hardly spoke to me, hardly acknowledged me even. Just put his head down and kind of grunted.'

'Do you think he and Cory got on?'

'Oh yes. Wesley idolised his brother.'

'So, you don't think they could have fallen out?'

Natalie squinted and regarded the question for a moment before answering. 'Maybe. There's definitely a change in Wesley. Like he's hiding something.'

Hmm … interesting.

33

DC Bradley Cooper was waiting for me in the hotel foyer when I stepped from the residential elevator. If his natural, cheery disposition didn't give you a lift, nothing would, but I also sensed something new in his demeanour as we shook hands. A hard foundation to his jolly tone, one that said, *I may be polite, but that doesn't mean you can fuck with me.* A product of maturity, perhaps after being demoted to uniform during the *X* case, then winning back promotion, and being a detective for a year. My first expression on our initial meeting was that the lad would need to toughen the fuck up if he were ever to make it in the police force. Well, he'd done just that. But kudos to him; all the knocks, frustrations and hardships of being a junior detective hadn't taken away his humility. Good on him.

'Scott.' He never called me Scotty.

'Hey, mate.'

'Sorry I'm late.'

'No worries.'

'Have you heard from Wesley?'

'No. He's not answering his phone. The concierge rang up to the apartment earlier, but no reply.'

'Okay.' He marched up to the concierge desk and produced his badge. 'Hi, I'm Detective Constable Bradley Cooper. We have some concerns about the safety of Wesley Cummings. When was the last time you saw him?'

The young concierge stood up straight and shrugged. 'A day maybe. Yesterday perhaps.'

'Right. Did he appear distressed to you in any way?'

'No, sir, but I paid little attention. Just noticed him passing through the foyer with his head down as usual.'

'We need to go up to the apartment.'

'I'll call up.' She punched a number into the phone on the desk and listened. After a minute or so, she shook her head and returned the handpiece to the cradle. 'Nobody there, I'm afraid.'

'That's okay. You can give us access, right?' With his badge still in hand, Bradley held it up as a reminder he was the police.

'Yes, sure. The young woman fumbled as she produced a key card from the top drawer, danced her fingers across a computer keyboard, then swiped the card. 'There you go. That will get you up to penthouse #2.'

Although I wouldn't be considering joining the police force again anytime soon, I have to admit, I missed having my detective badge and the privileges it provided. In a lot of instances, it was like having a key or a magic pass. My fame was both a blessing and a curse at the same time. Sometimes it came in handy in getting my foot in the door of certain places that would normally be out of bounds, other times because of the lack of anonymity, it would hinder any chance I had of lying low and blending in, something a good private detective depended on. Basically, without a badge, I was just a citizen.

Technically, the concierge could have turned down Bradley's request for entry to the apartment, and if the older guy from the previous day was on duty, that may have been the case.

Travelling up in the lift for the second time that morning, and knowing how quick the journey was, there was no time to engage in chat. Bradley and I remained quiet until the familiar *ping* and the rear door slid open.

The foyer was quiet as we stepped from the lift.

'Hey Wesley. You here mate?' I called out. There was no reply.

We crept quietly through the apartment as if we were about to discover a gruesome scene, but the place was spotlessly clean, with no signs of Wesley.

I wasn't about to waste the chance of taking another look through Cory's room, but there was nothing to be found.

There was another room almost identical to the suite on the opposite side of the bedroom wing. Our assumption that this belonged to Wesley because of its size proved correct when we found his clothes, mostly T-shirts, hanging in the wardrobe.

'Doesn't look like he packed,' Bradley said, opening and closing drawers that were full of socks, undies and shorts.

'So, we have the possibility of two missing persons.' The image of Mick Brennan marching through the Milton foyer came to mind and the warning I'd received from Knackers. "Stay away from Brennan, Scotty. You don't know what you're getting into."

Bradley thanked the concierge warmly as he handed back the key card. It was just after lunchtime, so we decided to grab a bite to eat.

'My shout,' Bradley said as we strolled into the Guzman y Gomez diner on Cavill Avenue.

'No way.' Being familiar with the salary of a DC, and even though I guessed Bradley didn't squander his money like I had, probably invested in Crypto or used it more wisely, I wasn't about to let him pay for me.

As I passed one of the brightly coloured stools, he forced me down onto it with a firm hand to the shoulder and said, 'What would you like?'

On first inspection, the enchiladas we munched on were identical, except Bradley's was vegetarian, mine was pulled pork. He drank iced tea. I had a ginger beer.

'I guess everything depends on the DNA results,' Bradley said, after taking a sip of his drink.

'Yeah, I spose.'

'If the body found in the car isn't Cory Evans. What then?'

'Well, it means we'll have two missing persons.' Unlike Bradley's refined etiquette of conversation, such as never speaking with one's mouth full. I spoke with a gob full of pork and Mexican rice.

'Perhaps they're together somewhere.'

The thought had crossed my mind. Of course, it had, along with other possible scenarios. Bradley was right. It all came down to the results of the DNA test. Until we had that, we were just guessing.

My phone rang. It was Jenny. After quickly wiping my mouth and hands with a napkin, I picked up the phone and answered it.

'Hey, Jen.'

'Hey. Where are you?'

'In Surfers with Bradley.'

'Okay. The results are back.'

'Oh ...' I would have liked to have put the phone on speaker so Bradley could hear too, but there were other diners around us, mostly Schoolies. 'And?'

34

Rather dramatically, Jenny refused to give us the results over the phone, insisting instead, we got straight to the police headquarters where she'd be waiting for us.

The zombies were back on the streets now, so with baseball cap pulled down as far as possible, sunglasses on and head down, I tailed Bradley as he blazed a trail through the herds.

Once we reached Ferny Avenue, we were clear.

Jenny was sitting at her desk, head deep in paperwork, when we approached the glass fronted office and knocked on the door. Without looking up, she called, 'Come in.'

We entered and took the seats facing her while she finished whatever it was she was working on.

'I'll get coffees,' Bradley said, rising and leaving the room.

'Won't be a minute,' Jenny said.

'No worries, take your time.' Nobody was more aware than me of the amount of paperwork a detective had to fill out each day. The majority of my career in plain clothes had been not much more than an admin role. That was one part of the job I didn't miss.

Bradley returned carrying three steaming mugs, just as Jenny completed her task with a scrolling flurry.

Bradley placed the mugs on the desk and reseated. It was refreshing to see that the Gold Coast police force had graduated beyond paper cups.

'Okay,' Jenny said, sitting back in her chair, closing the manila folder on the desk and clicking off the Parker pen I'd bought her for her last birthday. With one hand, she placed the manila folder in a tray to her left while retrieving another with the other hand. Opening it, she leaned forward and read silently, as if checking to make sure she had the correct document. 'Hmm … it's conclusive. The DNA sample taken from the body found in the burnt-out wreck was a match to the sample. It belonged to Cory Evans.'

'Wow!' Even though this was the news I'd been expecting, it came as no less of a shock. What a way for a young life to end.

'We haven't alerted the media yet, but we can't hold it off any longer.'

'The circus will be back in town,' Bradley said.

'That's right. Things are going to get pretty crazy again. Any news on Wesley?'

'No. The apartment's empty. I'm concerned about him.'

'You don't think he's done a runner?'

'Possibly, but …' I shared my concerns with them about the involvement of Mick Brennan and The Wasps.

Jenny suddenly appeared uncomfortable. Shifting in her chair, she attempted a sip of hot coffee.

'The thing is, if we're just talking about a hundred grand or so for Patty to launch an appeal, Brennan could come up with that kind of cash easily, surely,' I said.

'Right. I need to talk to you about that.'

'The appeal or Brennan?'

'Brennan. Listen, there's uhm …' She glanced at Bradley as if seeking support. 'We need to tread very carefully with The Wasps. There's an operation in place.'

'A sting you mean?' This wasn't meant as a pun.

'As you know, I've been trying to nail that bastard for some time. We thought we had him last year for importation and dealing in narcotics. Caught him red handed, but bloody Nash got him off on a technicality. Our evidence was ruled as unlawfully obtained.'

'Yeah, I remember. He walked free.'

'But he's been forced to keep a low profile since because he knows we're watching his every move.'

'Right, so he hasn't had the usual revenue coming in.'

'Not only that. When a large cargo of pure Columbian cocaine was seized, he would have already paid for it up front,' Bradley added.

'So, for Patty's appeal, he needs to get the cash to cover Nashie's representation and the court costs from somewhere.' Now it was my turn to take a sip from my mug. I don't know how Bradley did it, but even with the limited resources of the tiny kitchenette on the second floor of the police headquarters, he still produced barista level coffee.

'It's ironic when you think he was probably attempting to extort the money for the appeal from Cory, the defendant of the case,' Bradley said.

'Clever and *so* Brennan. Beneath that Palaeolithic exterior is an evil genius,' Jenny said.

'Being under threat from Brennan would definitely be a motive for suicide,' Bradley added.

'And now he could be after Wesley.' Replacing my coffee mug on the desk, I leaned forward. 'The Milton would have him on CCTV yesterday morning, entering and leaving the building. It shouldn't be too hard for you guys to find out from the concierge the reason for his visit. I'm guessing he was threatened to hand over the key to Cory's apartment.'

Jenny shuffled again in her seat and I could tell there was something else on her mind.

'What's up? What's going on?'

This time, the glance was reciprocal between the two detectives.

'The thing is, mate. We can't get involved with Brennan. We need to be really careful.'

My what-are-you-talking-about-Willis pout was a prompt for Jenny to continue.

'There's been another shipment.'

'Cocaine?'

'Yep, but twice as big as the last one.'

'You've seized it?'

'No ... yes ... well—'

Bradley interjected. 'We've infiltrated the gang.'

'An undercover operative?'

'That's right. A detective from New South Wales. We've known something has been going down for the last six months. All the assets owned by the gang, the tattoo parlours, bars, restaurants, brothels, the mechanic shops that we know of have been sold off.'

'Shit. How big is the shipment?'

'A shipping container.'

Once again, Jenny shuffled uncomfortably in her chair. 'And there lies the problem.'

'Well, have you seized it or not?'

'No, it's standing in a paddock out the back of Logan.'

Bradley took up the thread. 'We'd had a tip off about the shipment arriving in Queensland, one that was confirmed by our guy on the inside. We allowed it in but monitored its journey from the Brisbane docks with the expectation of nabbing Brennan and his gang when they received it. The only problem is, Brennan seems to have shied away. It's been standing there for a couple of months. We suspect he may have caught wind of our operation.'

'You think he's got someone in the police?'

'It's likely,' Jenny said. 'Either that or he's just leaving it there while he covers his tracks.'

'Or he hasn't got enough money to pay for it yet,' Bradley interjected.

'That would put him under massive pressure,' I said.

'We won't be seizing the narc. The agenda is to catch Brennan in the act,' Jenny added.

I knew exactly where this conversation was going. With such an enormous operation in progress and at such a sensitive stage, the Queensland Police showing up at The Wasps' headquarters and asking questions about the death of Cory Evan's could put the entire investigation in jeopardy. 'I understand.' Our detective minds were in sync. 'So, what do you suggest we do?'

'We can't do anything at the moment,' Jenny said. 'An inquiry will be opened into Cory's death as well as Wesley's disappearance, but we have to make sure there is no association mentioned with The Wasps. The media are going to be all over this.'

From my own experiences with the media during the *X* case when I was heralded as the saviour of the Gold Coast one day, then branded as the most hated man in Australia the next, it wasn't difficult for me to imagine the scenario that was about to play out. 'But I can …'

Their identical puzzled expressions said, 'You can what?'

'I can poke a stick into The Wasps' nest and stir it up a bit.'

'That's not a good idea, Scott,' Jenny said sternly. I don't think I'd ever heard her call me Scott before.

'It's the only way. Look, for all we know, it could just have been a coincidence that Brennan was at the Milton. Or he could have killed Cory and now has Wesley after finding out he has the cash. Either way, we're never going to find out if you can't investigate him.'

Jenny shook her head vigorously. 'No. I forbid it!'

35

Jenny Radford rose from the uniform division to become a detective constable right at the beginning of the *X* case. Apart from passing in the corridor now again, and the odd brief nod and g'days, we hadn't met properly. Then when I was promoted to Detective Inspector, she worked under me, and although I was her boss, we became mates, romantic for a brief time, but still occasional lovers. Now it was me who was the subordinate. And I didn't have a problem with that. Seeing her doing so well made me feel proud. But getting on the wrong side of her wasn't a good idea, and I realised that I'd need to come to terms with the fact that the feisty, tough little bugger who loved to surf, could drink me under the table and probably smash me in an arm wrestling match, would exercise her authority regardless of our friendship. Out in the surf, or during a Sunday arvo session at the Cooly Hotel, she was Jenny. During the working day, she was Detective Inspector Radford.

If I'd thought it through, I probably would have dismissed the idea as ridiculous, but I didn't. Tetley's pride and joy was parked in the back of the garage at Ruby Street, covered with an old doona. The little Pommy was always spouting about how reliable it was. Now was the time to find out. There was a thin layer of dust on the red paint, some of which slid off the curved contours as I wheeled the fifty-something-year-old machine out of the garage and into the sunlight. The classic Vespa was a far cry from the trial bikes

I used to ride as a young bloke, but apparently it was cool in some circles. At least Tetley thought so. There was just a single key with a 'V' on it. I remembered Tetley handing it to me the night before he left for the UK, solemn, like he was parting with a precious family heirloom. Perhaps he was. And he was right. It was reliable. After almost eight months standing, when I placed the key in the ignition, turned on the fuel tap and kicked it over, it started first time. *Bop, bop, bop, bop, bop, bop, bop* raced the little two-stroke engine. Small bursts of white smoke from the tiny exhaust rose into the air and formed a thick cloud. I'd only ridden the bike, *uhm, excuse me, the scooter*—that was Tetley's stern contradiction— just the once, and briefly, up and down the street. Not enough time to get used to the twist-grip gears on the left handlebar.

Putting on Tetley's helmet made me smile when I realised how big it was. He was a big-headed little fucker.

Stepping across the scooter, and grasping the handlebars with both hands, I flicked it forward and off the stand. There was a little skip when I found first gear. Then I was away.

Sticking to the smaller roads where possible, there was a sudden sense of panic when I realised that the only way across the Tweed River was on the M1 overpass. Taking the entrance just after Sexton Hill, I was at full throttle as I merged into the traffic. 'Fuck me,' I cussed out loud as cross winds belted the side of the chunky machine, causing me to wobble at a full speed of 80 kilometres per hour. Although I knew the area well, I hadn't given the bridge a second thought. Gee, was I glad when the Chinderah/ Kingscliff exit came up on the other side.

What appeared to be a large, corrugated iron shed at the end of a cul-de-sac in a non-descript industrial estate was, in fact, The Wasps club house. I never understood the endearing term 'bikies' that we Australians used for these gangs. It made them almost sound cuddly. And although most motorcycle clubs were run by legitimate motorcycle enthusiasts, usually cashed up retirees reliving their youth—the not-for-profit organisations who held regular charity rides and hospital runs leading up to Christmas— these weren't the bikies that made the news. The ones that made the news regularly were territorial, terrorist organisations, dealing in drugs, extortion, money laundering, prostitution, and all-out war with other gangs and the police. The flags they waved were the insignias on their backs. Their colours.

I wanted to have a good look first before approaching. Being on the little Vespa meant I was able to pull up inconspicuously between aparked van and a truck just down the street. From there, I had a reasonably good view of the building that dominated the top half of the circular turnaround point. There were two large roller doors. The one on the left was open, revealing a workshop with rows of motorcycles outside. The other was closed and there was a simple doorway to the right of that one. My guess was that the building was split in two. The interior of the right side would be the clubhouse, a plush, tasteless interior one would associate with a brothel, comprising a bar, illegal gaming and a meeting area. Above that I pictured a mezzanine floor with offices and sleazy bedrooms open for trade.

This was another one of those times when my extended fifteen minutes of fame was a pain in the arse. My task would have been much easier in the unlikely event that nobody recognised me, but I had to assume someone would. So, my plan was for the Vespa to be my way in.

Pulling slowly away from the kerb, the little front wheel wobbled. It was actually harder to ride the thing at a low speed. When I rode into the front gate and pulled up outside the open roller door, a mechanic looked up and grinned. Thickset, heavily tattooed, he appeared to be a bikie. Wiping his hands on a rag, he strolled out to meet me. 'Tetley, lad. When did you get back?' He had an English accent similar to Tetley's.

When I removed the helmet, his expression changed instantly.

'You're not Tetley.' He stood over me.

'No. He's still in the UK, but he's coming home soon.'

'You're that fucking detective.'

I'd become so used to the adulation expressed by most people who approached me these days, that it was unusual to experience a negative response. Of course, there was the odd occasion, jealous bucks wanting to exert their manhood, or the odd dodgy character who felt threatened by my presence, but nothing I couldn't handle. Until now. I guess in hindsight, me, the famous detective, stepping into The Wasps' nest, was like Batman walking casually into the Joker's lair. 'That's right. Scotty.' I held out my hand for him to shake, but he ignored it. 'Tetley's a good mate of mine.'

There was a slight nod of recognition. Depending on how well the guy knew Tetley, if he knew him well, chances are he'd know we were mates.

'I thought I'd get this old girl serviced and ready for his return.'

'When's he back?' There was a slight crack in the granite.

'He hasn't given me a date yet. But reckons he can't wait.'

A slight smile. 'It was that little bastard who got us the name 'whinging poms'. The smile widened, revealing uneven, smoke-stained teeth. 'What's he doing over there? I thought he was only going back for a couple of weeks.'

'Me too. Something to do with the family. Bloody whinging like you wouldn't believe.'

He threw back his head and laughed out loud. We'd struck on a mutual fondness for Sean Webster, aka Tetley. The little bugger was helping me even when he was across the other side of the world.

'So, what do you reckon? Is she serviceable?' I asked, peering down at Tetley's pride and joy.

'Nah mate, you've brought it to the wrong place.'

'Really?'

'Yeah, you need a sewing machine shop, or one that deals in hairdryers.'

I wasn't following until he burst into laughter again. 'Ahh, right. Sewing machine, hairdryer, that's funny.' I had to admit, they were both good analogies.

'Can you bring it back in the morning?'

'Sure.' What I had expected to be just a reconnaissance exercise had turned into much more than I could have hoped for. Not only was I invited back, but I had made a contact. The moment of smugness suddenly disappeared, though, when I overstepped the mark and asked, 'Is Mick around?'

His body seemed to inflate while his smile deflated at the same time. 'Mick who?'

'Mick Brennan.'

He shook his head warily. 'Don't know no Mick Brennan.'

'Oh right, sorry. I though he was the boss around here.'

'I'll be here at 7.30 tomorrow morning. You can drop her off any time after that. Should only need her for a couple of hours.'

'Okay, cool. I'll see you then,' I called after him as he marched back towards the workshop. *Damn!* Why did I have to push it? I was basically back to square one.

36

Of course, I didn't mention my trip to The Wasps' nest when I spoke to Jenny on the phone. And she had little else to tell me since our meeting that afternoon. I'd just finished watching the news. The story had broken. Australia was in mourning. That night almost every TV channel ran back-to-back Freckle movies, TV shows or docos. That little smiling face was everywhere.

The next of kin, Barry and Patty, were notified of Cory's death and Wesley's disappearance. One thing Jenny did mention, though, was that neither of the parents showed much emotion when they learned of the news. We arranged to meet up the following evening to share info at Burleigh Heads Surf Club.

Nobody needed to tell me that there was still bugger all surf the next morning. Experience and knowledge informed me it would be at least another day before the wind direction turned and the waves would be half decent again. I'd arranged for Elvis to follow me down to Chinderah so he could give me a lift back to the office once I dropped off the Vespa at the mechanics. Arriving on time at 7.30, the guy I'd spoken to the previous afternoon was already there.

'Good morning,' I said, unclipping Tetley's helmet.

The mechanic replied with a single nod.

'I'm sorry I didn't catch your name yesterday.'

'That's because I didn't throw it.'

'Right. Okay …'

'I'm Beau.'

'Beau. Good to meet you, man.' I offered my hand.

He reluctantly shook it. 'You can pick her up at lunchtime. Give me your number though, just in case.'

Now it was my turn to show reluctance. Did I really want to give out my phone number to a bikie gang? 'Yeah, no worries.' The last two digits of the number I gave him were false. I'd simply say he must have misheard me if he calls it and gets someone else on the other end. 'I'll see you later, mate.'

Elvis' Porsche was parked out front. When I climbed into the passenger seat, he pulled away before I even had time to put on my seat belt. 'They scare the shit out of me,' he said, driving a little over the speed limit.

A couple of minutes later, we were back on the highway, where we stayed until the Kennedy Drive exit.

'Hey, uhm, I meant to tell you …' Elvis said as we approached Coolangatta. '… I'm going down to Melbourne at the weekend.'

'Yeah? How long for?'

His nonchalant shrug was indecisive. 'Just a couple of days, maybe.'

'Okay … cool. Give you time to catch up with the olds.'

'Something like that.'

He dropped me off outside the office on Griffith Street, then pulled away to park the car.

I had nothing else planned for the day except to pick up the Vespa, but I wouldn't be going back at lunchtime as Beau had suggested. The whole reason for going down there was to figure out a way to infiltrate The Wasps' nest. To do that, I'd need a way into the clubhouse, which wouldn't be possible while it was closed. With the assumption that gang members would arrive at the club in the afternoon, my plan was to work my way in without getting my head kicked in. I wasn't sure how yet, but I'd think of something.

The whiteboard was due for an update. Confirmation of Cory's death meant everyone on the list were now suspects. I couldn't help feeling sad every time I looked into Cory's eyes. Using his real name rather than 'Freckles' had become my preference of choice. His photograph remained top centre, but I wasn't sure now if Wesley should have remained at the top of the list of suspects or placed at the side of his brother as a victim. My gut feeling was to leave it where it was for the time being.

One luxury I enjoyed since leaving the police force was time. Schedules, budgets and bureaucratic bullshit governed the day of a busy police detective. But since becoming a private detective, I was burdened with none of those constraints. Hours standing in front of a whiteboard ruminating, analysing, throwing around different scenarios, theories and what-ifs, was normal. The basis of my thought process was a watered-down version of the five journalistic codes: who, what, when, where, and why. However, my take only had two principles: who, and why. Answers are a by-product of questions. The more questions one asks, the more answers one will receive.

Mick Brennan had moved up the list. I'd yet to meet him, shuddered at the thought, but realised it would be inevitable sooner or later. Who knows, perhaps he'll be a Scotty Stephens fan.

After a long deliberation over each of the suspects, my eyes wandered back to Cory's younger sibling. There was something I was missing, I was sure of it—a piece of the puzzle that Grandad had inadvertently let slip down the side of his armchair when attempting a 1000-piece landscape of the Barossa Valley, meaning it would never be complete until the piece was found.

I was startled back to the present when I heard the door to the street open. As footsteps ascended the stairs, I flipped over the whiteboard. There was a knock at the office door.

'Come in.'

Bugger me. It was Wesley.

37

'Where have you been, mate?'

The shrug. 'Just out.'

'Out where?'

The bloody shrug again. He hadn't been back one minute and he was already annoying the shit out of me. When he approached my desk, he was trembling. 'Just needed to get away. To think.'

'Are you okay?' Rounding the desk, I placed a hand on his shoulder.

'No … I'm far from okay.'

'Have a seat.' Two steps to the little Aldi fridge and two steps back. I thrust a bottle of newly replenished water into his hand. 'Here you go.'

Breaking the seal and screwing off the top proved difficult for him. His hands were shaking that much.

'I'm guessing you've heard the news about Cory.'

With a mouthful of water, he nodded and closed his eyes.

'I'm really sorry, mate.'

'Thank you.'

'Where did you go?' My gentle approach was the caring parental kind that I'd mastered as a detective when breaking sad news to grieving families.

'Byron.'

It made sense, although Byron Bay had changed drastically over the last few years and was no longer the hippie haven it once was, it was still a good place to lose yourself.

I decided to take a punt. 'I know all about the threats.'

Wesley suddenly looked up. 'You do?'

'Yep. And I think I'd want to get away too if I had Mick Brennan after me.' The ADS monitor automatically kicked in. At first, there was nothing. It was almost as if he hadn't heard what I'd said, or was he regarding my words? 'I'm glad you came back. I can help you.'

He exhaled slowly and looked up at the ceiling.

'It's going to be alright, mate.'

The shrug.

I checked my watch. 'Come on. It's smoko.'

We wandered out onto the street and around The Strand, used the pedestrian crossing on Marine Parade, then approached the small coffee shop kiosk underneath Coolangatta Surf Club. Without asking Wesley what he wanted, I ordered two large takeaway coffees and two enormous blueberry muffins.

'Thanks,' Wesley said when I handed him the bounty.

'Sit or walk?' I asked.

'Sit.'

We found a shaded table and chairs. The kiddies' playground was a little noisy, but it didn't deter us.

'So, tell me all about it,' I said with a mouth full of muffin.

'Where to start.'

'The beginning.' There was an arsenal of questions loaded into the chamber, ready to fire with the safety off, but I wanted to wait and see how much he would open-up first without prompting. The shrug told me right away I was going to have to take charge. So, I fired off the first shot. 'When was the last time you saw Cory?'

'A week maybe.'

'And what frame of mind was he in?'

'The usual.' He wasn't about to make this easy.

'Look mate, I'm here to help, but you're going to have to trust me. Tell me what the hell's going on, eh?'

He took a sip of his coffee and was about to bite into his muffin when I grabbed his wrist.

'Do you want me to help you?'

'Yes. Yes. I need help. Badly.'

'Then help me to help you.' I fired a full round. 'I want to know why Cory signed over all his assets to you. What the relationship was like between you guys? How Mick Brennan got involved in all of this. And what do you think happened to your brother?'

He nodded thoughtfully as if dictating to a mental note pad. 'Cory was afraid. He didn't … couldn't trust anybody.'

He trusted you, I wanted to say but decided not to interrupt the flow.

'It wasn't just Mick Brennan. Barry, Patty. Even the personal trainer was into him.'

'Netty?' A gentle prompt to show I was listening. I already knew the answer.

'Yes. Not such a nice girl after all, apparently.'

'She threatened Cory?'

The nod. 'If you look into her background, you might be surprised what you find.'

Now it was me who was making the mental notes.

He told me about a message she'd left on Cory's phone. 'I'll fucking kill you if you think you're going to cross me,' she'd screamed, going on about how she'd borrowed her half of the money.'

Hmm. Cory's phone was destroyed in the fire, so there'd be no way of verifying this.

'Would she be capable of killing your brother?'

The bloody shrug again. 'Probably.'

'So, you mentioned Barry?'

'Barry. *Hah*. Barry, Barry. He ruined my brother's life. Regardless of what happened to Cory, it was Barry who killed him.'

'How so?'

'He strangled the life out of my brother years ago. Bled him dry.'

'But he's moved on now, surely. Successful business. Happily married.'

Wesley scoffed as he bit into his muffin.

I waited patiently while he chewed, swallowed, then took a drink of coffee.

'Barry had a secret and Cory found out about it. Cory hired a private detective to look into Barry's affairs.'

'What did he find?' I wanted to grab him by the shoulders and drive him into the chair to stop the inevitable shrug. Instead, I moved on. 'Tell me about your relationship with your mum.'

'Patty.' It was interesting how Wesley referred to his parents by their names and not as Mum and Dad. 'There *is* no relationship. They forced me to live with her. It was okay when we were in Currumbin.'

'Beachfront living.'

'The house was big enough for me to be alone. I was at school, spent most of my time playing video games. I didn't have a clue what she was doing. Didn't care.' He took a sip of coffee. 'But when we moved to the caravan park, she changed, started drinking. Then she met Mick Brennan.'

'How did Brennan act towards you?'

'At first, it was okay. Let's say they tolerated me. He lived in an enormous house down in Bilambil Heights. I went there once with Patty. Then she started going there a lot.'

'Leaving you alone in the caravan?'

The nod. 'Then before I knew what was happening, Mick moved in with us. And boy, was he angry like all the time.'

'Why would he move into a caravan when he had a house?' I averted my eyes to avoid the shrug.

A scenario was developing in my mind. Mick Brennan was involved with the biggest drug deal of his life—a shipping container full of pure grade Colombian cocaine, but for the deal to go down, he had to pay up front. To do that, he had to sell his assets, the house, the businesses, and whatever else he was involved in, but he still fell short. Then, when he was tipped off that the police were tracking the shipment, this created another hurdle towards getting his hands on the investment of a lifetime that sat in a paddock out the back of Logan. Moving from a big house, and the lifestyle of a crime lord and into a caravan, sure would have made him angry. But I'm guessing the only reason he was with Patty was because she was a potential cash cow. Cory Evans' fortune was within his reach.

'What were Patty's feelings towards Cory?'

'She hated his guts.'

'And what about you?'

'I loved him. Always did. Even when I was in the annex of that van listening to Brennan beating up Patty, I always knew Cory would come and save me one day.'

'What made you think that?'

'He was my brother!'

38

'Hey Jackie. Is the King around?'

'No. I'm afraid Elvis has left the building.' The smile was a wary one that did little to hide the concern.

'Gone home early?'

'No. Didn't he tell you?'

'Tell me what?'

'He's gone to Melbourne.'

'Already. When?' Elvis had mentioned that morning that he was thinking of going home for a trip. He didn't say he was going so soon. This was very unusual behaviour. We'd confided in each other in all matters since we were five years old. Even if he'd made a brash last-minute decision, he still wouldn't have left without at least calling me. 'Jackie, you've worked for him for what …?'

'Ten years.'

'So, you know him pretty well. Have you noticed anything different about him just lately?'

'Yes. He's depressed. My sister, Katherine, suffers from depression. I've seen a similar pattern in her.'

'Such as?'

'Mood swings. Bouts of silence, sadness.'

'What time did he fly out?'

'2.30 this afternoon.'

It was 3.30. This meant he would still be in mid-flight. I'd call him later that evening.

Uber was super cheap at that time of the day, and I didn't have to wait long for a ride. When the Indian driver dropped me outside The Wasps' clubhouse, I climbed warily from the Toyota Prius and strolled towards the mechanics' shop with Tetley's helmet under my arm. The little Vespa really did look like a hairdryer on wheels, lined up in a row of choppers and customised Harleys. Beau met me halfway across the forecourt and blocked my path as if he didn't want me getting any closer. It was only teatime, but the clubhouse next door was already heaving and there was a row of motorbikes outside. The roller door was open and heavy metal music punctuated the air. It wasn't the motorbike that I recognised, parked about three from the left with the fat rear tyre; it was the rego plate, Nak 666. It was Knackers' bike.

I'd been told to bring cash for payment. When Beau held out a greasy hand demanding $300, basically for a cup full of lubricant and an air filter the size of a fruit loop, I realised I'd been duped, but I was in no position to complain.

'She's running fine. Tell Tetley he'll need to replace the back tyre soon.' He handed me the key, then marched back into the workshop with my cash.

'I will, thanks,' I called after him.

The scooter started on the first kick, as usual. Pulling away, I side glanced to see if Beau was watching. He wasn't, so I cruised over to the other side of the building in first gear and parked at the end of the row of bikes.

'Scott. What the hell are you doing here?'

Pulling off the helmet, and looking up, I saw Knackers rushing towards me. 'Hey mate. How are ya?' My nonchalant greeting did nothing to ease the anger blaring from my old friend's eyes.

'What the fuck, man?' He'd lowered his voice. 'Get out of here.'

Mick Brennan strolled toward us from the clubhouse. The wing man behind him must have been 6ft 6, body of *Conan the Barbarian*, face like a burst sausage.

'Scotty Stephens.' Brennan didn't offer his hand.

'Hey. Mick, isn't it?'

He regarded me through narrowed eyes. 'Mick Brennan.' His voice was deep and gravely.

Knackers stood back and lowered his head as if in defeat. I also noticed that Beau was standing outside the workshop watching us.

'What the fuck are you doing here?'

'Just had a new cotton bobbin fitted to the Singer,' I said, gesturing towards the Vespa.

My humour didn't reach the desired effect.

'Follow me.' Mick turned and headed back towards the clubhouse. Conan and Knackers didn't move. Conan was watching me as if expecting me to bolt. Knackers' expression remained blank.

Following Mick into the clubhouse, I counted a dozen more bikies inside. Some played pool. The rest sat on barstools in front of a corrugated, iron clad bar spanning the back wall.

The curse of instant recognition showed on the faces of each Neanderthal as I followed Mick to the bar, with Knackers and Conan behind me like foot soldiers escorting a prisoner to the gallows.

Mick went around the bar, disappeared momentarily, then popped up with a stubby of Tooheys beer. He slipped it into a Wasps stubby holder, then pushed it over the bar towards me. There was an identical one already on the bar. He lifted it into the air and said, 'Here's to the condemned man!'

Although a simple "Cheers" would have been more welcoming and the pit of my stomach was hanging out of my arse, I had to admit, this wasn't the scenario that had played out in my mind since I'd disobeyed Jenny's orders. Mum's voice whispered once again, 'Be careful what you wish for, Scotty.'

'You're a lucky man,' Mick said after a long swig of beer.

'I am?'

'My little sister works in Surfers. When all them girls were being killed, she was shitting herself. I was about to take matters into my own hands when you stepped in and saved the day.'

'Glad to be of service.' We touched bottles and took another swig.

But when he lowered the bottle from his mouth, Mick's expression had changed. 'Now tell me why you're really here.'

The glance towards Knackers was inadvertent and dangerous for us both.

'I was just picking up me mate's scooter from next door.' Half-heartedly, I flicked a thumb over my shoulder toward the Vespa out front. 'Heard the music and—' I was about to say I knew Knackers, but something suddenly dawned on me. *What if Knackers was the undercover operative?* I knew nothing about him. We hadn't seen each other since leaving school. All I knew was that he'd moved down to Sydney. It all made sense. The warning to stay away. His uneasiness towards my presence. 'Just wandered in, really. Sorry about that.'

'Once a pig, always a pig, Mick,' Conan said, glaring at me now as if he was about to tear my head off.

'A private investigator,' Mick corrected the bigger man. 'Is that why you're here?'

It was no good lying. They'd see right through it. After all, I was pretty sure Mick had spotted me in the foyer of the Milton. I was up to my balls now. 'I'm working on the disappearance … I mean, the death of Cory Evans.'

Mick shook his head slowly.

As if being struck by a sledgehammer, searing pain turned out the lights momentarily, when a sudden blow to the side of my head sent me down to my knees. An enormous hand grabbed me under an arm and lifted me back up.

'And you just wandered in here, eh?' Mick said.

With heavy eyelids, I was about to nod when Conan twisted my arm up my back.

The rest of the gang had gathered around us. I was going to get a hiding, that was for sure, so I had nothing to lose. 'What was your involvement with Cory?'

'This is going to hurt me more than it hurts you. You're my sister's hero.'

Conan punched me in the nose. He must have followed up with further blows, but I don't remember any of them. I was out cold before I hit the floor.

39

My memory was split into fragmented recollections, as if I'd been randomly blacking out. Concussion maybe. Knackers holding me up and frog marching me out of the compound. Me whispering through sore swollen lips, 'The Vespa.' Knackers' reply, 'There is no Vespa.' A Muslim Uber driver, reluctant to let me into his car, but too intimidated by the bikie stuffing me into the back seat. Turning onto the M1, the roundabout off the Kennedy Drive exit, Coolangatta State School, Kirra. 'Get out, please.' Ruby Street.

After a shower and a beer, I crawled off to bed and slept like the proverbial bear with a sore head.

My inner surf clock woke me at 5.00 am. But there would be no riding the waves that morning. Lifting my head from the pillow was a mission. Thankfully, the light seeping into the bedroom was an early morning opaque. The throbbing through my temples, like electrical impulses shooting from point to point, needed little assistance in rendering me incapacitated.

Padding into the hallway, I immediately noticed that something was different, but I wasn't sure what. Heading into the kitchen, the silent pounding in my head made me nauseous. Then I realised it was the silence that was the difference. No snoring coming from Elvis' room. For the last twenty years, this ubiquitous sound was as familiar as the hum of the ceiling fan or the dawn chorus. I suddenly felt insecure, like I was no longer in a safe place. For the first time in my life, I was alone.

Surveying the damage through the bathroom mirror, I was relieved to see that the cause of the pain was mostly swelling around the eyes, the nose and lips, and a small cut on my bottom lip, but thankfully no need for stitches. Now it was me who had the face like a burst sausage. The only cure would be Panadol and time.

At first, the cool water from the shower *pit-patting* on my face was uncomfortable, but as the temperature rose, it eased the tightness a little. Towelling off was a system of gentle tapping.

There was a knock at the front door. I threw on a pair of boardshorts and opened it.

'Oh, my God. What happened?' It was Bradley. He lifted his hands to his mouth like a mother witnessing her darling little son's first hit on the footy field.

Stepping back, I gestured for him to enter.

'You don't have to tell me. I already know,' Bradley said, breezing into the house. 'And so does Jenny.'

I followed him into the kitchen.

'And she is livid, Scott.'

'Why? What do you mean?'

'We know you went to The Wasps' nest.'

'How?'

He didn't answer. Didn't need to, instead he went about preparing coffee. The inside operative had obviously contacted Jenny. Knackers, maybe.

'Do you realise the trouble you could have caused?'

'No. Me going down there has nothing to do with the investigation you guys are involved in—'

He held up his hand like a traffic cop stopping the oncoming flow. 'Save it. Jenny wants to see you.'

Even a slight shrug hurt like hell.

As always, the coffee Bradley handed me was perfection in a mug. Then he rifled through the kitchen cabinets until he found a box of Rice Bubbles, a bowl and the half-finished sliced loaf.

Without asking if I wanted breakfast or not, he threw two slices of bread in the toaster, poured the cereal into the bowl, sprinkled it with sugar, and drowned it with milk from the fridge. 'Here. You need to eat.'

'Thanks.' Elvis would be pissed if he'd known I was eating his beloved cereal, but he wasn't here.

After another quick search of the cupboards, Bradley found the jar of Vegemite. When the toast popped, he covered it with a generous layer of the yeast extract.

'Where's Elvis? I don't hear him snoring.' He was switched on, I have to say.

'Melbourne.' The word came out more as a blubber through my swollen lips.

'Melbourne?'

I nodded and immediately regretted it.

'So, you're here on your own?' He was talking to me like I was a school kid.

'Yeah. I'm fine.'

'You're far from fine, Scott Stephens.'

The Rice Bubbles were inadvertently a great choice of food for a sore mouth. The toast, not so much, and the salty Vegemite stung my lips and gums.

Bradley, reading my thoughts, said, 'Eat it.'

I persevered.

Unbelievably, I found myself missing the COVID mask mandate. The baseball cap and sunnies did a good job of hiding the top half of my head, but my swollen lips were flopping out there for everyone to see.

The drive from Kirra to Surfers in Bradley's SUV was a silent one. He didn't even have the radio on. Sitting in the passenger seat staring out the window, I suddenly remembered Tetley's Vespa. Would I have the balls to go back down there and get it?

When we arrived at the police headquarters, we went up to Jenny's office. It was empty. Bradley showed me in. 'Take a seat. I'll let her know you're here.' His immaculate suit rustled as he breezed away.

I was that kid again, waiting in the headmaster's office. Sitting there for ten minutes didn't help the anxiety.

When Jenny finally marched into the room, I was a bag of nerves.

'What the hell were you thinking, Scotty? I specifically told you not to go down there. Why did you disobey me?'

'I didn't. I just took Tetley's Vespa down for a service.'

'Tetley's Vespa? You mean that crushed piece of scrap that was dumped outside the Coolangatta Magistrate's Court?'

'They wrecked it?' My concern was genuine.

'Are you serious?' She shook with anger. 'You just may have jeopardised a multi-million-dollar operation and you're worried about a little moped?'

Ouch, they would be fighting words in Tetley's circle. I'd made the mistake of calling his pride and joy a moped once. 'It's a classic Italian-built machine!' But the dressing down I'd received then was nothing compared to the one I was on the end of now.

'Are you taking any of this serious, Scott?' When she called me Scott, I knew I was in trouble. 'What were you hoping to achieve?'

Suppressing a Wesley shrug, I remained quiet.

As if noticing my wounds for the first time, she sighed and lifted off my cap. 'My God.'

'I'm okay, Jen ... and look ... I'm sorry. I fucked up.'

'Yes, you did.' She rounded the desk and dropped into her office chair.

'And ... it was a waste of time. I should never have gone down there.'

'That's right. Don't make me put restraints on you, Scotty. We're supposed to be working together, remember?'

'I know. I'm sorry.'

<h1 style="text-align:center">40</h1>

I was hoping to call in and see Wesley but he wasn't answering his phone. Bradley dropped me off at home and fussed like a mother hen, insisting on making me some soup. There was a tin of Heinz tomato in the cupboard. Rather than just bunging it in the microwave, as I would have, he insisted on heating it up on the stove, in our only pan. Throwing in whatever else he could scavenge; the result was restaurant good. He'd also insisted I eat in bed, then get some sleep. I was feeling blessed to have him.

After Bradley left and the last spoonful of creamy soup had gently passed through my swollen lips, I headed to the bathroom.

The house was eerily quiet. It didn't feel right. Where were my mates? Again, like words from a recording that was stored in my mind and replayed on certain occasions, my mum's voice repeated, 'Be careful what you wish for, Scotty.'

Is that what had happened? Had my longing for change manifested this scenario? A year ago, the little house on Ruby Street was the bachelor's dream pad. Elvis, Tetley, Johnno; the place had rarely been empty. But I'd grown tired of all that. The partying in the man shed, the footy nights, I was over it and searching for a way to get away from it without actually leaving. And one by one, the mates disappeared—twinkling stars, snubbed out in the night sky. Could I have caused this? Looking at myself in the mirror, I was thankful that most of the swelling was already clearing. The black eye though was a beauty and would be around for a while.

While heading back towards my bedroom, there was a knock at the front door. Through the opaque glass panel at the top of the door, I could see someone about my height standing outside. But it was the sounds that stirred a feeling of guilt. It was the chatter of children.

'Bloody hell, Scott. Are you okay?' It was Josh, my elder brother. Standing in front of him and staring up at me through quizzical, shocked eyes were my niece and nephew, Juliette and Tommy.

'I've been better, mate.'

'Uncle Scotty.' Juliette, taller since I'd last seen her, but still only up to my waist, threw her arms around me. 'You look terrible!'

'Thanks munchkin.'

Tommy, also taller, about a foot in fact, offered a nod. I wasn't sure if the shyness was a preteen prelude of things to come or the lack of familiarity because he hadn't seen me for so long.

'Hey mate,' I said, offering him my hand.

He shook it and didn't let go.

Josh put an arm around my shoulder, pulled me in and we group hugged there on the front doorstep.

Yes, the feeling of guilt throbbed almost as much as my banged-up head. Estranged for most of our adult lives, Josh and I had finally made up at our dad's funeral last year. When this beautiful family—Josh's wife, Liz, and the two kids—let me into their lives, we'd vowed to not only keep in touch but interact regularly as close families do. But none of that happened. We got together at Christmas and again at Easter, but that was it. And it was my fault. Although I loved Liz and adored the kids, I hadn't invested the time.

'Uncle Scotty, we've come to look after you.' Juliette was beaming with anxious concern.

We retreated into the house and, as you do, wandered into the kitchen.

'I won't ask how you are,' Josh said. 'Is Elvis at work?'

'Nah, he's gone to Melbourne. Can I get you anything? Tea? Coffee?'

'No, you sit down. I'll get it,' Josh said.

While their father filled the jug, Juliette and Tommy, each holding a hand, guided me to the couch.

'Does it hurt, Uncle Scotty?' Juliette asked.

'No, I'm fine, darlin.'

'Who did this?' Tommy asked. 'Was it another murderer?'

'No, nothing like that. It's all good.'

'Far from good,' Josh said. 'You're coming home with us.'

'Eh?'

'You're coming to stay with us until you feel better.'

'Yay.' Juliette sprung up from the couch and jumped up and down on the spot as only an eight year old could. 'We're going to look after you.'

'You can have my room, Uncle Scott,' Tommy said. Dad said it will just be for a few days.

'Josh, I can't impose. I'm fine here.'

While the kids' attention was focused on me, Josh mouthed a single word nice and clear, 'Bullshit!'

'Honestly. I'm—'

'That's good. Means you won't take too much looking after.' He made tea, handed me a steaming mug and had one for himself. 'Why don't you kids go out and play in the backyard for a minute?'

Juliette huffed as they headed out the back door.

'Listen, Scott. I'm really sorry, mate. I promised we'd keep in touch, but we seem to have drifted apart again.'

'No mate, no. You've got nothing to be sorry for. It's me that should be apologising. What with work and everything. This bloody year's just flown by.'

Josh was nodding in acknowledgement of life getting in -the way. Of course, we both knew this wasn't the real reason, and neither of us understood what the barrier was between us.

'I'm okay here though, Josh. This is my home.'

'I know, but Juliette insists.' His smile reminded me of our mother. Genuine. Warm. 'It's school holidays, so it'll be a good opportunity for you to spend some time with the kids.'

'You won't take no for an answer, will you?'

'That's right. Pack a few things. You're coming home with us.'

I have to admit, the thought of staying with my brother in his comfortable suburban home in Broadbeach Waters was appealing, and although it would be absolutely awesome to spend time with the kids, I couldn't help feeling a little apprehensive, or awkward perhaps.

As if reading my thoughts, Josh said, 'It's okay. After Bradley rang me, I called Liz. This was all her idea. You can stay as long as you like.'

'But—'

'But nothing. You're not too big for a slap from your big brother, so unless you want a matching shiner on the other side, go get your things.'

'Okay.'

'Yay!' Two kids cried out in unison from the backyard. Little buggers must have been eavesdropping.

41

My head still hurt like hell, but it didn't matter. The rest of the day was pretty much in the hands of one Miss Juliette Stephens. Tommy was the wingman, who seemed happy to fall in line with the eight year old's agenda. They critiqued my colouring-in skills. Apparently, I could have done better. We played games, watched a little TV and went to the nearby playground. It was a great day.

Later that evening, while Liz showered the kids ready for bed, Josh and I sat out the back enjoying a quiet beer. The sun was setting over the mountains in the west. The sky was a fierce red and made the surface of the canal appear like a stationary river of molten lava.

'Red at night, shepherd's delight,' we said in unison, and I realised our mother's sayings were with us both.

A fish jumped, shattering the mirror of fire.

'So,' Josh said, breaking the silence. 'How's life treating you, Scotty?'

'I can't complain … but I do.'

'Still living the dream?'

'No.' I would have liked to have said yes. That would have beeen the easy way out, because nobody wants you to confirm that your life is as good as their misconception of it, so they'll quickly change the subject and swing the conversation back towards them. But my flat 'No' left me wide open for scrutiny.

'What's wrong?'

I spent the next hour opening up to my brother, sharing my concerns about the changes in my life and how they appeared to be at the cost of friendships. Now I'd even pissed off Jenny and Bradley. 'I've grown tired of the bachelor lifestyle.'

'Be careful what you wish for, Scotty.'

I was momentarily stunned into silence, but then realised Mum's memory was embedded in Josh's mind too. Why wouldn't it be?

'But you can't blame yourself for any of that, mate. Sounds like Elvis is dealing with his own problems.'

'Yeah, he is. I might go down and see him.'

'To Melbourne?'

'Yep.'

'Sorry I couldn't make it this year for the anniversary.'

It had been an annual pilgrimage I'd undertaken every year without fail since I first earned a wage—the anniversary of our mother's death. It was something I'd been doing alone all these years This year, though, Josh and I had decided to travel down together, but it didn't eventuate. He couldn't get away from work. I didn't mind. I'd grown used to spending the time alone with Mum as a way of apologising for being the architect of that dark day that took her away from us in a car accident.

The next day, Josh was back at work, so he left early. Liz had organised a day for herself and the kids to go to Currumbin Wildlife Sanctuary. I turned down the invite to join them. It would have been nice, great even, but I needed to keep busy. I was supposedly working on a case, but so far, the results of my investigation were disappointing. Sore head or not, I was determined to get out there, dig deep and get some answers.

When Liz and the kids left, the house was quiet. I'd made the rookie mistake at the dinner table the evening before of not choosing the correct words when I attempted to compliment

Liz on her beautiful home. I'd meant to say she was a great homemaker, or words to that effect. The words I'd actually used were: 'You're a good housekeeper.' Luckily, she seemed to realise what I was trying to say and didn't take it the wrong way. But boy did the family give me a ribbing over dinner.

After making a mug of tea, I sat out the back and enjoyed a wonderful, quiet moment. The canal was like a liquid cul-de-sac. Some of the neighbours had boats moored at private jetties at the end of their gardens. There was no feeling of familiarity. I wished there was. The house belonged to my brother, but I'd only been there a handful of times. I was a guest—and that's exactly how I felt. The square patch of garden leading to the water's edge was mainly filled with a swing set. There was a kayak lying face down against the fence. A footy ball on the grass looked like it hadn't been kicked in a while. The hardwood deck beneath my bare feet was warming in the morning sun. The outdoor area was a far cry from the man shed out the back of Ruby Street. A six-burner, stainless steel barbeque with a rotisserie hood. Hardwood outdoor furniture. My brother and his wife had created the perfect family home. Was I jealous? Heck, yes. Not in a nasty way, though. More envious, I guess. Perhaps a reality check was underway. My brother had everything I didn't: a beautiful family, a waterfront home, a steady job as a civil engineer. What did I have? A surfboard and a dilapidated old VW Beetle I kidded myself was a classic. *For fuck's sake, Scotty. Pull yourself together.* Sipping tea was a great medium for reflection. Sitting by a canal somewhere in Broadbeach Waters, watching a pelican as it slowly paddled across the water, also helped. Was this the life I was secretly craving? I was forty-four years old. Marriage had never been a consideration. I'd never had a steady girlfriend. Why was that? I could no longer blame the job. The career with the Queensland Police. The long unsociable hours. That was all in the past now.

42

It was time to get back to work. Josh had insisted on driving me to his place the day before, but I'd put my foot down and followed him in the Dub. I needed to maintain my independence. The good thing about being in Broadbeach was that I was only minutes away from Surfers Paradise. Wesley was on my mind, so I'd decided the night before to pay him a visit in the morning. Realising he'd probably be meeting Cassie early, I purposely waited until later when he'd be back at the Milton.

Schoolies was still in mid flow. It was Thursday but it seemed like a long week. By mid-morning, the zombies were stirring, but not in the herds as yet. Wesley had two parking spots with the apartment. The Porsche Cayenne took up one; the other, where the MINI would have stood, was vacant. He'd given me a key on our last meeting, which meant I could now not only park in the underground basement but go up to the apartment any time I liked. As a courtesy, though, I called him first to let him know I was coming.

'Scott. I was just about to call you!' Wesley said after answering the phone on the first ring.

'Really. Why?'

'I need to tell you something. Something I should have told you before.'

Not having to navigate the zombie gauntlet was a relief. Parking in the heart of Surfers and riding the lift from the basement to the penthouse apartment was a luxury. Wesley was anxiously waiting for me in the kitchen when I arrived.

'What's up, mate?' I asked, joining him at the large marble clad island.

He remained seated on a stool, so I climbed on the one next to him. We didn't shake hands. Like a typical nerd, Wesley launched straight into business, skipping the awkwardness of social interaction. He didn't even enquire about the black eye. 'It's time I told you what's really going on but … I'm afraid.'

'Afraid of what?'

'Not what. Who?'

I raised my eyebrows, prompting him to continue.

'Brennan. Mick Brennan.'

'The biker. So, he is involved.'

'Yes. He killed Cory!'

'Really? Have you told the police?'

Wesley shook his head and lowered his gaze to the countertop. 'They questioned me for three hours yesterday. I couldn't tell them, I—'

'Why not?'

'He said he'd kill me too.'

'Okay. Let's start from the beginning, eh?'

He took a deep breath and exhaled slowly.

'It's alright. Take your time.' I placed a reassuring hand on his shoulder.

'He was blackmailing Cory. Demanding more and more money.'

'For what?'

The familiar shrug. 'I don't know. He obviously had something over my brother.'

'Did Cory tell you this?'

'No.'

'Then how do you know he was being blackmailed?'

'It was Brennan who told me. He came here. Said there was an overdue debt and that it was down to me now to pay it.'

'How much did he want?'

'Two million.'

'Hmm … you said it was Brennan that killed Cory?'

Wesley nodded, avoiding eye contact. 'He said if I didn't give him the money, I'd be toast like my brother.'

'He said that?'

'Yes.'

'Okay. You need to make a full statement to the police—'

'But I can't. He'll—'

'He won't be doing anything. You'll be safe.'

The nod again, as if he knew what I was saying made sense.

My phone rang. The number was Patty Cummings. 'Excuse me for a minute, mate. I've got to take this.' Rising from the kitchen stool, I padded back into the foyer. 'Hello, Patty.'

'Scott. Where are you?'

'I'm in Surfers. Why?'

'I'm at your office. Need to talk to you right away.'

'Oh, okay. Is everything alright?'

'No, it's not. Can you come right away?'

'Sure.' I checked my watch. It was just before lunch. 'I can be there in about thirty minutes.'

'Right. I'll be waiting.' She hung up.

When I returned to the kitchen, I noticed Wesley's complexion was a sallow white except for his cheeks and ears, which were red. Had he been eavesdropping?

'Who was that?'

'Your mum.'

'Patty?' A stupid question because I'm sure he only had one mum. He seemed more agitated by the call from Patty than when he was telling me about the threat from Mick Brennan. 'What did she want? Why would Patty be calling you? Where is she?' The questions were quick fire, shot from a nervous revolver.

I wondered if my use of the shrug annoyed him as much as his did everyone else.

'Is she coming here? Is she—'

'Whoa, mate. Take it easy. Why are you getting all worked up over Patty?'

'Because she's in it with him.'

'Brennan?'

'Yes.'

'Don't worry about that. Listen.' I placed a hand on his shoulder again. 'I'm going to call DI Jenny Radford—'

He flinched, and the tension in his body hardened.

'It's okay, it's okay. I want you to tell them everything. I'll insist they offer you protection.' Gently squeezing his shoulder, I leaned in. 'It's going to be alright.'

Driving south towards Coolangatta, I called Jenny.

'Hey.' Her voice sounded distant over the trundle of the Dub's engine.

'Hey. Listen, I've just left Wesley. There's been a new development. He needs to talk to someone.' I went into detail about the conversation we'd just had.

'Mick Brennan? Bloody hell, Scotty. I told you we can't get involved with him.'

'We can't ignore the fact that he may have killed Cory Evans and is threatening to do the same to his brother.'

'I know. I know. Shit!'

'It's a tricky one.'

'You're not wrong.'

'At least talk to Wesley. Give him some reassurance about his safety.'

'But what if he's making all this up? What if he killed Cory? If we approach Brennan now, we'll spook him.'

'What's more important? The drug bust or justice for a young bloke's murder?'

'You bastard.'

'I'm sorry. Like you said, it's a tricky one. We agreed to share all information, but—'

'We did. Thanks for bringing this to my attention. I'll get Bradley out to see Wesley now.'

'Thanks, Jen. Meanwhile, I'm on my way to see Patty.'

'Patty? Why?'

'She just called me. Said she needs to talk urgently.'

'That's strange. She wasn't willing to open up to us at all.'

'Me neither. Got the call a few minutes ago out of the blue.'

'Okay. Keep me informed.'

'Will do, boss.'

43

Patty hadn't said where she'd meet me. I wasn't sure if she'd be waiting out on the street, so parking out the back of the building in Elvis' car space, I continued on foot through the side alley to Griffith Street. Patty was nowhere to be seen, but to my shock, her ex-husband, Barry Evans, was. He was standing outside the door to my office. After checking his watch, he looked up and saw me approaching.

'Scott, thank goodness you're here,' he said, marching towards me with his hand out.

We shook hands.

'Barry. What can I do for you?'

'Sorry to just show up unannounced. Can we go up to your office?'

'Sure.' The door to the street was unlocked. Once inside, the entrance to Elvis' accountancy suite was quite apparent. The stairway to the left of this, which led up to my little office, was less so. Producing keys from my pocket as we ascended the stairs, I unlocked the door and showed Barry in. 'Can I get you anything? Tea, coffee?'

'No, I'm fine.' Although dressed in an expensive sports jacket, designer jeans and highly polished shoes, he was looking a little dishevelled—ruffled hair and a heavy five o'clock shadow.

We sat at my desk. 'How can I help?'

'I've just come from the police headquarters. They've been questioning me all night.'

'That's perfectly normal, mate. Doesn't necessarily mean anything.' We hadn't parted on the best of terms after our last meeting, but he had approached me now. So in an attempt to keep him on side, I used the sympathetic friend routine. 'Police procedure is to talk to the next of kin first up.'

He shook his head wildly. 'No, no. They think I did it. They think I killed Cory.'

'Did you?'

'No, of course not!'

'And you want me to *prove* you didn't. Is that correct?' It wouldn't be the first time I'd represented a prime suspect. Bestselling author Ben Fisher hired me to prove his innocence after he'd been accused of killing a young woman in Tallebudgera Valley earlier that year.

'That's right. You're the best.'

'I can't do it, I'm afraid, mate. I'm already working for Wesley.'

'Wesley? But he's the reason I'm here.' The arrogant confidence of the second-hand car salesman was nowhere to be seen. Instead, Barry's voice broke with a nervous fear.

'It is?'

'Surely, you're starting to put two and two together?'

'How do you mean?'

'It's obvious. Wesley had Cory killed.'

'I don't understand.'

Barry ran a shaky hand across the top of his head. 'You know he's a member of the bikie gang?'

'The Wasps?' My smirk would have done little to hide the surprise in my voice.

'Yes. He and that thug were bleeding Cory dry. When Cory finally had enough, they killed him.'

'That's a bit of a stretch, mate.'

'Is it? Do you really think Cory invited Wesley to stay with him?'

'Uh … yeah.'

'He didn't. He had no choice. Whatever Wesley had over his brother, he was using it to his advantage.'

'But how would you know this?'

He shrugged off the question as if it were irrelevant. 'Ask Patty.'

'I intend to. In fact …' I checked my watch. 'She's supposed to be here anytime now.'

'Patty's coming here?' The reaction was identical to the one I'd witnessed from Wesley earlier that day. 'Why would Patty be coming here?'

If I was still a copper, I wouldn't be divulging such information, but being a private detective meant I could use situations like this to my advantage. 'She reckons she knows who killed Cory.'

'And she's going to tell you?'

'Yep. So, I guess if what you're saying is true, she'll be corroborating your story.'

Now it was Barry's turn to check his watch. The shiny Breitling. 'I've got to go.'

'No, hold on a minute, mate. You can't just lob in here throwing around accusations like that without any way to back them up.'

'Well, that's the thing. I don't have any proof. That's why I need to hire you.'

As far as I knew, there was no ethical code of practice stating that more than one party couldn't hire me in a case. It was cheeky, probably immoral, but if the end result was a conviction, what harm could it do? 'Okay. I'll help you, but I'll need to know all the facts.'

I was hoping this would have come as a relief to him, relaxed him a little, but it didn't. He stood and inadvertently glanced at his watch again. 'Okay, that's good, but I need to be somewhere else right now.'

'What's more important than being here? Don't you want to prove your innocence?'

'Yes, yes … yes, of course. I just need to do something first. Can we meet up again, later perhaps?'

The Wesley shrug was my tool of choice. 'Whatever.'

'Okay, I'll call you.' He rushed out of the office, no handshake, not even a glance back over the shoulder.

Hmm. Interesting. I picked up the phone and called Jenny. After a dozen or so rings, I was about to hang up when she answered.

'Hey.'

'Hey. What did you do to old Barry?'

'Barry Evans?'

'Yeah, you've scared the shit out of him.'

'Good. The little bastard's hiding something.' Jenny wasn't the kind of girl to mince her words. 'Trouble is, we've got nothing on him yet. We're going through his accounts, but he's a *phlippery widdle phucker.*'

'He's just hired me to prove his innocence.'

'What? I thought you were working for Wesley?'

'I am.'

'Now who's the slippery little sucker?'

'Me, I guess.'

I knew exactly what was going through Jenny's mind. *That can't be legal* would have been her initial thought, and she'd be searching her memory right back to the academy days for a piece of information that would back this up, but like me, she wouldn't find it. Then she'd be sifting through her realms of reason. Was it right? Or was it immoral? What would be the advantages and disadvantages?

I told Jenny how Patty had been a no-show but suspected that this may have been because she saw Barry. I also confided in her the reaction I'd received from Barry when I told him I was meeting with his ex-wife, and how it was exactly the same reaction I'd received from his son, Wesley.

'It sounds like Patty knows more than she's been letting on,' Jenny said. 'We had her in for most of the day yesterday. She chose the "no comment" routine. Can you believe Nash is her brief?'

'Sounds like she's found enough money to hire him, after all.'

'We'll bring her in again.'

'Why not let me talk to her first? It was me she contacted. Even went as far to say she knew who'd killed Cory.'

'Hmm … makes sense. Sounds like she'll open up to you.'

'That's right. I'll go down to Tweed this afternoon. Might be yet another case solved by the amazing Scotty Stephens by the end of the day.'

'Tosser!'

'Thanks Jen. Let's catch up tonight for a drink.'

'We'll see. Call me as soon as you know anything.'

'Yes, boss.'

44

The boom gate was down, so I was forced to park the Dub in the visitors' parking out the front of the caravan park. Patty's trailer was on the other side of the property, so it was a leisurely late afternoon stroll.

'G'day, Scotty,' an elderly woman, who was hosing a small patch of lawn in front of her mobile home, said, as if she knew me.

'Afternoon.'

I'd rang Patty a couple of times before making the trip down to the Tweed, but her phone rang out. I even had a quick look around Cooly to make sure she wasn't waiting around, perhaps for Barry to leave, but she was nowhere to be seen.

'Hello, Patty. Are you there?' I called out, stepping under the awening.

The only noise was the sound of a lawnmower somewhere across the park.

'Patty, it's Scotty Stephens.' There was no reply. The flimsy fly screen on the caravan door rattled when I knocked, and it creaked when I opened it. Wrapping on the thin aluminium front door caused the van to shake. Call it a detective's impulse, but I tried the handle and it opened. Was she inside? Hoping I'd go away, perhaps. 'Patty. Are you there?'

There were no family photos on the small side dresser, only a stack of bills, a Coles magazine, and a bunch of keys. A worn tan, leather sofa dominated the square room. A thirty-inch TV and a coffee table were the only other items of furniture. From where

I stood there was a clear view of the basic kitchen—off-white Formica cabinets, a grimy, freestanding stove, a stainless steel sink full of dirty dishes.

There was a vinyl, faux wood concertina door hanging open on a ceiling track, leading to a narrow corridor.

'Patty. Are you there, love? You wanted to talk to me?'

The matching bathroom door was also open. A shower, a toilet, a sink, a linoleum floor. Old Patty obviously wasn't the house-proud type. The place was far from clean.

The remaining closed door at the end of the short corridor must have been the bedroom. It rocked on its track when I knocked on it. Patty didn't seem to be at home, but I looked anyway to make sure. The door squeaked as I slid it across.

'Fuck me dead!' I cried out loud.

Patty was lying on the bed. There was blood everywhere. I didn't venture any further into the room. The massive wound on her head, gaping mouth, grey complexion, sullen, empty gaze towards the ceiling told me she was beyond help. Closing the door, I backtracked out of the van, and called 000.

A police squad car and an ambulance arrived at the same time. Jenny and Bradley were also on their way. I'd called Jenny after calling 000. Detectives Geoff Reynolds and Kelly Blake arrived just after the first response. Reynolds manhandled me towards his car.

'What the hell are you doing?' I growled.

'Detaining a suspect. What do you think I'm doing?'

'But I called this in.'

'So?' He swung open the back door of his car. 'Do I need to cuff you?'

Remaining calm, I climbed into the back seat.

Leaving the door open, Reynolds said, 'Right, tell me what happened.'

Aware of the procedure, I told him everything from Patty contacting me to arrange a meetup, her not showing, to me finding her body.

'When was the last time you spoke to her?'

'About lunchtime.'

'Did she seem … worried about anything … or?'

'No, she just said she had some important information for me.'

'What kind of information?'

I didn't want to tell him what Patty had said, but I knew if I didn't, it would look bad on me later when it came out.

'She knew who killed her son?'

'Yes. Apparently.'

'So why was she telling this to you and not to the police?'

'I don't know.'

'And now she's dead. Wait here. We'll need to talk to you.' He slammed the car door shut, and I watched him pulling on a pair of rubber gloves as he made his way towards the caravan. Stopping to have a word with one of the uniformed constables, he nodded in my direction—ordering the young bloke to keep an eye on me, no doubt.

More squad cars arrived, and the area was cordoned off.

I didn't spot Jenny's MINI. There were so many police cars there, she must have parked further up the lane. It was Bradley who spotted me in the back of Reynold's car. When Jenny saw me, the pair marched over, but the young constable blocked them. Jenny produced her badge, but the guy shook his head and stood firm. We were just over the border in Northern New South Wales. Out of Jenny's jurisdiction. A reassuring glance and a nod in my direction told me to be patient.

Tweed Heads Police Station was a large modern facility on Wharf Street. Jenny and Bradley had followed in Jenny's car. I was taken in the back way—thankfully, still uncuffed.

'You okay?' Jenny asked, as Detectives Reynolds and Blake led me into an interview room.

'Yeah, no worries.'

Over an awful cup of police coffee, I relayed the sequence of events once more and answered all the questions the two detectives threw at me, accurately and clearly. Jenny and Bradley, obviously grateful to sit in as bystanders and unwilling to overstep the mark, remained silent, but I was glad of their presence.

'You said you've spoken to both Mrs Cummings' son and her ex-husband today?' Detective Blake asked.

Detective Reynolds was silently analysing me. This was normal practice. While one detective asked the questions, the other monitored the responses. Some of us could do both at the same time. Others couldn't.

'Yes.'

'And what were their reactions when you told them you were meeting up with Patty?'

'Defensive, angry even. Scared perhaps.'

'Scared?'

My firm expression must have told the detectives I was a worthy opponent when it came to a game of analytical tennis.

'Do you think either of them could have killed Mrs Cummings?'

'It's possible. Wesley would have had plenty of time. Barry not so much, but he was already in Coolangatta. It's only a few minutes' drive to the Tweed.'

'Why would either of them want to kill her? Start with Wesley.'

'If he had anything to do with the death of his brother, and Patty knew about it, he'd get scared when he found out she was going to meet me.'

'Did you tell him why Patty wanted to meet you?'

'No. But he could have put two and two together.'

'And Barry Evans?'

'Exactly the same motive if he had anything to do with the death of his son.'

Although the interview was being recorded, Detective Blake scribbled down notes.

'So, what motive would Scotty Stephens have for smashing a helpless, middle-aged woman's head in?' Detective Reynolds said.

'No motive at all. In fact, I was desperate to speak to her. If she really did know who killed Cory, it would have been case solved.'

'And Mick Brennan?'

'What about him?'

'Could he have killed her?'

'If she was about to tell me he'd killed her son, absolutely.'

'Is that a feasible scenario?'

'Yes. There is a connection between Brennan and Cory. I suspect he was extorting money from him and has continued to do so with Wesley.'

'How'd you get the black eye?'

Side glancing Jenny, she nodded.

'Brennan. I foolishly went snooping around The Wasps' nest.'

Sharp intakes of breath from both detectives told me they agreed with my self-description of foolish.

Detective Blake ended the interview at 8.30 pm. I was told to remain accessible, as it was likely we'd be speaking again.

'Of course. No worries.'

45

There was little to say during the ride back to the caravan park that evening. Seated in the back of the MINI, Bradley resembled a polar bear squeezed into a clown's car.

When we pulled into the gravel car park, I immediately regretted my decision to fetch the Dub and not leave it until morning. The media circus was back in town. The bitumen compound was full of identical four-wheel drives. Parked either side of the little Beetle were two chunky white Land Cruisers. One had the *9News* logo on its doors. The other *7News*.

Around the Gold Coast, the Dub was almost as famous as I was. When I left the police force just over a year ago, I was offered large sums of money for my story from the networks and magazines, which I shamelessly sold to the highest bidders, but I also did several lucrative TV and social media commercials, one of which was for VW Australia. When the giant car manufacturer heard I drove a classic Beetle, one of their savvy marketing execs came up with the idea of the man of the moment, arguably the most famous person in Australia at that time, driving into the VW showroom at Robina in the Dub, and driving away into the sunset in a brand new Golf GTI. This was at the beginning of my new business venture as a PI. I'd quit my career in the police force with very little to show for it. The money thrown at me was enough to set me up in business, so I pretty much took whatever was sent my way.

Now I was living to regret it. Of course, I didn't trade in the Dub, which meant it was recognised and even photographed from time to time by the tourists. The Land Cruisers parked just close enough so I couldn't open the doors on either side, meant the drivers knew who the little car belonged to. When Jenny's MINI pulled into the car park, two sentinels, posted just inside the entrance, were already on their phones. And before Jenny could march over to the two young guys and demand they move the vehicles, a pack of camera crews appeared from inside the caravan park, filming as they ran.

'Scotty, Becky Bishop, *10 News First*. Is it true you found Patty Cummings' body?'

Realising it was pointless even attempting to get into my car, but trying anyway, I wandered towards the mob and was surrounded. Memories of the *X* case came flooding back. 'Yes, that's correct.'

'Was she murdered?'

Jenny stepped in. 'Okay, move back.'

'Is Scott Stephens a suspect, Detective Inspector?' A young man wielding a *Sky News* microphone asked.

'No comment at this time. This is a police investigation. We'll be releasing information as it comes to light.'

'What the hell is going on here?' It was Detective Geoff Reynolds forcefully wading through the crowd.

'Relax your teeth, Geoff. We're just trying to get out of here,' Jenny said.

'Don't say another word.' He turned towards the crowd of reporters. 'There will be a press conference tomorrow morning. Until then, you can all get out of here.'

'Is it true you'll be laying charges against Scott Stephens?' a faceless voice called out.

Ignoring the lorikeet chatter, Reynolds turned to us. His face was scarlet with anger. 'Get the fuck out of here. I'll be talking to your superiors, Radford.'

Knowing Jenny, she wanted nothing more than to deck him. And she could do it too. But ever the professional, she lowered her head and gestured with a nod to the Land Cruiser blocking the driver's side of the Dub. The fact that both killings had taken place over the border in New South Wales meant it was their case, their jurisdiction. Jenny would need to tread lightly. We had to keep them on side.

'Get this heap of shit out of the way. NOW!' Reynolds demanded, pointing to the four-wheel drive without turning or taking his eyes from Jenny.

A few minutes later, I was able to get into my car. Before I did, Jenny whispered into my ear, 'See you back at Ruby Street.'

Yes, it was just like the height of the X case all over again, I thought, while driving along Minjungbal Drive in Tweed Heads, with Jenny's MINI and the procession of news vehicles behind me. *How did I get myself into this situation again?* Just when I was thinking things couldn't get much worse, I was wrong. This became apparent when I pulled up at the house I'd shared for over twenty years with my best buddy to find a 'For Sale' sign outside. 'What the hell?'

Because the house had a single garage, which was the domain of Elvis' car; as usual, I had to park on the street. Jenny pulled up behind me with a Hollywood screech of tyres and we rushed into the house before the pack could settle.

'You didn't tell me Elvis was selling the place,' Jenny said once we were safely in the kitchen.

'That's because I didn't know, Jen.'

'What? He didn't tell you first?'

'Nope. I just found out the same time as you.'

'Wow. There really is something up.'

'He's not answering his phone. I spoke to his mum. All she said was this wasn't a good time. She couldn't get off the phone quick enough, but she promised to call me back when she gets the time.'

'Awkward,' Bradley said.

'You obviously need to talk to him,' Jenny said, placing a reassuring hand on my shoulder.

'I know. I will.'

'Okay, we better get out of here. It's like old times, eh? The media camped outside your door on Ruby Street.'

'You're so celebrity,' Bradley threw in.

'Yeah, right. Now bugger off.'

'You'll need to come into the station in the morning,' Jenny said.

'Sure. No worries.'

She kissed me on the cheek. 'Stay safe and stay off the street. See you tomorrow.'

Bradley did a kind of bow before leaving.

Once they had gone, I noticed a Ray White Real Estate brochure on the kitchen counter. There were pictures of not only the exterior of the property, but inside too, including my bedroom. Elvis had obviously given them full access. We'd been best mates for most of our lives. Why hadn't he told me about this? In the bottom, right-hand corner of the brochure was a picture of a young blonde woman dressed in a nice business suit. Underneath this was the name and phone number of Ingrid Schmitz.

Ingrid answered on the first ring. 'Ingrid Schmitz.'

'Oh hi, my name is Scotty Stephens. I—'

'Scotty. I've been expecting your call.'

'You have?'

'Yes, of course.'

'Right. I'm calling about the house on Ruby Street.'

'Of course, you are.'

'Well, what can you tell me?'

'Uhm ... the vendor approached me last week—'

'Last week?'

'Yes. Didn't you know?'

'No.' Needing to sit, I plonked myself down on one of the kitchen counter stools.

'Oh. Well, look, it's going to auction, but the vendor is open to offers prior to that.'

'How much will it go for, do you reckon?'

'Two. Two and a half. Maybe even three. A developer will buy it. They're queuing up for large blocks like this.'

'Three hundred grand seems pretty reasonable.'

'Three million!'

'What?' I was glad I'd sat down, because I'd probably be picking myself up off the floor about now. The house was little more than a three-bedroom fibro shack. 'Will it really go for that much?'

'My oath it will. I've got a dozen developers who'd write the cheque tomorrow. It's not the house, you understand, that'll be demolished. It's the land. A savvy architect could fit up to eight luxury villas on that size block.'

'Really?'

'Are you interested in buying it?'

'Me?'

'The vendor said he would consider all offers prior to the auction. You're a friend of his. Maybe he's waiting to see if you make an offer.'

'Hmm. Interesting. Well, thanks for your time, Ingrid.'

'If you got this for the right price, it would be an amazing opportunity. But I'd get in sooner rather than later. There's a lot of interest.'

'Cheers. I'll consider it.'

Remaining seated, I called Josh's number. As much as I wanted to, I'd decided not to go back to his house in Broadbeach. The media would follow me and I didn't want them exposed to all of that. After a brief chat, Josh understood, and told me to take care of myself. We arranged to meet up soon.

46

The polished concrete floor was cool under my bare feet. The corridor was quite long. Identical stainless steel doors on either side, like cabins of a starship, were spaced opposite each other every couple of metres. My faithful old wetsuit was silver for some reason, and so was the surfboard under my arm. As I increased my speed, I noticed a figure up ahead, facing me in the middle of the corridor. A little beyond this was the familiar front door of Ruby Street from the inside.

I didn't need to see his face to know who it was. Not just a chubby little kid. As I got closer, I noticed the chocolate around his mouth. Melted Tim Tam. That cheeky grin shone like a beacon as bright as the Byron Bay lighthouse.

Of course, the original Tim Tam ad wasn't set in an ultra-modern building. It was on the verandah of a Queenslander on a summer's day. His mum would appear at any moment. She'd produce a handkerchief, roll up one corner, lick it to moisten the cotton, then dab away the chocolate from around the little lad's mouth.

'What the fuck, Scotty?'

Hearing an expletive from the mouth of the little cherub shocked me.

'Are you so worried about yourself that you've forgotten about me?'

I didn't speak. Couldn't. Starstruck, I guess.

The boy suddenly burst into flames, but he didn't yell out. Instead, with his eyes fixed on mine, he went through a kind of metamorphosis, like melting in reverse. He passed through the stages of his growth: the not so cute kid anymore, the awkward puberty phase, the young man who everyone felt sorry for. Then, like a magician's stage show, there was a puff of smoke and the figure disintegrated. The black charcoal stump appeared momentarily, but then it was gone.

Now I was standing naked on Ruby Street, looking back at the house. Not your show pony Queenslander, but an icon nowadays, just the same. A flaky green front door, with a window on either side of it. Dirty pink fibro walls, a mission brown corrugated roof. Ugly as hell, but home for my entire adult life. Sanctuary.

The dented, wheelless body of Tetley's Vespa stood in the middle of the small patch of grass that was the front yard. A Bougainvillea grew from where the seat once was. In front of this was a small wooden cross with a dog collar resting over it. An inscription in the wood said 'Romeo'.

The roar of a full capacity footy crowd rose from somewhere at the back of the house—from the man shed, no doubt. As if startled by the sudden noise, the recycling wheelie bin, the one with the yellow lid, flipped over and empty beer bottles and pizza boxes spilled out onto the street.

I was in the middle of the road. A pale green Holden Kingswood drove towards me and stopped within millimetres. The parents I remember from my childhood were in the front seats. Dad was driving. He didn't smile, just looked at me as if to say, 'What the hell have you done now?' Mum made up for the smile, that regardless-of-what-it-is-you've-done-I'll-always-love-you smile I missed so much.

Stepping back and allowing the car to pass, my heart rate pounded when I realised the *X* killer was sitting in the backseat. The monster grinned at me as the vehicle pulled away and, holding up a small, hooked knife, the figure made the mark of an *X* across its throat. I wanted to cry out but couldn't find my voice.

The giggles of children echoed as if from a vast hall. The Palm Beach Currumbin High School year of 1996 had gathered at either side of the road. Among them were the young versions of Elvis, Tetley, Johnno, and Knackers. Everyone was pointing at my nakedness and jeering. The girls giggled. 'For Fuck's sake, Scotty. What are ya doin, lad?' Tetley called out.

Then all eyes averted to the sound of a whining differential. The Kingswood was reversing back towards me at speed … but this time, it didn't stop.

I didn't think I'd gotten any sleep. If it wasn't for the dream, I would have said I'd been lying awake all night, thinking about Elvis and the house on Ruby Street. And what a bloody day I'd had. Finding Patty's body. Learning that my life would change forever once the sale of my home went through to a developer. 'Be careful what you wish for, Scotty,' my mum whispered again as I paddled out to the back off Kirra Point.

'Bloody hell, Scotty. What's with the mullet, mate?' It was Chilly, my barber.

I took offence at the word mullet. I didn't have a mullet. The problem was, just lately my hair at the front had receded a little, not noticeably. It just meant it grew quicker at the back nowadays, so if I didn't keep up with the maintenance routine, it resembled a mullet.

'We've spoken about this, remember?' Along with a dozen or so other surfers, Chilly was sitting on his board, waiting for the next set. His post-Covid business was given a much-needed boost in the arm when the media learned he was my barber. Chilly, being the shrewd businessman, exploited the exposure. I didn't mind one bit. The picture of me sitting in his chair while he trimmed my fringe was my idea. The caption, "While keeping the Gold Coast safe, Scotty still needs to look good!" was Chilly's. He even invented a name for the hairstyle—The Scotty #1.

'Sorry, mate. I've been a bit busy. Just haven't had time to come around to the shop.'

'Well, make sure you get around as soon as you can.' He was concerned that people would see my unkept appearance as a reflection of his business. I'd created a monster.

The first wave of a new set rolled towards us. We dropped onto our stomachs, and let it pass beneath us. When the second one approached, we were ready for it. And so began another day.

I didn't talk to anybody else for the next hour. Just surfed. Thinking. Contemplating the case. My future. The welfare of my best mate. When I finally got back to the house, showered and poured a bowl of Rice Bubbles, my phone rang. Accompanied by the lyrics, 'I like big butts and I cannot lie', the image on the screen was of a wide, slightly hairy, bare backside. It belonged to Elvis. The picture was a product of a night on the piss a couple of years ago. Tetley, Elvis and I had taken selfies of our bums and used them as the profile pictures in our phones. This meant that when Tetley rang either of us, a little white, scrawny arse would appear. When I rang them, I like to think they felt a little intimidated by the taut, tanned posterior that adorned their screens. Childish, pathetic, and all of the above, such was the life of a bachelor.

'Hey bud.'

I could only just hear his voice. I wanted to yell at him, demand some answers. *Why did he bugger off to Melbourne without telling me? Why hasn't he been answering my calls? Why did he put the house up for sale?* But he sounded terribly down, as if he were on the verge of tears. 'Hey, mate. How's it goin?'

'Ah … been better.'

'What's goin on, Elv?'

'I don't know. Wish I did. Things have just been getting on top of me lately.'

'So, are you staying in Melbourne? Or …?'

'Don't know yet. Just got to think things through, ya know?'

'But you've put the house up for sale.'

'Yeah.'

There was an awkward silence until I said, 'What would you think if I bought it?'

'I was hoping you'd say that.'

'Really? So why didn't you offer it to me first?'

'I don't know. I've not been thinking straight just lately. Hiding from responsibilities, I guess. I don't know if you can afford it though, bud.'

He was my accountant. He knew I could. 'What do you want for it?'

'Give me two and it's yours.'

Two million dollars was a hell of a lot of money, but even with my limited knowledge of the real estate industry, I knew that for an 800 square metre block a street back from the beach in Kirra; it was a once in a lifetime bargain. 'Can I think about it?'

'Of course you can. The auction isn't for a couple of weeks, but I can take it off the market at anytime.'

'Has there been much interest?'

'Ballistic. Developers want to demolish it. At least I know if you buy it, you'll preserve it, eh?'

I didn't answer, choosing to change the subject instead. 'Listen, mate. I'm thinking of you, missing you, and I want you to know I'm here for you. If there's anything you need.'

'I know. I know. I've just got to get my head right, you know?'

'Yeah, and you will.'

'Alright. Got to go. Let me know as soon as you've made a decision, and we'll talk soon.'

47

There was so much going through my mind I hardly remembered the drive to Surfers. Giving a statement at the Gold Coast police headquarters would be the first point of call. This would act as a double whammy because it meant I'd also be able to seek Jenny's opinion on the situation with the house.

Then I wanted to visit Wesley, see how he was getting on. The first week of the Schoolies festival was drawing to a close, which was the Queensland week. Unbelievably, there were still another two weeks to go. The New South Wales graduates next week, then Victoria the week after that. Poor old Wesley would have to carry on with his life of stealth for a little longer yet.

Depending on the situation, I also wanted to pay Barry Evans a visit. I'd need to check with Jenny first, though, to make sure that was okay. I wouldn't have been at all surprised if he was being held in custody. Wesley was also under suspicion, so I'd be playing by the rules from now on.

The boom gate leading to the underground parking beneath the police headquarters opened by itself as I approached. That famous little Dub.

Bradley met me at the lift, took me up to the third floor, showed me into interview room number one, then breezed away to get me a coffee. While I sat waiting, memories of the interviews with the Monroe children during the X case came to mind. The twins were under suspicion after CCTV footage showed one of them fleeing the scene of one of the murders, but we couldn't determine which one it was. None of us could have imagined the outcome.

Bradley returned, carrying two coffees. As he placed them down on the table in front of me, Jenny entered the room.

'Hey, boofhead,' she said, instantly softening the mood.

'Hey Shrimp.'

'Can I get you anything else, ma'am?' Bradley asked.

'Did you eat all the Tim Tams?'

Bradley appeared shocked and ruffled. 'No, I did not!'

'Good. Go and get them then.'

He bowed his head and rushed out of the room but was back before Jenny even had the chance to sit down.

'Uh, caramel flavour. Fancy shmancy,' I said when he placed the open packet on the table.

'Save me one, eh?' He left the room.

The interview was standard procedure, one that both Jenny and I had conducted hundreds of times. Waiving my right to have a solicitor present, I told her everything from being approached by Maria Constanta, the concerned house maid, through to finding Patty's body.

Like Detective Blake, Jenny also took notes even though the interview was being recorded. 'Do you think the same person who killed Cory, killed Patty too?'

'Possibly, but I can't help thinking there's more to this case. Something we're missing.'

'So, who do you think killed Cory Evans?'

'Hmm ... good question. There are four prime suspects.'

'Four?' she didn't look up from her pad. 'Interesting. Can you list them in the order of relevance?'

'Sure. Although the motive isn't a hundred per cent clear yet, I'd place Mick Brennan at the top of the list.'

'Why's that?'

'I believe he used Patty to get to her eldest son.'

Jenny nodded in agreement as she scribbled down my words.

'The drug deal you intercepted would have cleaned him out. He'd already sold off most of his assets to fund it, now it's sitting in a paddock in Logan getting a zero return.'

'Why would he kill Patty?'

'Because I think she was about to crumble. Come clean. She'd asked to meet me the afternoon of her death. Maybe she feared for the welfare of Wesley. It appears as if Brennan's focus had switched to the younger son, who just happened to have recently taken control of the fortune.'

For the audio recording, Jenny's silence was remaining impartial, but the nods and facial expressions told me she was agreeing with just about everything I'd said so far.

I was well aware of the extra difficulty surrounding the case if Brennan was involved to the extent I believed he was. The fact that he was a New South Wales resident, though, meant Jenny couldn't just arrest him or bring him in for questioning. She'd have to run everything by Reynolds and Blake first.

'Who's next on your list?'

'Barry Evans, the father.'

The nod again, the scribble, the absence of eye contact prompting me to continue.

'Barry supposedly lost everything when his son sued him for loss of earnings.'

'You believe he stashed some of the fortune away?'

'Most of it, I reckon.'

'So, where's the motive? He seems to be doing alright.'

'That's right. He's doing very well in such a short period of time. I think Cory was planning on going after him again. Would Barry be able to account for his success?'

'And third on your list?'

'Until yesterday, I would have said Patty Cummings.'

'Could she have killed Cory? Or had him killed?'

'Absolutely. This is where the link with Brennan is important.'

'In what way?'

'Well, think about it. What interest would Brennan have in her? He had to have had an angle. So, although she may have had nothing directly to do with Cory's death, she was heavily involved.'

'Which takes us back to Brennan.' I could tell that Jenny was itching to end the interview so that she could throw in her own two cents worth, but for now at least she remained quiet. 'Who's next?' As if she didn't know.

'Wesley, of course.'

'Motive?'

'He'd have you believe he idolised his older brother. That he was rescued from the caravan park, and his life changed for the better. But when you realise it was *because* of Cory he ended up in the caravan park, you can look at it from a different perspective. He had a comfortable life in Currumbin. Nice house, good school. He'd shown no interest in the life his brother had led, never really even been a part of it. We have to remember that when Patty lost everything after the court case, Wesley did too. Then, out of the blue, his brother plucks him from the depths of poverty and brings him to Surfers. He's a hard character to read. I suspect there may have been some jealousy, resentment even, which is understandable.'

'Enough to make him a killer though?'

'Well, there's a new theory that he may have been working with Brennan.'

'What?'

'Something Barry said yesterday.'

'Wesley and Brennan?'

'Hard to believe but worth looking into. I want to spend some time with Wesley. Buddy up. See if I can learn more about him.'

Jenny inhaled, sat upright, and took a sip from her coffee cup. 'That might not be possible.'

I was about to ask why when she cut me off.

'And number four?'

'Netty.'

'Annette Slater, the personal trainer.'

'Yep. High profile but another individual who is on the brink of losing everything because of Cory Evans.'

'Hmm.' Jenny's note keeping was swift. 'And the cleaner?'

'Maria? Doubtful.'

'Cassie Evans?'

'Not sure…' I knew Cassie should have been on the list, but it wasn't computing, she was just a kid. *But what if her mother, Josie, was involved too?* This was a thought that had only just come to mind.

'Okay. There's another suspect that you seem to have overlooked.'

My puzzled frown begged an explanation.

'Geoff Reynolds has another suspect he is investigating and is insisting that we include in our investigation too.'

'Who?'

'You.'

'Me. That's ridiculous. You know that.'

Once again, for the sake of the recording, the sigh Jenny let out was a silent one that said, I know, I know. 'Tell me again why you went to the caravan park yesterday afternoon and what happened when you got there.'

48

It was lunchtime when Jenny finally ended the interview. 'Hungry?'

'What kind of a question's that?'

'A stupid one. You're always hungry. Come on. I'll shout you lunch.'

We ate at an all-day Aussie breakfast café on Chevron Island. Jenny had no need to apologise for the awkward questions. She knew I understood the job.

'So did you speak to the real estate agent?' Jenny asked before biting the end off a sausage.

'Yep.'

'And?'

'It's going to auction in a couple of weeks. Developers are queuing up for it, apparently.'

'You need to speak to Elvis. See if you can buy it from him.'

'Already have.' Taking a bite of toast, I chewed it loudly.

'…if you make me say "and?" one more time you're going to be wearing that fried egg.'

'He said I could have first dibs.'

'He did? Wow! That's awesome. Oh … how much does he want?' She screwed up her face as if I were about to deliver some devastating news.

'Two mill.'

'Ouch. That's a lot of money.'

'A bargain, so I'm told. He can expect upwards of three if it goes to auction.'

'Really?'

'Yep.'

'So, what are you going to do?'

'I was hoping you could help me decide.'

'Me? How?'

'Well, you're the level-headed one, Jen. After all you went to uni and that.' There was a hint of sarcasm in my tone. Part of the banter.

'Do you have that kind of money?'

'Sort of.'

'So buy it, then sell it to a developer and make a million dollars.'

'I couldn't do that to Elvis. He'd be expecting me to keep it.'

'It wouldn't have anything to do with him.' As if realising she was coming down hard, she softened her tone. 'How is he?'

'Not good. I reckon he might have had some kind of nervous breakdown or something.'

'I'm sorry to hear that, but it sounds like he's in the best place. With his parents.'

'Yeah. I said I'd give him a decision soon.'

'Right, so you wanted to talk to me first. Get my advice?'

Nodding while piling a fork full of baked beans into my mouth was well within my skill set.

'Then go for it. That would be my advice.'

Jenny dropped me back at the police headquarters. As we walked towards the Dub, she reminded me that Reynolds would likely contact me soon with more questions.

'What do you reckon to that guy?' I asked.

Her slow intake of breath was bated with calculated caution. 'You know about what happened in Brisbane?'

'No.'

'He was a detective with the Queensland Police. There was an incident with an informant. A young prostitute. She blew the whistle, said he'd been taking bribes, turning a blind eye. That kind of thing. But instead of getting booted off the force, as he should have been, they reassigned him to New South Wales. Spent a couple of months in Sydney, but then came up to the Tweed.'

'I knew there was something about that guy.'

'I know you did because I did too. It wasn't until I did some digging that I learned all of this.'

'This could complicate things even further.'

'That's right, if he's on Brennan's payroll, that would explain how The Wasps can remain one step ahead of us.'

'What about our inside man? Reynolds obviously doesn't know we have one.'

'That's right. This is why we have to be so bloody careful. We've worked hard to infiltrate them.'

Is it Knackers? I wanted to ask but knew perfectly well that even though we were friends, and I was an ex-copper, she was bound by law and duty not to divulge such information.

As I drove the short distance across town, I wondered what the locals of Surfers Paradise really thought about the Schoolies festival. Did they see it as a good thing, earning much needed revenue for the area, or was it one big pain in the arse? Sitting at the lights on the corner of Cavill Avenue and Surfers Paradise Boulevard, watching a group of teenagers monkeying around on the tramlines in the middle of the street, while being cheered and jeered by their peers, I suspected the latter.

Once again, I was grateful to Wesley for the loan of the parking spot under the Milton. The passkey made it easy for me to enter and exit without being caught up in the zombie herd. I'd called him before leaving Chevron Island. He'd sounded happy to hear my voice. When I let myself into the apartment, I realised why. The police had confiscated his computer, so rather than gaming all day, which had been helping him get through the quarantine necessary to avoid the Schoolies pandemic, he was basically sitting around moping.

'You alright, mate?' I asked, trying to inject a little enthusiasm into him.

He was sitting at the kitchen bench, nursing a can of Pepsi. 'No. It's pretty shit at the moment.'

'Yeah, I'm sorry to hear about your mum.'

The Wesley shrug made an appearance.

'First Cory. Now Patty.'

'I don't give a shit about Patty. Good riddance, I say.'

'Come on, mate, you don't mean that.'

'I just got back from the Tweed Police Station. They held me overnight, asking the same questions repeatedly.' The hand he lifted to his mouth was shaking. 'They're trying to say I hated Cory, and that I was jealous of him and that I ... I killed him.' Tears streamed down his cheeks. 'I'm on my own, Scott. Why would I want to hurt the only person who ever cared about me?'

'I know, mate. I know.' I placed an arm on his shoulder. 'If it's any consolation, they're questioning me too.'

'You?'

'Yep. They reckon because it was me who found your mum's body, I could have had something to do with her death.'

'That's crazy, isn't it?'

'My oath.'

Wesley pulled away from me and paced the room. 'There's something else I haven't told you, Scott,' he said without making eye contact. 'Something about Barry.'

'Barry?'

'Yes. He's been harassing me. Well, first Cory, now me.'

'Harassing you? In what way?'

'At first, I didn't know what was going on. He showed up a couple of times when Cory was here. They asked me to leave the room, but I could hear them shouting and arguing.'

'About money?'

'Yes. Well, I know that now because he's since directed his focus on me.'

'What's he doing?'

'Demanding money. Says it's rightfully his.'

'How much?'

'Thirty million.'

I'd never been a great whistler, always came out as more of a blow, but an attempt seemed appropriate at this time. 'Wow!'

'But there's more. He seems to assume that since moving in here I'm the benefactor of a secret he shared with Cory. Something so big that if he went to the press, it could change everything.'

'And what is this secret?'

'I haven't got a clue. He's been calling me, ranting on about how he's going to go to the authorities and tell them everything. He said I'll be back on that caravan park quicker than it would take to wipe away the tears. He's a nasty piece of work, Scott. Before Cory disappeared, he hardly even acknowledged my existence. Hasn't for years. Now I seem to be very important all of a sudden.'

'So, you think he may have been blackmailing Cory?'

'Yes ...' he continued to pace the room. 'The thing is, Scott, like I said, I'm all alone here. I can't even step outside without being set upon by a pack of Schoolies chasing Toolie blood. I've had the bikie thug up here, Barry, that fucking personal trainer chick, and now the police. All wanting a piece of me. I don't know how much more I can take.' He cried into his hands.

'Now then, mate.' I put my arm around him. It seemed as if depression was all around me at the moment. 'That's all right. You're not on your own.'

'My dad hates me. My mum's dead. My brother's dead. I'd say that's pretty much the definition of being alone.'

'No. You've got Cassie, and … you've got me. Go and pack a few things.'

'What for?'

'Go on, a couple of days' worth of clothes and whatever else you'll need.'

'Why? Where am I going?'

'You're coming to my place. I'm feeling just like you at the moment. No parents, no mates.' I didn't let on that I had a brother and his family who cared about me, but I fully understood his fear of being alone. 'Come on. I insist.'

There was a definite change in his demeanour as he marched towards the bedroom wing. Purpose in his stride, more positive than I'd seen him, excited even. He was a complex character. Having him close over the next couple of days would allow me to analyse him without him even knowing it.

49

It was hard to understand how trading a multi-million-dollar penthouse in a five-star hotel resort in Surfers Paradise for a fibro shack could bring on such excitement to a usually un-abstractive disposition.

'This is it?' Wesley asked climbing from the Dub on Ruby Street. His expression was filled with excited wonderment, as if I'd just handed him the keys to a Boystown prize home. 'This is where Scotty Stephens lives?'

'This is the old girl.'

'But it's for sale?' he said, noticing the large sign out front.

'Yeah, don't worry about that.'

'Why are you selling it?'

'I'm not. The owner is.'

'But you're going to buy it right?'

The Wesley shrug worked for him so why not me?

Since we'd met, Wesley had mainly displayed a mono-solemn expression—a head down, don't-look-at-me or don't-talk-to-me demeanour. I'd only noticed a slight smile on a couple of occasions, but never the genuine kind that lights up a person's face. Standing on Ruby Street admiring the old beach house like it was the Disney castle, there was a definite twinkle in his eyes. 'You have to.'

'Do I?'

'If you don't, I will.'

Hmm, interesting. 'Come on, let's get you inside before one of the neighbours dobs us into the press.'

Each unspectacular room in the house seemed to be a source of wonder for the lad. He crept quietly through the rooms like he was in a museum or if he'd stepped back in time to an era when people lived a lot differently. 'This is your TV?' he asked pointing to the cheap 40 inch. A stupid question by all accounts, so I assumed he was asking if it was the only TV we had.

'There's another one in the man shed.'

He swung around to face me, mouth agape, eyes wide. 'You have a man shed?'

'Yeah, come on, I'll show you.' I led him out to the back yard.

'Wow! This place is amazing,' he whispered as he followed me across the bindi infested lawn. 'A pool table. A bar. A dartboard. A beer fridge. A wall mounted TV. Can I stay here forever?'

'You can stay here as long as you like, mate.'

'Cool.'

I checked my watch. It was beer o'clock somewhere. 'Grab a stool.' I pulled out two XXXX stubbies from the fridge, twisted off the tops and placed one on the bar for Wesley.

Just like a kid, he jumped up onto the stool and let it swing around. 'This is awesome.' He took a massive swig of beer. It was the most animated I'd seen him since we'd first met only a few days ago.

'Do you follow the footy?' I asked, even though the football season had finished some weeks ago.

'Yeah.'

'Who do you follow?'

'The Lions, of course.'

Although a till-I-die supporter of Essendon, I did have a soft spot for the Brisbane Lions. 'Shame they just got rid of Coxie.'

'Nah, it was time for a change at the back. There's a young bloke called Gilly coming up the ranks.'

I was impressed. Until today, I thought Wesley's only interest was computer games. He seemed to have a knowledge of Aussie Rules Football, which I liked.

'What happened to Essendon last year?'

I didn't tell him I was an Essendon supporter. My life was pretty much in the public domain, he could have done some research on me, but as if reading my thoughts he added, 'You have a poster of Mark Harvey on your wall.'

My bedroom was still very much a teenage sanctum, but I guess having posters on the walls was something millennials no longer did. The old footy posters, as well as Rambo and Oasis, showed my age a bit. 'Ahh, we're just regrouping. Next season's all ours, mark my words.'

'Cool. Let's have a bet. Who finishes highest, Lions or Essendon?'

'I'll be in that,' I said, lifting my stubby and taking a swig.

'10k?'

I almost choked on the mouthful of beer. 'What? Ten thousand dollars?'

The shrug was back, only this time it was quicker, more zestful.

'Steady on, mate. I'll go hungry.'

'A hundred dollars then …?'

We shook hands.

'Listen. You'll have to sleep on the couch, I'm afraid. There is another room, but it belongs to my housemate.'

'Elvis.' He really had done his homework. 'No worries. I'll sleep out here if that's okay?' he said, pointing with his stubby to the old leather couch.

'Sure.' The Vinnies couch had been the choice of rest for my mate, Tetley, on many occasions.

'This is so cool. Thanks Scotty. These last couple of days have been … well, you know.' His expression cooled, and he lowered his head.

I needed to remember what a traumatic week this would have been for the young bloke. It had started with him being beaten up by a bunch of Schoolies, then learning that his brother had been killed, and now his mum. I wondered if his feelings towards his mother were genuine or if a part of him still cared for her. All of this would have been feasible to a normal mind. But unfortunately, or fortunately for me, I didn't possess such a thing. My cognitive function was that of a detective. For every action, there was a reaction. For every scenario, there was a parallel but-what-if situation.

Wesley's mood was reverting to his usual self. I needed to bring back the new happy version who might just open up if the correct lubricants were applied. 'Fancy pizza for dinner tonight?'

'Are you kidding me? Have I died and gone to heaven?'

'Pizza it is. But wait, there's more.' I reached under the bar, pulled out a box, placed it in front of Wesley, and blew off a layer of dust.

'What's this?'

I didn't quite get the reaction I was expecting when he opened it and looked inside.

'Is that a …?' He pulled out a black cable and a plug. 'Is this like an antique?'

'Antique? It's Elvis' PlayStation.' Sate of the art I thought.

'Wow, this is probably worth money now.' He lifted the console from the box like it was a lost relic.

'We'll bang it on later. I'm shit hot at Mario.'

Wesley burst into laughter. 'That'll be fun. How about another one of these for now?' He lifted his empty beer bottle into the air and wiggled it from side to side.

50

As usual, my inbuilt surf alarm clock woke me just before dawn. It surprised me to see Wesley sitting at the kitchen table eating a bowl of cereal. 'Bloody hell, did you shit the bed?' Another one of Tetley's English sayings.

Wesley, obviously not averse to our kind of banter, looked back at me horrified.

'It's just a saying, like if you arrive early for work.'

'Oh … no. I'm just keen for my first surf lesson.'

'Oh, that's right.' I remembered last night's PlayStation wager. If I won, Wesley would teach me how to play golf. If he won, I'd have to teach him how to surf. He won. Well, destroyed me I should say. But the golf was a bit of a surprise. I didn't realise he played. He didn't seem the sort.

Joining him at the table, Elvis' box of beloved Rice Bubbles finally yielded. As the last little puffed rice kernel landed on top of the small pile in my bowl, I couldn't help feeling this was a poignant moment, the end of an era.

'You okay?' Wesley asked.

'Yeah, mate. Just … you know. Life's changing.'

'You don't have to tell me.'

He was right. Here's me carrying on about my insignificant problems when this poor fellow had lost half of his family in the last couple of days. And although he was acting cool about it all, I was sensing there was some deep hurt in there. During our time together last night, laughing, joking, getting to know each other,

I learned a lot because I was still very much working. Like tickling a trout, I was slowly gaining his confidence.

'I reckon you'll be a natural surfer.' A lie, but the encouraging kind you understand. Living by the beach for most of his life, if he wasn't affluent at the sport at his age, he never would be. I hoped I was wrong.

'Yeah right.'

'You've obviously tried though, living on Currumbin Beach.'

This seemed to throw him, as if I'd just breached the over familiarity mark. There was a pause, and he shook it away. 'Tried a couple of times when I was a kid. Didn't take to it. Had a bit of a tumble.'

'Well starting today, mate, you're gonna be riding with the riders, hanging with the hangers, and shaggin' with the shaggers.'

This made him laugh. There was a definite childish side to his personality that I suspected he fought hard to hide. My plan was working. He was letting down his guard. So far, instead of the awkward, stereotype nerd he portrayed, I was enjoying the company of an intelligent, fun kid whose life experience seemed to be very limited. Oh, and on top of all that, he was harbouring a big fat secret. I had no idea what it was, but after spending quality time with him, my superhero detective senses were telling me it was there. Like opening a delicate oyster, I just needed to prize it out of him.

Elvis would have been a little heavier than Wesley so his surfboard, that was gathering dust in the garage, would be perfect for the young lad. When I pulled up the rusty panel door of the garage, I was amazed to find that Elvis' Porsche was gone. I hadn't bothered checking before, I'd just assumed it was there. Had he driven all the way to Victoria? Or did he sell the car before he left?

I was due to call him with my decision about the house. Had I been subconsciously putting it off? There were many questions, but few answers. There was one important one though that needed answering right away.

Padding back into the house with Elvis' board under one arm, I handed it to Wesley along with a bar of Sex Wax. Better give her a good going over, mate. It's been a while since she's been out there.

'Cool.' Wesley took the board out to the backyard, placed it on the grass and began to scour it with the wax.

Sitting down at the kitchen table, I lifted my phone and called Elvis' number. Unlike the previous hundred or so attempts, he answered this time, and I wondered if the picture of my butt on his phone made him smile.

'Hey, bud.' His tone was as lifeless and flat as it had been the previous day.

'Hey mate, how's it going?'

'Good.' The standard reply. *Good* meant *shit* in this case.

'Hey, you'll never guess who's staying at the house for a few days.'

'Uhh, let me guess. Jenny?' There was a spit of resentment in his tone. Had I inadvertently stuck a dagger in the heart of the problem? Was my relationship with Jenny the cause of his depression? Although I didn't think it was, I guessed it didn't help.

'No, not Jenny. Wesley Cummings.'

'Who?'

'Cory's brother.'

'Freckles' little brother is in our house?' A glint of excitement.

'Yeah.'

'Is he paying rent?'

I wasn't sure if he was joking or not but laughed it off anyway.

'So, have you decided? About the house I mean.'

'I have, mate.'

'And?'

'I'll take it. Two million, yeah?'

'Two million. Congratulations. Yet another milestone in the wonderful life of Scotty Stephens. I'll get the contract drawn up. Send me your solicitor details.' He hung up.

I couldn't work out what was going on. The call was all about business, no friendly chat, none of the usual banter. What on earth had I done to piss him off so much? His inaccurate perception of my lifestyle was obviously a factor. It wasn't a word that I wanted to use but it kept warring its ugly head. Was he jealous of the lifestyle he thought I had? A week ago I would have dismissed that as ridiculous, but our world had changed.

51

Wearing only board shorts and thongs, with our surfboards under our arms, we made our way across Musgrave Street towards the beach. The surf was reasonably decent, but I realised I wouldn't be enjoying it as much as usual. Today I was an instructor. 'Just do as I do, and when I tell you,' I said as we approached Kirra Beach Surf Club. The esplanade was already busy with early morning walkers. The Good Old Boys were chatting while waiting patiently for the kiosk to open.

Wesley suddenly stopped in his tracks.

'What's up, mate?' Following his gaze, I realised he'd a spotted a large bikie standing at the entrance to the beach like a sentinel. His Harley Davidson, parked in the surf club car park, glistened under a red sunrise. It was Knackers. 'It's okay, Wes. I know him.'

'You know Knackers?'

'Yeah. Since school.'

'Scott,' Knackers said as we approached. His gaze towards me was brief. His eyes rested on Wesley.

'Knackers. What can we do for you?'

'I'm sorry about what happened the other day. There was nothing I could do.'

'That's alright, mate.'

He stepped menacingly towards me. 'Well it's not, because I told you to fucking stay away.'

At this point I was ninety-nine per cent sure he was the cop working undercover, but that wasn't enough to mention it, because if I was wrong, and he wasn't, I'd be alerting him to the fact that the police had infiltrated the gang. 'You did. I'm sorry. I should have listened to you. Wes, do you wanna just wait for me on the sand?'

'Sure.' The old Wesley was back, head down, lack of confidence as apparent as the zinc on his face.

'You're lucky you're still alive, Scott,' Knackers said when we were alone. 'These guys don't mess around.'

'I realise that now. How deep are you in?'

'What do you mean?'

'Well, I wouldn't have thought you'd be the kind of guy to get involved with drugs and prostitution and anything else Brennan is involved with.' And I meant it. Although I knew nothing about his adult life, I remembered the lad from school. I remembered his mum, Linda. He was from a good family background. Sports orientated.

'You know nothing about me,' he said, mirroring my thoughts.

'I remember the Knackers from school. Knackers, the good mate.'

'We were never mates, Scotty. You and that Elvis ponce, and the little Pommy. You guys were tight.'

'You were a good bloke. Still are I reckon.'

'You're wrong. I'm not here off my own back this time, I've been sent to warn you.' He stepped in even closer.

'About what?'

'The Cummings kid.'

'Wesley?'

'You know who I mean.' He pointed to Wesley, who was practising the stomach to standing exercise I'd showed him earlier in the backyard. 'Things are about to heat up. You don't want to be getting in the way.'

I wasn't brave by any accounts, but during my many years in the police force, I'd had to face dangerous situations. This was one of those occasions. Now it was my turn to lean in and lower my voice. 'Why don't you go back to Brennan and tell him to get fucked?'

Knackers shook his head warily and exhaled.

'Oh, that's right, you can't,' I continued. 'Because he's in hiding after killing Patty. First Cory, then his mum. Are you seriously involved in this shit, mate?'

'If you get too close, Scott, you'll be next. But it won't be at the hands of Brennan.'

'If not Brennan, then who?'

Knackers glanced towards Wesley.

Following his gaze, I noticed Wesley was watching us, but when he realised our attention was on him, he suddenly looked away and carried on with the exercise.

'Wesley? What's he got to do with it?'

Knackers narrowed his eyes. 'I've said too much. You're supposed to be the detective. Go figure it out, eh?'

'Point me in the right direction. What do you know?'

He pointed to the silhouette of Surfers Paradise in the distance. 'That's the direction you want to go. Take the kid back to the Milton, drop him off and walk away.'

'You know I can't do that, mate.'

'I know.' He shook his head gravely.

'What made Brennan think he could just walk in and take away Cory's fortune?'

'What? It wasn't like that. Cory owed Brennan a lot of money.'

'Owed him? For what.' *Shit, was Brennan supplying Cory with drugs? Did Cory fall behind with his payments?*

'Listen, if I tell you, you've got to swear none of this will be repeated. Do I have your word?'

'My oath, mate.'

'They were partners. Let's say Cory committed himself to a large investment, but then at the last minute he pulled out. You don't do that to Brennan.'

'Right, so he killed him.'

'No, of course not. We're talking millions here. Brennan needed Cory alive because that money was the pivot keeping the deal together. Without it, it didn't just mean the deal was off, it was too late for that, Brennan was fully committed, balance of payment pending.'

'So, you reckon that while Cory was still around, Brennan still had a chance of getting the money.'

'That's right. There's a nest far more venomous than The Wasps' nest that you might want to consider looking into.'

Watching the big man stroll back toward his motorcycle, I realised he wasn't the undercover cop, and I was glad I said nothing.

As I trudged through the sand towards Wesley, the thunderous roar of Knackers' Harley ripped through the air but did little to interrupt my thoughts. There seemed to be a pattern forming with Cory's business deals. First Netty Slater entering a lucrative venture only to pull out at the last minute, leaving her on the brink of ruin. The scenario with Brennan was almost identical, only highly illegal.

'Everything okay?' Wesley asked when I reached him.

'Yeah. How do you know Knackers?'

'Huh?'

'Knackers. You asked me if I knew him. Well, how do *you* know him?'

'He came around looking for Cory a couple of times.'

'Did he find him?'

'I don't think so.'

'Wes, I need you to be honest with me, mate. I get the feeling there's something you're not telling me.'

The shrug made its first appearance of the day. 'I think I've told you everything I know.'

Now wasn't the time or place. I'd quiz him more on this later. 'Okay, let's get them balls wet,' I said, heading towards the surf.

52

Wesley had some funny little ways. He seemed to be obsessed with his hair. Not obsessed with keeping it tidy, quite the opposite, making sure it was unruly. Regular scuffs with a hand would ensure this. Unlike his brother, who made a living from being stared at, analysed and adored, he grew noticeably uncomfortable if anyone looked at him for more than a moment. When we were out in the surf and Chilly pointed out how much he looked like Cory when his hair was wet, he blushed to the extent that I thought he might storm out of the water. The only conclusion I could come to was that although he outwardly gave people the impression he adored his elder sibling, he'd been forced to live in his shadow for so long that he desperately wanted to have his own personality without being compared to Freckles. He confirmed this during our walk back to Ruby Street.

'You alright, mate? You've hardly said a word since we met Chilly.'

The familiar shrug.

'I get the impression you don't like being compared to Cory.'

'Being compared would be okay. It's the *pity* that hurts. "Such a shame you didn't have the golden hair or the freckles like your brother" are the usual comments. "Never mind, you'll get by." I get sick of it.'

'I bet.'

'I'm my own person, Scott, always have been, but whenever I get close to achieving something by myself, it's always looked down on. "Ahh, bless him. Nice to see he's trying to get on in life."'

'I can imagine that's hard. Did you ever get angry with Cory because of this?'

'No, never!' After expecting the usual shrug, the rapid-fire answer took me by surprise. The delivery was a little *too* quick. 'I had my chance. When I was little, Barry was pushing, pushing, pushing, you know. Sent me to drama school, dance, music, you name it. But when I showed no interest or, more importantly, no talent, he completely lost interest in me as if I no longer existed in his life.'

'That must have hurt.' In the capacity of a police officer and later a detective, I'd been working with people long enough to recognise trauma. Wesley had deep emotional scars that he worked hard to hide. These core lesions were usually the cause of depression and anxiety, which could manifest into bigger issues if not diagnosed early enough.

'When you're only six years old, yes, I guess you could say that. The older brother you idolise is taken away from you. Your father appears to hate you. Your mother treats you like you're a nuisance who is impeding on her lifestyle. I've actually been on my own for most of my life.'

As we crossed Musgrave Street on the way home, I placed a reassuring hand on his shoulder. 'But you never complained once, right?'

The shrug. The rant was over. Wesley was back. Good old not-quite-right Wesley. He'd opened up to me but closed down just as quickly.

The therapy sessions would need to be short but regular and conducted without the knowledge of the patient. For now, this was the closest foot in the door I had to the Evans/Cummings ethos, so I needed to capitalise on it as much as possible.

'Fancy a pie?' This once morning ritual was now a thing of the past. Since leaving the police force, I'd been watching my health, but enjoying a steak and bacon pie now and again was one of those welcome treats. Giving Wesley the full surfer lifestyle experience seemed like a good idea, so when I led him to Kirra Beach Bakery and asked him to choose the pie of his choice, the excited kid made a reappearance.

He chose steak and onion, and when I grabbed two chocolate flavoured milks from the fridge, I thought he was going to jump up and down with joy. *Changeable moods, easy transition from sad to happy, self-sorry to proud,* were the words I was scribbling down in the mental notepad. The side note would have said, *hard personality to read, constantly changing.*

And for the full experience, we carried our tucker back over the road and sat at a bench under the shade of a Pandanus tree overlooking the beach.

'You've got the best life, Scott,' Wesley said before taking a large crispy bite from his pie.

'Yeah, well it certainly looks that way, I know, but believe it or not, I've wished all this away.'

'What do you mean?' He took a swig of milk.

Resisting the urge to tell him how much he looked like his brother with chocolate around his mouth, I continued, 'Well, you can have too much of a good thing, mate. Just over a year ago I had a simple job that took no brain power at all, I lived in a house with my best mates, we partied most weekends like we were teenagers, watched the footy, surfed most mornings, didn't give a stuff about anything else. But deep down I was over it. Subconsciously craving for change. Are you familiar with the principles of positive thinking, Wes?'

'You mean when you decide to do something, focus on it, put it out to the universe and make it manifest?'

'Exactly. Well, my mum always used to say, "Be careful what you wish for." I hadn't given it any thought at all, just decided I needed certain things in my life to change. And bugger me, that's exactly what's happened.'

'You got promoted, but then quit your job. Started a successful business instead. Sounds pretty positive to me.'

'It was more about the lifestyle. First Tetley going to England. Elvis swanning off to Melbourne. The house is up for sale. And … let's not forget … they demolished the bloody pub.'

'You poor bastard,' Wesley said with a sarcastic chuckle. 'And I thought my life was shit.'

Changing the subject completely. 'Do you think Cassie's been affected by all of this too?'

'Little miss princess? Nah.'

This reaction surprised me. I thought they'd grown close. With a mouthful of pie, I frowned.

'No, that's not fair. I don't really know her that well. Only met her this week.'

'But you've always known about her?'

'Yeah. The other kid that my dad loved more than me.'

Oh yes, definite signs of resentment in his tone. Although he usually displayed a nonchalant attitude when asked about his father, I was sure there was emotional hurt there. Good work, Scotty. Albeit, in painful increments, he was finally opening up to me.

53

After hot showers, we climbed into the Dub and travelled the short journey to Coolangatta. During all this time, I'd been gently quizzing Wesley, mostly superfluous mundane stuff like which subjects did he prefer at school, who was his first love (it was no surprise to find out he'd never been in love). Every now and again, I'd drop the little bombs. 'Bet there were times when you hated Cory, weren't there?' As if picked up by his early warning radar, he mostly answered with the shrug or the shake of the head, so I needed to keep delving without alerting him to the fact that I was prying. 'I used to hate my brother. He and Dad were always off fishing or camping, leaving me at home.'

'And how did that make *you* feel, Scott?'

The little shit had turned the tables and was analysing me. I was happy to play that game.

'Not good, mate. It made me feel inferior to my brother. Why did Dad love him more than me?' I parked the Dub on Griffith Street.

'So, did you hate your father too?' Wesley asked after we'd climbed out of the car.

'I thought I did.'

'Did you ever feel like hurting your brother?'

'My oath I did.'

'And did you?'

Taking a leaf from the tree of Wesley, I shrugged and shook my head.

'What did you do?'

'I sometimes wish I'd taken my fate in my own hands and done something about it. If I had, perhaps I'd be living a more normal life now, instead of being the over forty bachelor.' As far as I was concerned, this was role play, but something in the last phrase seemed to hit a nerve.

'I understand that. This is why I wanted to get to know Cory. To learn to love him, instead of resenting him.'

Break through. This was the first time Wesley admitted to feelings of resentment towards his brother.

'And did you? Get to know him? Learn to love him?'

'Oh yeah, from the moment I moved in. He showed me nothing but love and affection. He was a great guy. I loved him so much.'

'Who do you think would have wanted to hurt him?'

'Barry.'

'Just Barry? Not Patty and the bikies?'

'No. It was Barry. Cory was going to double dip but this time take everything. Barry knew it and panicked. He's a nasty man, Barry Evans. Not to be crossed.'

We reached the entrance to the office that was shared with Elvis' accountancy firm.

'What the hell?' There was a 'For Lease' sign outside.

The door was locked, which was unusual. Alisha, Elvis' receptionist, was normally there at that time of the morning. Once inside, peering in through the glass door on our way to the stairs, I realised the office was closed, and that Elvis was serious about moving back to Melbourne.

We went up the stairs, clonking on the cheap, wood-effect, linoleum flooring.

'There's a jug in there, mate,' I said, pointing to the small storeroom cum kitchenette. 'I just need to make a couple of phone calls.'

The shrug was followed by a mournful traipse to the storeroom. It was almost like an act. A way of reverting into himself to avoid too much interaction with the outside world.

Stepping back out onto the stairs, I called Jenny. She was very interested to hear what Knackers had shared with me.

'So, Cory was an associate, not a victim of The Wasps?'

'Sounds that way. Until he crossed them that is. Any luck finding Brennan yet?'

'No. He's gone underground. Unless he sets foot in Queensland, we're in the hands of the New South Wales Police.'

'Maybe he's already here somewhere.'

'Hmm, we're keeping a look out.'

I also mentioned that Wesley would be staying with me for a couple of days.

'You have Wesley there with you?'

'Yes.'

'No wonder we can't find him. He's not answering his phone.'

'Do you need him?'

'Yes, something's come up that we need to discuss with him. Keep him there, Bradley and I will be there shortly.'

By the time I stepped back into the office, Wesley was standing in front of the whiteboard. To my horror, he had flipped it over so that the investigation notes were in full view.

'Hey, that's private, mate,' I said rushing towards him.

'You have me down as one of the main suspects.'

'Yeah, of course. I didn't know you then as well as I do now,' I said, turning the board back over to face the wall.

'Do you think I did it?'

My phone rang. It was a number I didn't recognise. I made my way to the window alcove before answering it. 'Hello.'

'Hi Scott, it's Ingrid.' It was the real estate agent informing me that Elvis had withdrawn the property from the market. Her congratulations didn't sound too convincing. A fair bit of lost commission, I guess, letting it go this cheaply. We arranged a meeting at her office in an hour so that I could sign the contract. As she spoke, I was peering out the window and noticed Barry Evans marching along the street towards us. 'Okay, I'll see you then,' I said before hanging up. 'Wesley. Your dad's here.'

'What?' His shocked expression took me by surprise. 'Barry is here?' He paced like a caged bear.

'Yeah, is that a problem?'

'A problem? Damn right it is. He can't find me here, Scott. He can't even see me.'

'No worries. Why don't you step into the storeroom, close the door behind you.'

An industrious nod replaced the nonchalant shrug. He rushed into the storeroom as if escaping an approaching tide of stormtroopers.

The familiar sound of the front door opening and closing, followed by the *clump-clop* of footsteps told me Barry was in the building. There was no knock. The door to my office flew open. 'Oh good, you're here,' Barry said, marching into the room.

'Barry. Good to see you.'

'I've been with the police again all night. They are harassing the hell out of me, Scott.'

'Have they got anything on you?'

His back straightened and his chin rose into the air. 'No. Not a thing.'

'Well, that's good then. Have a seat, mate.'

He didn't sit. Like his son only moments earlier, he paced the room. 'They're going to blame me for this regardless of whether they have anything or not.'

'They can't do that.'

'I've told them everything now. All about Wesley and that bitch, and what they were up to.'

'Wesley and … Patty you mean?'

'Yes, yes. It'll only be a matter of time now before he's arrested.'

Wesley would have been hearing this loud and clear from the storeroom.

'What did you tell them?' I asked, gesturing for him to take a seat.

'Everything. How that scheming little bastard wheedled his way into Cory's life.'

'But it was Cory who reached out to Wesley, surely?'

'No, it was Wesley who contacted Cory. He told him his mother and her new boyfriend regularly beat him, and that his life wasn't worth living. Cory took pity and rescued him.'

'Wesley was being abused?'

'No, of course he wasn't. It was all a part of the master plan concocted by the three of them.'

'Wesley, Patty and Brennan?' I wasn't purposely aiming to appear thick, I just needed Barry to spell everything out for me. The phone in my pocket had been on record since he entered the room.

'Yes.'

Using the old that-doesn't-make-sense-mate frown, I prompted him to continue.

'Think about it, Scott. Patty Cummings, the once socialite queen of the Gold Coast, is suddenly thrown into poverty with her useless son. All because of Cory. And her new boyfriend just happens to be the king of the bikies. They hatch a plan to get Wesley into the penthouse, and then the next minute, Cory's fortune is signed over to Wesley and Cory turns up dead. You couldn't write this stuff.'

Among others, it was a scenario that I'd been throwing around, but did Barry have genuine knowledge or was this just his fanciful opinion. 'Can you prove any of this?'

He pulled out a memory stick from the pocket of his sports jacket and placed it on my desk. 'This is a copy. I've just given the police the original.'

Within minutes we were watching footage of Brennan marching into Barry's car dealership. Captured on various CCTV cameras, and although with no audio, the situation that played out was clear. Brennan was demanding and threatening.

'When they realised they were getting nowhere with Cory, they switched their focus to me.'

'Because they know you still have most of Cory's fortune.'

Barry looked away and stroked a hand through his thinning hair.

'Did Brennan kill Cory?'

'Yes, but on the instructions of Wesley.'

'Surely Patty was the instigator.'

Barry laughed. 'Patty couldn't organise shit. It was all Wesley. Always has been. Seems like he's just as good an actor as his brother, eh? Had us all fooled. You included.'

I checked my watch. Jenny and Bradley would arrive anytime now. Without asking, I took a copy of the footage, then handed the memory stick back to Barry. 'Thanks, mate. This is really helpful.'

'No worries.' There seemed to be a sudden need to leave. 'There's just one more thing. It's in the car. Can you come down with me?'

'Sure.' I was reluctant to leave Wesley in the storeroom but this sounded important. 'Lead the way,' I said, opening the door at the top of the stairs.

54

I didn't understand the relevance of a signed photograph of Freckles. That was Barry's reason for insisting I walk with him to his car.

'I thought you'd appreciate this, being a big fan and all,' he said, handing me the framed picture as if he'd just awarded me the keys to the city.

'Thanks.' I tried to appear grateful, but why the hell did he make me leave the office for this? 'I better get back. Take care, Barry.'

He climbed into his Mercedes and merged into the traffic.

No shit, Sherlock. By the time I got back to the office, Wesley was gone. After a quick search of the building and out the front, he was nowhere to be found. He'd obviously heard the full conversation between me and Barry. Had he panicked? Or was it guilt that cast him adrift?

Jenny and Bradley arrived. I told them about my meeting with Barry, and about Wesley's disappearance.

'Bugger,' Jenny said. 'We need to speak to him.'

'So, you believe Barry?'

'No … not for a minute. We've received intel that Brennan is back in town and he's looking for Wesley.'

'Would Wesley know that do you think, Scott?' Bradley asked.

'I don't think so. He's been with me for the last day or so.'

'Could Brennan have got to Wesley while you were preoccupied?' he asked glancing at the framed picture in my hand.

'You know, there was no reason for Barry to give me this.' I held up the picture.

'If he wanted to give it to you, why didn't he bring it up?' Jenny said.

'Exactly.'

After Jenny and Bradley left, I revisited the whiteboard. The list of suspects was growing shorter. Rearranging the pictures, I moved Cory and Patty to the bottom of the board. The key players now were Wesley, Brennan and Barry, but I still had Netty and Cassie in the peripheral view.

After exchanging contracts, you would have thought my mind would be filled with the thrill of purchasing my first house, but no, it was Wesley who occupied my thoughts. It was crazy to even consider going back into The Wasps' nest, but there I was, driving down towards Chinderah.

Parking a little back from the cul-de-sac among the usual trade vehicles, I had a view of the building. The gate was open, but the mechanics' shop and clubhouse were closed up.

When I strolled into the compound, I didn't have a clue what I was looking for. The CCTV above the main roller door was the concealed kind, but I was pretty sure it was trained on me and someone was watching my every move.

At the back of the building, there was nothing but garbage, empty beer cartons, bottles, and abandoned motorcycle parts. After completing the circumference, I was about to head out when I heard an electrical buzz followed by a click. To the right of the second roller door was a plain, discreet doorway. The door now sat slightly ajar.

'Hello,' I called out, gingerly opening the door and peering into the dark interior. 'Anybody here?'

The overhead industrial style lights hanging in the rafters flickered in a random chaos then ignited. After double checking my surroundings, I entered the building. 'Mick? You here?'

There were empty beer bottles along the bar. Like an abandoned Western saloon, there was a table with cards strewn over it, and glasses with varying levels of spirits in them. A couple of the chairs were lying on the floor as if the game had come to an abrupt end.

'You here, Mick? It's Scotty Stephens.'

The place was deadly quiet. There were stairs leading up to a mezzanine level. While constantly looking over my shoulder, I climbed them tentatively. 'You up here, Mick? I just wanted to have a chat.'

Upstairs was a series of rooms that were probably once offices in some kind of business. Now they were decked out with king-size beds and the kind of décor you would associate with a brothel: reds, velvets, leather. Very tacky.

After checking all the rooms, it became obvious there was no one there. Did this mean the security was monitored offsite, and that someone was on the way? This was a likely scenario, so not wanting to be caught snooping around, I made my way back downstairs. But it was too late. Detective Inspector Geoff Reynolds was waiting for me at the bar.

'What the hell are you doing here, Scott?' He went around the bar, grabbed two cans of beer from the fridge, and opened them. 'I would have thought that after your last little visit, you'd be keeping well away.' He gestured for me to join him at the bar.

'I just wanted to speak to Brennan.'

Reynolds threw back his head and laughed. 'Brennan doesn't just speak to anyone. He's a vicious killer. You were lucky to get out of here alive last time.' He took a sip of beer.

I didn't join him. 'What do *you* know about that?'

'Show me your phone.'

'What?'

'Put it on the bar here so I can see it.'

I knew the reason for his request; he wanted to make sure I wasn't recording our conversation, which I would have been if I'd known he was coming. When he was satisfied I wasn't, he came around the bar and we sat side by side on the barstools.

'He's not here. And neither should you be.'

'You seem to be very familiar with the place.'

'You don't understand what's going on here, Scott. This business with Cory Evans is an annoying distraction from a case we've been working on for some time now.'

'Operation Wasp Sting.'

'You're familiar with the case?' He appeared to be surprised.

'Uhm, well, only what I've been able to pick up here and there.' I wasn't about to disclose to him that Jenny had allowed me full access to the case details.

'We were so bloody close, then in you waltz like fucking Magnum PI. Do you have any idea how far you've put us back on this?'

'Sounds like the deal had stalled, anyway. Brennan didn't have the money for the cargo.'

'But he was close to getting it?'

'From whom?'

'Never mind that.' This time he sculled half the can. 'You need to back the fuck off or I'll have you arrested.'

'Arrested for what?'

He exaggerated a scan of the room. 'Break and entry to start with.'

'Why are you here, now?'

'I was just passing through, keeping an eye out for activity when I noticed your little banger parked out there. It's not very conspicuous, Scott.'

'You seem to know your way around this place.'

The laugh again. 'What, so you think I might be in cahoots with Brennan?'

'Are you?'

'Right up to my fuckin balls, mate!'

55

The security system that Elvis used was a simple one. A standard app gave me access to the CCTV footage taken over the last day or so. I wasn't expecting to see much, just Wesley slipping out of the property, but that's not what I saw. When Barry and I exited the front door and made our way down the street, someone crept into the building. It was Cassie. Four images were on a constant loop. After the street was the inside entrance, and by this time Cassie was at the top of the stairs. Annoyingly, the next image was of the interior of Elvis' offices. By the time the shot of my office appeared again, it was empty, but when the loop began again on the street, Cassie and Wesley were outside. After cautiously checking their surroundings, they headed off in the opposite direction that Barry and I had taken.

Did the relevance of the signed photograph of Freckles make sense now? Had Barry wanted me out of the way so Cassie could get into the office and whisk Wesley away? But why would Wesley go with Cassie? Perhaps he didn't know she was with Barry. Maybe she wasn't even with Barry. Either way, Wesley had left with her. Did Cassie have her car waiting around the corner? Likely.

I had Cassie's number, so I called her. It was no surprise when she didn't answer.

It was late afternoon by the time I got back to Ruby Street. Wesley's things were still there. A quick rifle through his bag turned up only a change of clothing. Good to my word, I called Jenny with my latest findings.

'Cassie?' Jenny said. 'Do you think Barry set it up?'

'It certainly looks that way.'

'Is there anything unusual about the picture?'

My phone buzzed. There was an incoming call. The dialler ID told me it was Barry Evans. 'Got to go, Jen. Got another call. It's Barry.'

'Barry? Okay, keep me up to date.'

'Will do … Barry. How's it going?'

'Not good, Scott. I think Cassie may have gone missing.'

'Isn't she at Schoolies?'

'No, she came home last night. Said she was sick of it.'

'But it's only an hour or so since she came to my office then legged it with Wesley.'

'What? She was at your office? When?'

'When you insisted I follow you to your car. She ducked in and left with Wesley. But you already know that, Barry.'

'I can assure you I didn't. What would she be doing in Coolangatta?'

'I was hoping you could tell me.'

'I wouldn't have a clue, honestly. This is the first I'm hearing of this.'

'Why the photograph, then? Why insist I follow you all the way to your car, just to give me a picture of Freckles?'

Ignoring my question, there was desperation in his voice. 'I need you to find, Cassie, Scott. She's the only thing important to me now.'

'What's she driving?'

'A late model BMW 125i. It's a little hatchback, white. Rego, Cass 06.'

'Why do you think she's missing? Like I said, she's only been gone an hour or so.'

'She's not answering her phone. She's always picks up when Daddy calls.'

Retrieving the trusty notepad from my back pocket, I jotted down some notes. 'Is there anywhere she'd go that you know of?'

'I've checked with the friends she went to Schoolies with. They haven't seen her since she left.'

'Anyone else?'

'Not that I'm aware of. They must be at the Milton.'

'Hmm, maybe. I'll call you back, Barry, as soon as I hear anything.'

'Right. Make sure you do that, please.' He hung up.

I wasn't planning a drive to Surfers Paradise and the late afternoon traffic did little to make the trip any less appealing. Once again I was grateful for the key pass Wesley had loaned me, but, I was surprised that it still worked. It would have been a simple task for Wesley to arrange with the concierge to change the code.

The apartment was spotless and quiet. Maria's cleaning routine was obviously continuing because there was a vase of fresh lilies on the kitchen countertop.

'Wesley. You here mate?' I knew he wasn't but felt the need to call out anyway. Looking around the spacious penthouse, an idea came to mind.

Jenny answered her phone on the first ring. 'Anything?'

I filled her in on the latest conversation I'd had with Barry. 'What time are you knocking off?'

'Uhm …' In my mind's eye I could see her seated at her desk, checking her watch. 'Soon I guess. Why?'

'Fancy a night in Surfers?'

'What with all of those kids? No, I bloody don't.'

'I've got a room. An apartment. Well, a penthouse. It'll be like old times when we were hiding out in the Q1 building.'

'You are seriously not suggesting we stay the night in Cory Evans' place.'

'Yeah.'

'Are you serious? I'm not that cheeky little surfer chick anymore. I'm Detective Inspector Jenny Radford.'

Life, it seemed, was no longer as simple as it once was.

'Are you there now?'

'Yes.'

I heard the door to her office open and the familiar voice of Bradley. 'You better come right away, Jen.'

'What's going on?' Her voice lowered, and I realised she'd moved the phone from her mouth.

'Reports of a shooting out at Nerang.'

'Scotty, I've got to go.'

'Yeah, no worries. I—' The phone went dead.

<h1 style="text-align:center">56</h1>

Having that little bit of fame and a knowledge of security had to work in my favour sometimes. It did when I approached Gold Coast Security Solutions in Coolangatta. This was the company who manned the local CCTV cameras as part of the safety camera network, monitoring the streets from North Kirra to the Coolangatta border. Cameron Davey, a bloke who, I guessed, enjoyed the odd pie, was more than obliging when I asked to view the footage of the northern end of Griffith Street in Coolangatta between 10.00 and 11.00 am that morning. He didn't ask for ID, but I got the impression he thought I was still a detective with the Queensland Police.

'Of course you can, Scott. Come in, come in.' Like a mate he'd known forever, he ushered me into the back office of the indiscreet shop building facing the Twin Towns Services Club in Tweed.

The room resembled a police control centre, but with Cameron the only security guard on duty. He sat down at a console, pointed to a screen, then went to work tapping on a keyboard. Griffith Street appeared. Time lapse figures raced up and down the street, zig-zagging across a steady stream of traffic, while a time signature in the bottom left corner ticked over. When it reached ten o'clock, Cameron jabbed his finger on the keyboard as if he were ceremoniously adding the final full stop to a novel.

'Great work, buddy,' I said.

'Thank you.'

'Can you move it on until someone enters or leaves the building?'

'Sure.' He sped up the image again but not as fast as before.

'There,' I said, pointing to the screen when Barry and I exited the front door to the office.

The image returned to normal speed. Cameron switched to the next camera down the street, which changed the image to one in front of us.

'No, go back to the office please. I want to see what activity took place during the few minutes I was away.'

'No worries.'

With a clear view of the street, Cameron zoomed in so we could read the fine print on the 'For Lease' sign.

'That's awesome. Now just pan back a bit. We shouldn't have to wait long.' And we didn't. Cassie appeared on the screen. Stopping outside the office door, she peered along the street in the direction that Barry and I had strolled. Then she rushed inside the building.

Minutes later, she reappeared with Wesley in tow. After cautiously checking the street, the duo headed north along Griffith Street.

'Can you follow them?'

The image switched to about fifty metres ahead and showed them marching towards the intersection of McLean Street. When they turned the corner, they crossed the road to where Cassie's BMW was parked across from the Coolangatta Sands Hotel.

'This is great work, Cameron.'

'Thanks, that means a lot coming from you.'

Cassie and Wesley climbed into the car. They stayed there for a few moments.

Cameron zoomed in as close as possible and we could see that the couple were involved in a heated discussion. The conversation seemed to end when Cassie shook her head, started the engine and looked over her shoulder in readiness to pull away from the kerb.

'Hello,' I said under my breath.

Just as the BMW was about to pull away, a bikie riding a customised chopper pulled in front of her. Two more appeared from behind, blocking in the car. The front rider climbed from his bike and removed his helmet. It was Mick Brennan. He hammered on the driver's side window with the side of his fist. At first Cassie didn't respond, so he hammered again. When Cassie lowered the window, Brennan leaned in.

Gee, I wished we had audio. It was impossible to tell what was being said as Brennan had his back to the camera.

After a few minutes, he stood upright and put his helmet back on. He returned to his motorbike, climbed aboard and kicked it over. Like a procession, the little cavalcade pulled away and turned left at the end of the street onto Marine Parade.

Without asking for instructions, Cameron daisy-chained the camera images as the procession travelled north around Kirra Point then along Musgrave Street towards Bilinga. The final shot showed them on the Gold Coast Highway heading north past Gold Coast Airport.

'That's as far as we go, I'm afraid. Tugun traffic have it from there. I could contact them if you like. It'd be possible to follow them all the way up the coast.'

'I might just ask you to do that, Cameron, if that's okay.' It didn't surprise me that Brennan was directing them north. The Wasps' nest would have been the obvious location, but the New South Wales Police obviously had the place under surveillance. Brennan had been in hiding since Patty's death. It was pointless to call in the sighting. The footage was almost two hours old.

My phone rang. It was Jenny. 'Scott, don't ask questions. Just get yourself to the address I'm about to text to you.' She hung up. Moments later, the familiar *ding* rang out and I checked my messages. The screen displayed an address in Nerang.

Turning into a typical suburban street west of Nerang, I was met by a police roadblock. Seeing Jenny and Bradley among a group of armed police officers, I parked the Dub at the end of the street.

The constable standing at a taped off police line didn't question me as I approached. Instead, he held up the tape, allowing me to enter the area.

'Hey, Jen. What's going on?'

'It's Brennan, him and a few of his mates are held up in that house there.' She pointed to a lowset brick and tile house at the end of a cul-de-sac. There was a line of motorbikes outside. On the driveway was Cassie's BMW.

'A siege?'

'According to the neighbour, they've got an arsenal in there. We've checked the rego of the BMW. It's registered to—'

'Cassie Evans.'

'That's right. It looks like they have her.'

'Not only Cassie. Wesley too.'

'What? How would you know that?'

I relayed my movements over the last couple of hours, including the security footage I'd viewed.

'So you think Cassie was with Barry? And they what, kidnapped Wesley from under your nose?'

'Wesley seemed to go with her willingly but I'm not sure if Cassie was with Barry or if Barry knew she was there.'

'And then Brennan sweeps in at the exact right moment.'

'Hmm. It seems a bit coincidental, doesn't it?'

'You're not wrong.'

The bikie that I only remembered as Conan appeared on the driveway. 'You can all fuck off!' he yelled. He didn't appear to be armed.

The armed police taking refuge behind the parked squad cars focused their aim on the figure.

'If you want a war, we've got enough fire power in here to fucking annihilate you bastards.'

Bradley handed Jenny a crowd control speaker.

'This is Detective Inspector Jenny Radford. Put down your weapons. Come out of the building and we can talk.'

'Fuck you, bitch.'

'We need to speak to Mick Brennan.'

'Who?'

'We know he's in there. We also know you have Cassie Evans and Wesley Cummings.'

'That's right. And if you don't back off …' He aimed an imaginary gun to his temple and pulled the trigger.

'We have the shot, ma'am,' a voice crackled from the radio that was in Jenny's other hand.

'No, stay alert, but do not fire. I repeat, do not fire.'

Conan strolled nonchalantly back into the building.

57

'Scott, Scott, over here.'

Turning towards the familiar voice, I saw Barry Evans standing behind the police line.

'Let me through, Scott. My baby's in there.'

A glance at Jenny was enough communication. She waved to the constable on guard, allowing Barry to come through.

Barry rushed towards us. 'What's happened. Where is she?'

'Take it easy Mister Evans,' Jenny said, standing in his path. 'As far as we know, nobody's been hurt.'

'Is it Brennan?'

'We believe Mick Brennan is in the building, yes.'

'Let me speak to him. If it's money he wants, I can give it to him.'

'That's not a good idea.'

A *9News* helicopter hovered overhead.

Conan appeared on the driveway again. Without speaking, he pointed to Barry and waved him forward with his fingers like a lollipop man ushering school children over a pedestrian crossing.

Barry lunged forward.

Jenny and Bradley stopped him. 'We need to speak to Brennan,' Jenny said into the tannoy.

'We need to speak to Barry Evans,' Conan said. 'Send him through.'

'That's not going to happen. Send Brennan out.'

Barry broke away and ran towards the house.

'Halt!' one of the armed personnel yelled.

'Hold your fire,' Jenny called out.

When Barry reached the driveway, the enormous bikie grabbed him by the scruff of his neck.

I still have the shot, ma'am.' The voice again on Jenny's radio.

'Don't shoot,' Jenny said. 'What's your name and what do you want?' She yelled through the tannoy.

Conan sneered and with Barry held firmly in his grasp, he backed up and disappeared into the house.

Senior Sergeant Don Chapel lowered his gun and marched over to us. 'Great work, detective. Now they have three hostages in there.'

Detectives Geoff Reynolds and Kelly Blake from the New South Wales Police arrived on the scene. 'What's happened so far?' Reynolds asked, glaring at Jenny.

Jenny told him what little information we had.

'Do we even know if Brennan and the kids are in there?'

'No, we don't. We've only seen the one guy so far.'

'I count ten motorbikes,' Kelly said. 'But that doesn't mean there are ten riders in there.'

'The one there …,' I said, pointing to one of the choppers. '… the green one. That's Brennan's. Or the one he was riding this afternoon.'

'And the BMW is registered to Cassie Evans.'

'Okay. I'm going in,' Reynolds said, pulling out his handgun and handing it to Jenny.

'I'm afraid that's not possible,' Jenny said, ignoring the gun.

'I know Brennan. I can find out what this is all about.'

'We've just given them a third hostage. I'm not about to give them another.'

Conan appeared on the driveway again. This time he pointed towards someone else. Me.

'No way, Scott. That's not happening,' Jenny said.

'We're ready to negotiate,' Conan said. 'But we'll only speak to Stephens.'

'I can do this, Jen.' Still analysing, I couldn't help it, the mixed expressions on Jenny's face were ones I'd never witnessed before, not with Jenny. They were fear and uncertainty.

'Okay, but I'm coming with you.' She handed her gun and radio to Bradley.

'But—'

Jenny placed a finger on his lips. 'We'll be okay.' Then, looking at me, she said, 'You up for this?'

'My oath.'

'Scott Stephens is coming in but I'm coming with him,' she said through the tannoy before also handing that to Bradley.

Conan smirked as he nodded.

Jenny stepped forward first, with me right behind her.

Conan backed into the house.

'I can't believe I'm allowing this to happen,' Jenny said under her breath.

'She'll be right. We're just going to talk to them.'

At first, when we reached the door at the side of the house, the interior of the building was dark and foreboding. It took a moment for our eyes to adjust after the afternoon sunshine outside.

Conan led us through a very 1980s archway and into the kitchen. The room was still gloomy but lighter than the entrance. There was a group of bikies. I didn't see any guns. Standing in the middle of the room was a small figure, arms on hips, and a wide stance that reminded me of Peter Pan. The dyed blond hair with dark roots. The Black Sabbath T-shirt. Painfully thin arms that barely had the room to display the faded tattoos. Blue jeans and pink thongs. All belonged to Moe Brennan, Mick's mother, who was widely believed to be the matriarch of The Wasps.

'As oy live and breathe, if it isn't Scotty Stephens standing in me own kitchen.' Her accent was Irish, Belfast if I wasn't mistaken.

'Hello Moe.' I'd never met her before, but I knew all about her.

'Come on in lad, come in. And who moight this be you've brung to visit?' She was looking at Jenny.

'This is Detective Inspector Jenny Radford. Jenny.'

'Welcome, Jenny. Would ya like a cup of tea, love?' Moe spoke as if we'd just popped around for a visit.

'That would be nice, Moe,' Jenny said. Sometimes our brains worked as one. She would have been assessing the situation in the same way I had since we entered the house. Counting the bikies, noting the absence of weapons.

Barry Evans was sitting at the kitchen table with a protective arm around his daughter. There was no sign of Brennan or Wesley. Knackers sat beside them tapping at an open laptop.

'Take a seat,' Moe said, gesturing with a shaky arm towards the table. Between nicotine-stained fingers was a half-smoked cigarette that had gone out. 'It just so happens that we have some other guests today too.'

'Is Mick, here, Moe?' I said, taking a seat across from Barry and Cassie. 'I was hoping we could catch up.'

'Mick. No. Mick's not here.' Moe filled the jug from the tap and plugged it in.

'Do you know where he is?' Jenny asked.

'Yes.' She wasn't about to offer any more information. Instead she reached up to an overhead cabinet and pulled out two mugs.

'And what about Wesley?' I asked.

'He's with Mick. They have some business to attend to.'

'What kind of business?'

'Secret business. Nothing for you's to be concerned about.'

'Moe, can we let Barry and Cassie go, please?' Jenny said.

'Sure we can.' She placed a tea bag in each of the mugs as the sound of the boiling jug increased in volume. 'We also just have a little bit of business to finish first.' She looked over at Knackers.

Knackers nodded and slid the laptop over to Barry. 'Username and password. Then you know what to do.'

Barry removed his arm from Cassie's shoulder and typed slowly on the keyboard. When he'd finished, he slid it back towards Knackers, who immediately went to work on the keys.

'Would ya be wanting sugar?' Moe asked.

'No thank you,' Jenny and I said in unison.

'What's happening with the laptop?' Jenny asked.

'Unfinished business, that's all,' Moe said. 'Nothing to worry yourself about.'

'Okay, it's ready,' Knackers said, sliding the laptop back to Barry.

Barry looked up at Moe. 'Are you really going to make me do this, Mrs Brennan?'

'Nobody's making you do anything, Barry lad, you've just got to do what's right,' Moe said, focusing on her task of pouring boiling water into the two mugs.

'You know what will happen if you don't,' Knackers said, leaning in.

Barry looked at his daughter then tapped the keyboard.

Knackers grinned as he took back the laptop. 'All done, Moe.'

'Good. And about time ya thieving heathen,' Moe said, turning to face Barry.

'Can we go now?' Barry said.

'You's better before I throw ya's out!'

Barry, looking around bewildered, stood slowly. Cassie joined him and the pair walked across the kitchen with their heads low.

'Ya have the rest of the day to clear out your office ... excuse me, moy office,' Moe said as she handed the two mugs of tea to Jenny and myself.

'Yes Mrs Brennan,' Barry said.

Conan led them out.

'What was all that about?' I asked, taking one of the mugs.

'Barry's been a naughty boy. He defaulted on his loan, so we've taken back his assets.'

'Barry owed you money?'

'Aye. How do ya think he started his business? His lad took him for every penny he owned.'

Jenny and I side glanced each other as we sipped our teas.

'So, you wanted to speak to me, Moe?' I said as she took a seat next to Knackers across the table.

Moe relit the half-smoked cigarette with a Bic lighter. 'Ya see, the thing is, Scotty,' she spoke through a plume of cigarette smoke. 'Ya think you're a smart detective, right?'

My shrug was non-committal.

'Well ya know fuckin nuttin.' Her brow knitted with a sudden anger. 'You's are meddlin around in stuff that doesn't concern ya.'

'Drugs, kidnapping, murder. I think all of those things might concern us a little, don't you?' Jenny said.

Moe looked at me and grinned. 'A feisty little one, Scotty. I bet she's a handful.' She reached across and nudged me with a bony elbow. 'The thing is, Detective inspector Jenny Radford. Look around. Do ya see any guns? Any drugs? This is my humble home.'

'Why are we here, Moe?' Jenny asked. 'Is this all a distraction so Mick can get away?'

'I guess ya don't get to be a DI at such a young age for nuttin. She's a keeper this one, Scotty.'

'She's not bad, Moe.'

Jenny shot me an annoyed glance.

'A distraction? Maybe.' Moe took a drag from the cigarette.

'You lay siege just to tell us this?'

'There is no siege here, love. Ya shouldn't be listening to no crackpot neighbours. She's as batty as a cane toad is old Stella next door.'

'We can't just walk away from here, Moe. You know that.'

'Aye. I do. No doubt we'll be having a little chat in Surfers Paradise, but it won't be going much further than that.'

'You said you wanted to talk,' I said.

'Aye. And we have.' She glanced up at a Brisbane Broncos clock on the wall. 'The deal will be done now. We can all relax, get back to normal.'

'What do you mean?' Jenny asked.

'The Wasps are going back into hibernation. No more trouble.'

'Do you seriously think we'll be turning a blind eye to all of this?' Jenny said.

'Aye. I do. Now drink ya tea while it's still hot.'

58

Along with Barry and Cassie, Moe, Knackers, Conan, and the other bikers were transported to Surfers Paradise Police Station for questioning. Moe, Barry and Cassie were placed in separate interview rooms. The rest were put in cells to be brought out for questioning later.

Jenny allowed me to sit in on the interviews. We started with Barry.

'Are we to understand that you just signed your business over to The Wasps?'

'Yes, but under severe duress. You guys were there. They threatened me. My daughter. You saw that.'

Jenny and I remained non-committal.

'So, you borrowed the money from the Brennan's to open the dealership?' Jenny asked.

I was a guest; it was my place to let her handle the questioning.

'Yes. All those rumours of an overseas bank account were just bullshit.'

'You didn't mind people thinking that, though. All part of the image, eh?'

'All publicity is good publicity.'

'But you fell behind with the payments. Why was that?'

'When Cory heard I was doing okay, he believed the hype about the secret bank account and went for me again.'

'He was going to take you to court again?'

'Yes. And that's an expensive game. Especially if you lose.'

'But surely you realise that if you borrow money from a bikie organisation, you don't renege on the repayments.'

'I've already paid those bastards ten times what they loaned me. But they keep coming back for more.'

'So you killed Cory to reduce the threat?'

'No, that's ridiculous. I never killed anyone.'

'Then who killed him?'

'Wesley obviously!'

'What makes you say that?'

Barry shuffled in his seat. 'I want to see my solicitor.'

'Sure. We'll resume this later.' Jenny closed the manila folder she had before her and stood. 'Let's see what Cassie has to tell us, eh?'

'You can't speak to her without me present. My solicitor will represent her too.'

'No worries, she's an adult. I'll mention that to her.'

We filed out of the room.

Bradley met us in the corridor. 'As you know, we've been monitoring Wesley's bank account since we learned of his windfall. Well, guess what?' He didn't wait for a reply. 'Twenty million dollars was just transferred from his account.'

'What? Twenty million?' Jenny said.

'Yep.'

'To where?'

'To an untraceable offshore account.'

'So it looks like Brennan finally got what he wanted.'

Cassie Evans was sitting on her hands at the nondescript table in Interview Room #2.

'You alright, Cass?' I asked as Jenny and I took our seats.

'You're not under suspicion or anything like that, Cassie,' Jenny said. 'We just want to ask you a few questions if that's okay.'

'Should I have a solicitor here?'

'You can have a solicitor present if you like, but we'll be done in a couple of minutes,' Jenny said, exaggerating a glance at her watch.

Cassie nodded and looked down at the table.

'Did you arrange with Barry to pick up Wesley from Scott's office in Coolangatta?'

Cassie shook her head. 'No. Dad didn't know I was there. Wesley texted me earlier that morning. Told me to come to Coolangatta and get him.'

'So how did you know he'd be at my office?' I asked. Jenny seemed happy to let me handle the questioning this time.

'He told me to park as close to your office as possible but out of sight.'

'And what happened then?'

'I got another text. Come to the office right away. So I did, and Wesley was waiting for me.'

'Did you know Barry had just been there?'

'No. We came straight out and headed for my car, but just as we were about to drive away, those horrid motorbikes stopped us.'

'Were they looking for Wesley?'

'No. It was me they wanted.'

My leaning forward was an inadvertent response. 'Why would they want you?'

'So they could get to my dad.'

Jenny and I shared a knowing sideways glance.

'How would they know you'd be at Coolangatta?' I asked.

'Wesley told them.'

'Wesley? Why would he do that?'

Cassie shrugged. 'He seemed to be friendly with the big guy.'

'Brennan. Mick Brennan?'

'I don't know if that was his name, but he was in charge.'

'What did Wesley say to him?'

'He just introduced me, but the big guy wasn't interested. He instructed me to follow him and said if I didn't he'd fucking kill me.'

'You followed him to the house in Nerang?'

'Yes.'

'What happened to Wesley?'

'He went with them. I heard some trucks pulling up outside the house. Most of them left, including Wesley, and I heard the trucks pull away.'

'Trucks, as in big trucks or—?'

'Yes, big trucks. Diesel, loud brakes.'

Jenny was scribbling down notes.

'Were there any guns present or—?'

'No, after they'd taken me into the house, the old lady, Moe, insisted on making me a cup of tea. Not long after that the police arrived. And then my dad.'

Jenny stood and closed off the interview.

Following her out of the interview room, she grabbed Bradley in the corridor. 'Get a team out to the paddock in Logan, the container. Scotty, you can come with me.'

Within minutes, we were racing across Chevron Island towards the back highway. There was no need for an explanation. Once again, our detective minds came to the same conclusion. Brennan had found the money to finalise the drug deal. The contraband in the container had been released to him, hence the need for the trucks that Cassie heard earlier.

Jenny corresponded over the radio with the SWAT team she struggled to keep up with. Behind us was a convoy of police cruisers. There were no sirens.

'Before turning into the road, I want to do a drive by first. Make sure they're actually there before going in. Over.'

'Copy that, ma'am.'

'The container's been under surveillance all this time, obviously?' I said.

'Sort of,' Jenny replied. 'At first, we had surveillance officers working shifts, monitoring the place. After there'd been no activity for over five months, it was decided, against my better judgement, that a CCTV would do the job.'

'And did it?'

'When it was working. But it somehow kept mysteriously malfunctioning.'

'Hmm, funny that.'

Pre-empting a problem with traffic, we travelled north on the side roads off the highway as much as possible still with the sirens off.

We didn't need to do a drive by. As soon as we turned into the rural street in Jenny's MINI, we saw two large trucks backed up to the paddock. An army of bikers were loading them from the container. Jenny pulled in at the side of the road and gave the command over the radio. The SWAT team was quick to swoop in and take charge of the situation.

59

Like Wimbledon, the seeded players were moved around. In Interview Room #1, Mick Brennan now held the centre court. Moe Brennan was in #2. Barry Evans #3. Conan #4, and Knackers was in #5. Cassie was sent home with her mother, who had been waiting outside the building anxiously chain smoking.

When Jenny and I sat facing Brennan, it was no surprise when the only words he uttered were, 'I won't be saying anything without the presence of my solicitor.'

'You just did, dickhead!' Jenny said.

Brennan's scowling face turned scarlet. He obviously wasn't used to being spoken to in that way. Jenny knew that, using the technique to provoke a reaction.

'Some good that will do you. We've got you, mate. Possession of what could be Australia's largest drug haul, and two counts of murder.'

Just as Jenny finished speaking, in breezed the high-profile Gold Coast defence lawyer, Craig Nash. True to form, he took charge of the situation and dismissed Jenny and myself from the room so he could speak privately with his client.

Brennan grinned at Jenny as we rose from the table.

'I'll be wiping that smile of that ugly face soon enough,' Jenny said.

Moe Brennan welcomed us with a smile. 'Hello again, you two. Gee, you's make a lovely couple.'

Jenny blushed a little.

'G'day, Moe,' I said as we took our seats opposite her. 'Is everything okay. Did you get a coffee or—?'

'Aye, but it was shite.'

'Aye.' Her accent was rubbing off on me.

'Moe, we've just brought in Mick,' Jenny said. 'Caught him unloading a container full of cocaine out at Logan.'

'I don't know anything about that.'

'Are you sure?'

'Positive. Oy understood that the only reason oy'm here is because moy stupid neighbour called the police again. Said something was happening at the house. But nothing *was* happening, was it?'

'You were holding a young girl against her will.'

'No, oy wasn't. She drove herself to my house. Could have left at any time.'

'We both know that it isn't true, Moe.'

'Look, there were no guns found in the house. Ya's came out there expecting a siege situation. If there *was* a siege, you lot created it arriving like Starsky and bloody Hutch. Oy welcomed ya's in and gave you a cup of fuckin tea for God's sake.'

'You're a very clever lady, Moe.'

'Thank you. And so moight you be one day.'

'We have two witnesses who will testify against you. And Barry Evans is claiming that you forced him into signing over his business and all of his assets.'

'*Phf,* Barry Evans.' Moe leaned forward in her seat and lowered her voice. 'We're all friends here, right?' Her eyes flickered between me and Jenny.

'Of course we are, Moe,' I said.

'You's haven't got the time to be worrying about no false kidnapping claims. No. Ya want to know who killed that poor little mite and his mother. Am oy right?'

'Cory Evans and Patty Cummings?'

'Aye. Freckles. God bless his little heart. Can you imagine anybody wanting to harm that child?'

'Do you know who killed them, Moe?'

'If oy was to tell you, oy'd want to be walking out of here tonight along with me lad.'

'Mick won't be going anywhere, I'm afraid, but I won't have a problem letting you go,' Jenny said.

The door suddenly swung open and in marched Nash. 'Don't say another word, Moe.' He turned to Jenny. 'I'll be representing Mrs Brennan along with her son and the members of his legitimate motorcycle enthusiasts.'

'Legitimate motorcycle enthusiasts?' Jenny's smirk was fuelled by as much anger as it was mirth. 'You mean The Wasps bikie gang who have been terrorising the Northern Rivers and the southern Gold Coast for the last ten years. You really are a piece of work, Nash.'

'Leave us,' Nash demanded.

Jenny's right hand clenched into a fist as she jumped to her feet. It was completely childish on my behalf, but if she'd belted him one there and then I would have cheered like a school kid.

Moe stood. 'Have you checked the boat?'

'Say nothing else, Moe,' Nash said, ushering her back into her seat.

'The boat?' Jenny asked. 'What boat?'

'My client has no comment. Oh, and that goes for the rest of the people you're holding too.' Nash took the seat Jenny had occupied, facing Moe. 'Close the door on your way out, detective.'

'The arrogant prick,' Jenny said as I closed the door behind us.

'That's Nashie.'

'What do you think Moe meant? About a boat I mean.'

'Maybe Mick has one?'

'What's the relevance? Does she mean there's a boat waiting to be loaded with the drugs?'

'I don't think so,' I said as we strolled along the corridor towards Interview Room #4. 'She's claiming to know nothing about the drugs. But she was about to tell us who killed Cory and Patty.'

'That's right, until bloody Nash came barging in.'

'He'll have her hiding behind the "no comment" wall when we go back in, along with Mick and the rest of them. The only person he won't be representing is Barry.'

In Interview Rooms #4 and #5, it seemed Nash's words had spread quicker than the Coronavirus. Neither Conan nor Knackers would speak without his presence. And of course, we knew that once he'd spoken to them, the only words would be,

"No comment". I was familiar with the procedure. It was typical Craig Nash.

So, we found ourselves back in Interview Room #3.

'Barry, do you know anything about a boat?' Jenny asked as we took our seats. It was a long shot question.

'Boat?' Barry shrugged. 'The only boat I know of is Cory's.'

'Cory had a boat?'

'Yeah. we bought it a few years ago. Well, I bought it for him.'

'You used his money you mean,' Jenny said.

'The company's money. It was purchased as a company asset. We only went out on it a couple of times. Used it mostly for entertaining guests. Gosh, I'd pretty much forgotten about it.'

'Cory didn't sell it?' I asked.

'Not as far as I know.'

'So, it's still here moored somewhere on the Gold Coast?'

'I suppose.'

'Come on, Barry. Don't fuck us around,' Jenny growled. 'Where's the boat moored?'

'Marina Mirage of course.'

'Of course it is.' Jenny tore off a page from her pad, slid it across the table and handed Barry a pen. 'I want the name of the boat and the berth number.'

'Sure.'

Jenny and I watched as Barry scribbled on the sheet: *The Tim Tam Kid*, followed by the berth number, 123.

'Cory owned a boat. So what?' Jenny asked as we stepped back into the corridor. The question was rhetorical. Jenny's detective mind worked exactly the same as mine. She was throwing around questions and scenarios, not expecting anyone to answer them but herself. I was doing the same thing.

'What's the relevance to the case?' I threw in.

'How would Moe know about a boat that Cory owned?'

'And why would she go out of her way to mention it?'

'There's something here we're missing.'

'My bloody oath.'

'We need to find the boat.'

'We do. Let's go.'

60

Although Surfers was only a few kilometres away, and the Schoolies festival didn't reach as far as The Spit, it seemed it was still too close for comfort for the locals and tourists who would usually patronise the area. It was 9.00 pm by the time Jenny's MINI pulled into the Marina Mirage car park. The place was dark and unusually quiet for a Friday night.

Jonathon Went wasn't your Tetley tea bag kind of Englishman, more your Earl Grey. Wearing a typically expensive polo shirt, beige chinos and boating shoes, he met us at the entrance of the marina. On Jenny's orders, Bradley had called through to tell the manager we were on our way. A security gate led through to a stainless steel grid of floating walkways that ran between the berths. Boats of all types and sizes were moored side by side—multi-million-dollar yachts, catamarans, sailing boats with masts that rose into the air like javelins, commercial fishing and diving boats, half cabins for hire, barbeque pontoons, and even the odd tinnie, gently rose and dropped with the incoming tide.

'Do you mind me asking what this is all about?' Went asked.

'It's police business. Nothing to alarm yourself about,' Jenny said.

'Did Cory Evans use his boat much?' I asked.

'He came here often, but never took the boat out. Let's say he liked to entertain guests.' Went unlocked the gate, and we followed him through it.

'Guests? What kind of guests?' Jenny asked.

'The pretty kind that you pay for.'

'Oh. Okay. Point us in the right direction, please Mister Went and we'll take it from there,' Jenny said.

Went pointed straight ahead. 'Go to the end of here. Turn left, then keep going. Mister Evans' yacht is the one at the end on the right. *The Tim Tam Kid*. You don't need a key to get back out, but my office is over there if you need me.'

'Thank you Mister Went. You've been very helpful.' Jenny led the way, her mid height heels clonking on the stainless steel walkway.

The evening was calm and still. A star-filled, cloudless sky sat overhead like a veil of pearls. The gentle lapping of the water, the rise and fall of the boats, rubber against steel as the walkway moved with the motion. Our way was lit by pedestal lights on either side every few metres. Most of the boats were dark and quiet. Some residents sat on back verandahs drinking wine. A family was having a barbeque on another boat.

By the time we reached *The Tim Tam Kid*, the sound of muffled rap music pulsated through the air. The enormous yacht was easy to spot; it was the one with all its lights on.

'Wow! Got to be at least five mil,' I said as we approached the twenty-five-metre-long boat.

'And the rest?' Jenny said.

There was a gangplank leading across to a shelf where two jet skis sat. Steps on either side led up to a large verandah. Sliding doors into the first level were open, and although the interior was illuminated giving a good view of a palatial lounge area, there didn't appear to be anyone inside.

'Hello Wesley, are you there?' Jenny called out.

I had given up calling Wesley's phone. After ringing him constantly throughout the day, he hadn't picked up once.

Cautiously, we crept across the gangplank. Female laughter coming from somewhere in the bowels of the boat halted us momentarily.

Climbing the few steps to the first deck, the verandah was as big as a modest apartment balcony and it was furnished with expensive outdoor furniture.

'Wesley, you there, mate?' If he was below deck, I doubted he would have heard me over the loud music, but I felt the need to call out anyway rather than just arriving unannounced.

The lounge area was spacious with a white circular leather sofa in the middle of the room. There was a TV on the right-hand side wall, a bar on the left, and a substantial kitchen, or galley, at the far end. To the right of the galley was a staircase leading up to the next level, and to the left of it was a staircase leading below deck.

More laughter rang out. It sounded like there was some kind of party taking place below us.

When Jenny looked at me, her expression said, 'What do you reckon? Shall we go down there?'

My nod was enough of a reply and I took the lead.

A corridor at the bottom of the staircase led to a series of doors, which I guessed were cabins. The door at the end was the only one open. The music was louder now and a groaning of the erotic kind accompanied the female laughter.

'Wes? You there, mate?'

We approached the door tentatively.

'Bloody hell!' I wasn't expecting what we saw.

Wesley was lying on a king-size bed with a young naked woman straddling him. There was another naked girl sat on the bed beside them. She was gently stroking Wesley's face and it appeared to be the source of the laughter. A third naked girl was leaning over the dressing table snorting a line of coke. When she saw us at the doorway, she stopped mid snort.

'Wesley.' The music was too loud for me to be heard so I stepped into the cabin.

'Fuck!' Wesley yelled, opening his eyes and catching sight of me. He sat bolt upright, pushed the girl off him and covered himself with the sheet. The three girls scurried away to the ensuite bathroom. 'What the hell are you doing here, Scott?'

'I've been calling you all day, mate. I was worried about you.'

With a face redder than a fire truck, the lad became physically flustered. It was as if his eyes were desperately searching for an escape route.

'Why don't you compose yourself. We'll be upstairs waiting for you,' I said.

His erratic nod was a product of desperation and fear.

Jenny and I retreated to the lounge on the main level. A few minutes later, the three girls, now dressed and ready for the next party, marched off the boat with their heads down, each barely managing to stifle a giggle.

'See you girls,' I called after them playfully.

One of them looked back over her shoulder. 'See you, Scotty. Any time, mate. On the house.'

My smirk soon disappeared when I realised Jenny was watching me.

'On the house, mate,' she said, mimicking the girl's seductive voice.

Wearing the usual black T-shirt and shorts, Wesley appeared at the top of the stairs.

'Hey mate, how's it going?' It was the only thing I could think of saying.

A frown was his choice of response.

'Having a bit of a party?'

'No.'

'Looked like a party to me. What do *you* reckon, Jen?'

'Oh yeah. Party, party.'

61

On the way over to the marina, Jenny and I discussed the best way to handle this. If we found Wesley at the boat, which we had, we decided we'd interview him there first before taking him back to the police headquarters, where Craig Nash would likely take over and shut down all communication.

'Why don't you have a seat?' I said, pointing to the expansive sofa.

Wesley, the awkward geek, was back. His movements resembled those of a sloth.

Jenny and I pulled out chairs from the dining table and placed them opposite. Wesley sank into the centre of the curved sofa.

Once again, there was no need for communication between me and Jenny. I was the one most familiar to the lad, so I steered the questioning.

'What happened to you this morning?'

'I was kidnapped.'

'Kidnapped? By whom?'

'Mick Brennan.'

'Did he take money from you?'

'No.'

'Thing is, mate, we've been monitoring your bank account.'

The shrug again, but this time there was a slight wince.

'A lot of money was withdrawn this evening.'

Silence.

'Strange time to throw a party when you've just lost twenty million dollars.'

Silence.

I don't believe in first impressions. First impressions can be manipulated by the host or misinterpreted by the beholder. In my experience, it took time to build a profile. You needed to dig deeper. Like any other practised skill, the ability to do this would eventually become second nature. In my case, I'd been doing it for so long that I was analysing people without even knowing it. Making mental notes of their mannerisms, their expressions, changes in their appearance. This had been the situation since first meeting Wesley not even a week ago, but I had to admit, for the first time ever, I had nothing. Until that night I was swayed by the impression he'd projected, awkward post teen, slightly overweight, no fashion sense, little experience in the real-world, lacking social skills, but possibly harbouring an intelligence that was common in the IT world. Having him stay at my place did show me another side to him, but not much. Even after a few beers, when we chatted casually at the bar in the man shed, there wasn't that much to learn. He was like a turtle that would retreat to his shell each time a situation arose he couldn't, or didn't want to, deal with. Or perhaps his brother, Cory, wasn't the only actor in the family.

I kicked on. 'Maybe it was a relief to finally have Brennan off your back.'

The shrug.

'Listen, Wes. We're mates. I can help. If Brennan was threatening you, we can nail him.'

The silence was worse than the "no comment" scenario that we'd likely face once Nash got a hold of him.

'Or maybe you were partying because you were just involved in the deal of a lifetime.'

'I want to speak to my solicitor.'

Jenny and I side glanced quickly as if checking we were still on the same page.

'Of course you do. But to do that, we'll need to take you into the station for questioning. Is that what you want to do? Wouldn't you rather stay here? Talk to us in comfort.'

'No. Get the fuck off my boat!'

Whoa, the side glance again. This time, a slight frown supplemented Jenny's expression. She rose to her feet and gestured for Wesley to stand. When they were eye level, she said, 'I can arrest you, read you your rights, and cuff you, or you can come with us willingly for questioning.'

I watched him closely as the options filtered through his mind.

'Do the right thing, mate. If you've got nothing to hide, there's nothing to worry about,' I said, also standing.

This brought on a very brief change in Wesley's expression. A harried flicker of uncertainty and fear passed across his face like a brief shadow. *Was it something I'd said? What the hell was he hiding?* There was something about this boy that I just couldn't put my finger on. Like one of those annoying little splinters that, as much as you try, you just can't get it out. This is how I felt. There was something there. Something he was hiding. But prizing it out of him, so far, had proved impossible. 'Unless that is … you do have something to hide. Either way, mate, we can do it here or we can do it down the station.'

'I need to see Craig Nash. He was Cory's solicitor.'

'Okay,' Jenny said. 'Are you happy to accompany us at your own free will?'

The shrug was back.

The walkway back to the marina entrance wasn't wide enough for the three of us to walk side by side, so Jenny led the way.

'You alright, mate?' I asked as we strolled past gently bobbing boats.

The shrug.

'It's all good. They have Brennan in custody. If he forced you to hand over the money, that's corruption, plus with what else is going down, he'll be going away for a long time, so he won't be bothering you again.'

'With what else is going on? What do you mean?' Gosh. He strung together two sentences.

If I was still a detective in the Queensland Police, I wouldn't be divulging information about the case, but reading my mind as usual, Jenny turned her head and gave me a slight nod as if to say, "I see where you're going with it and it's okay."

'We've just busted him for what might be Australia's largest ever drug haul.'

No shrug. A searching frown instead.

'Looks like he used your money to complete the deal. Good job *you're* not caught up in any of that, mate. It'd all come out then. Every *last* little secret.'

Jenny walked with her head down, listening.

'I just want to go home and be left alone,' Wesley said.

'That's not going to happen just yet, I'm afraid. But if you help us, Wes. I'll make sure your life gets back to normal as quickly as possible.'

We reached the entrance to the marina. Pressing a green button opened the gate.

'Is there anything you want to tell us before we get back to the station?' I asked as we walked towards Jenny's car.

This time, a shake of the head accompanied the familiar shrug.

'Okay, mate. But be aware. There is something you're hiding. I'm sure of it. And I'm going to find out what it is. Do you hear me?'

The silence was expected, but the slight grin wasn't.

62

Although we suspected Moe's little street party that afternoon was a decoy to make us believe Brennan was in the house, we had no proof. And as she rightly pointed out, there were no guns found on the property, Cassie drove herself to the house, and so did Barry. Apart from an investigation into Barry's business dealings, there was nothing to hold them for. We literally had a truckload of bikies in the cells, arrested on the spot in Logan, including Brennan. We also had Wesley, so Moe and Barry were released, each with a 'don't leave town' order. Knackers and Conan would be held at the watch house for at least twenty-four hours.

Brennan was in Interview Room #1. Wesley was in #2. Nash had briefed them both, so we pretty much knew the response we would face.

'Is he putting on an act, do you think?' Jenny asked as we stood peering at Wesley through the two-way mirror.

'I can't work him out, to be honest, Jen.'

'He's definitely hiding something. I think Wesley Cummings has a big fat secret.'

'Yeah. I know what you mean.'

'Fancy a bite to eat?'

'Yeah, why not?' I suddenly realised I was bloody starving.

We headed out to the corridor. Bradley joined us and the three of us made our way downstairs. When we walked through the reception towards the front exit, Moe Brennan was there, receiving a final brief from Nash.

'There will be a car here for you in a couple of minutes,' I heard Nash say. But I don't think Moe was listening. Her attention had switched to the three of us, or more specifically, me. She stepped away from Nash and blocked our path. 'A good day's work for ya's all,' she said.

'A great day,' Jenny said. 'Not only for the Queensland Police, but for the people of Australia.'

'Aye, aye, a great day. Ya have been a formidable adversary, Detective Inspector Jenny Radford. I take my hat off to ya.'

Jenny didn't reply.

'But what of you, Scotty Stephens?' Moe continued. 'You're not a member of the police force anymore, so what the hell were you doing getting involved in all of this?'

'Just looking for justice, Moe.'

'Justice, aye … justice, that's a good word, is that. Not unlike revenge. Very appropriate under the circumstances.' Her eyes were fixed on mine like she was about to read my fortune. 'You see, the thing about a gypsy curse is that ya won't know when, and ya won't know how, but you'll know it's going to happen. It moight be next week, it moight be next year, or it could be tonight. In many cases, it's the anticipation of the curse that drives people to the brink of hell. Living their lives in fear, knowing that they are being followed by a black dog that is just waiting for the moment to pounce.'

'You're putting a curse on me, Moe?' My attempt at a casual smirk proved in futile.

'Aye, 'tis already done.'

'Thanks.'

'Ya can thank me when the pain ya are about to endure is over. Or ya can come and see me to beg for my forgiveness. You'll decide when the time is right.'

'Righty oh, then.'

'I think that's enough, Moe,' Jenny said, pushing past her.

The elderly woman, who was dressed like she was heading to a heavy metal festival, stepped to one side, tipped an imaginary hat and lowered her eyes to the floor.

'You okay?' Jenny asked as we waited to cross Ferny Avenue.

'Yeah, of course. Why wouldn't I be?'

'You've just been cursed by a gypsy,' Bradley said.

'The queen of the gypsies, you mean.' Now it was Jenny's turn to smirk.

'Leave it out.'

'You're not worried?' Bradley asked, jabbing at the button on the pedestrian crossing.

'Nah, don't be daft. Why would I be?'

'I wouldn't like it,' Jenny said.

'It's not nice,' Bradley added with an air of authority.

'What do you know about being cursed?' I shot back at him as the *beep, beep, beep* of the pedestrian crossing sounded and we stepped onto the road.

'Darling, I'm gay. I've been cursed every day of my life … just kidding!' Bradley slid into a fit of giggles. He'd come a long way from that lad who was bullied by Super Intendant Andrew Ripley when he was assigned as my assistant during the *X* case. Open with his sexuality, confident, funny, but when required, an intensely good detective, I really appreciated his attempt at softening the fact that I'd just become the recipient of a gypsy curse. Of course, I didn't believe in any of that mumbo-jumbo crap, but if that was the case, why did I feel like I'd just received word that the headmaster wanted to see me in his office?

We didn't go into the heart of Surfers. The Schoolies festival was still in full swing. In fact, it was reaching the climax of the first week, after which it would all start again for the second phase.

We ate at a little Indian restaurant on a side street close to the Q1 building.

'Here's to Detective Inspector Jenny Radford for bringing down the biggest drug haul in Australian history,' I said, holding up a Corona beer.

Three identical bottles clinked together, and we all took a swig in unison.

'Congratulations, Jenny,' Bradley said. 'Well deserved.'

'Thank you, but I couldn't have done it without you guys.'

'That's very kind.'

We placed our order.

'We've still got the matter of Cory and Patty to clear up,' I said before taking another swig of beer.

'Maybe we have the killer in custody,' Jenny said.

63

When we arrived back at the station, there was no hurry to speak with Wesley. Nash was sticking by his side like a Siamese twin.

With the effects of a slight curry coma, I went to use the bathroom. While standing at the urinal, the white wall tiles morphed into my whiteboard and my mind automatically summarised the case so far.

Although I hadn't ruled out Barry Evans, Cassie or Netty Slater completely, we were down to the two main suspects, the two finalists in the latest Scotty Stephens reality TV show.

Mick Brennan was involved in both Cory's and Patty's deaths, but did they die at his hands or did he get someone else to do it? The man was easy to read. A thug with a hard exterior, but inside was an entrepreneur, a leader, and possibly a criminal mastermind. However, the same could be said for Wesley. The only difference was his exterior was soft, but having said that, it had proved impossible to penetrate so far, even for a seasoned detective like me. And right there was the route of my problem. There was something about Wesley that was scrambling my mental devices. Something that I couldn't pin down, like trying to program a radio station that was almost there but not quite. *Wesley, Wesley, Wesley, how are you doing this?* Of course, this could all have been my imagination. Perhaps the lack of leads in the case was making me so desperate. That I was looking in the wrong place, focusing on something that wasn't there.

The door to the men's toilets had a distinctive screech, which made the whiteboard on the wall instantly dissolve, rendering my thoughts back to the current moment. I didn't have to turn my head to know who it was that joined me at the urinals. The expensive aftershave, heavy confident steps, the forceful *zhripp* of his zipper.

'Scotty.'

'Mister Nash.' I wasn't sure why the formal greeting. 'How's it going?'

'Good.' Like his movements, and unlike my no-hurry dribble, his stream was a heavy flow. He guided it over every inch of the porcelain as if it were his duty to clean it. 'How's the private detective business working for you? I see you smashed the Kathy Brown case out at Tallebudgera.'

'Yeah, it's going good.'

'You were a good copper. The Queensland Police lost a good one when you left the force.'

'Thank you. Looks like we're going to be up against each other again.'

'What do you mean?' He leaned forward to check his progress. 'You might be called up as a witness for the prosecution, but that's about all.'

The cheeky bastard. His attempt at belittling me now that I was no longer a police detective was all a part of the intimidation game. I was better than that. 'I'm a part of the Cory Evans' murder investigation. I'll be the one fighting to bring the killer to justice.'

The patronising laugh that he'd honed over the years was a major piece in his toolkit. 'Good luck with that. But I'm sure Detective Inspector Radford will allow you to hang around.'

'Let's not do this, eh, Craig.' There was no longer a need for formality.

'Do what?'

'Comparing dicks.'

At my unconscious choice of metaphor, his eyes inadvertently lowered to my side of the trough.

'We both know I'm a competent detective, which means your little mind games won't work with me.'

'Really? I thought we were just having a friendly chat.'

'Okay. If that's the case. What do you make of Wesley?'

'I'm not about to discuss my client with you.'

'Friendly chat, remember?'

After an exaggerated shake, he zipped up and turned away from the urinal. 'I don't really know him yet. He seems to have shut down.'

My shake was less exaggerated but more carefully executed to ensure there were no lingering drops to flower the front of my trousers.

Everything Nash did had a sense of drama and authority. He forcefully pressed the handwash device, turned on the tap and washed his hands.

'I've been trying to delve below his surface for the last week,' I said, joining him at the sinks. 'And I have to admit, I still don't have a clue who he is.'

'I know what you mean. It won't be easy, but hey, I'm Craig Nash. He'll open up to me.' Choosing the paper towels over the automatic hand dryer, even ripping off the sheets, was a performance. 'Listen, can we get this over with?' He dried his hands and checked his watch. 'It's getting late.'

'Sure, we'll come in now. I suppose you've versed him with the usual routine?'

His wily smile reminded me of the cunning fox.

'It shouldn't take long then.'

'Good man. I haven't eaten yet and they're holding a table for me at Room 81.' Even the usual squeak from the door hinges seemed to rise to the occasion as he marched out of the men's toilets leaving a cloud of aftershave in his wake.

Bradley monitored the interview via CCTV from another room. Jenny entered first, with me close behind. After placing a rather thick file on the table, she took her seat across from Nash and Wesley. I took the chair by her side.

Jenny switched on the recording device and started the interview with the usual formalities—noting who was present, etc.

My eyes were fixed firmly on Wesley and there they would remain for the entire interview. Each "no comment" would be closely analysed. Every twitch of the face, eye movement, every flicker of emotion was mentally recorded. My first impression was of how tired he looked. The day had begun with me giving him a surfing lesson, which seemed more like a week ago now. And when I put that into perspective, the fact that it was less than a week since we'd first met, a hell of a lot had happened in that time. No wonder he looked buggered.

'Wesley Cummings, can you share with us your movements on October 29th please?' Jenny asked politely. This was the date that forensics had estimated to be the day of Cory's death.

Wesley glanced at Nash for support.

Nash nodded and raised his eyebrows as if to say, "Go on, remember what we discussed."

The dark rings around Wesley's eyes were evident when he returned his gaze to Jenny and said, 'No comment.'

Jeez, I could have reached across and banged their bloody heads together. This was so typical of Nash and was the same ploy when he briefly represented me a year ago.

Still, my focus remained fixed on Wesley. His hair was more unruly than normal. His body language was slow and tired. If there were cracks to be found in his armour, my continuous scrutiny would find them. When he glanced in my direction, something caught my eye.

And that's when *it* happened. At first, I wasn't sure what *it* was. I only knew it was something important.

Taking a leaf from Nash's book of intimidation, I sat forward and narrowed my eyes.

Wesley shuffled in his seat, and there it was again … a flash of gold.

What did it mean? What did it mean? The voice in my head demanded. A flash of gold?

Then it all fell into place. *A flash of gold.*

Sitting as if momentarily frozen in time, my mind systematically checked and rechecked the permutations like a lottery machine, and the answer came up the same each time. The reason for the murders became clear. But more importantly, I knew who the killer was!

With my first ever epiphany, I suddenly felt like a magician about to deliver the most amazing magic trick ever. I was the only one who knew how to perform the trick, and everyone would be baffled and amazed, their minds filled with the question, "How on earth did he do that?" But once the trick was revealed, the audience would say, "Ahhh … right. I see. Not that good after all, really."

Jenny knew right away that I was on to something. God bless her. She didn't say a word, she just sat there watching me, allowing me the time to prepare.

Nash also realised something was happening. He straightened his back and looked at me expectantly.

Wesley's body language was the opposite. It was as if he was melting into the chair. After the last glance my way, when I'd leaned forward, he must have noticed something in my eyes. Something that told him I knew.

'Why did you do it, mate?' I asked calmly.

Once again, the glance in Nash's direction, but this time there really was no comment.

'Why did you kill your brother and your mum?'

64

Now it was Jenny and Nash's eyes that were focused directly on me. Wesley hung his head low as if he knew the game was up.

I'd delivered the first part of the magic trick perfectly. But before revealing how I'd done it, there was the second, and final WTF moment, which would lament my performance as truly remarkable. The big reveal was upon us. The grand finale. 'Why'd you do it … Cory?'

Jenny and Nash's puzzled frowns were identical. It was time for me to reveal the science behind the magic. I leaned across the table and ran my hand through the lad's hair. 'Looks like you're ready for a top up, mate. Your roots are showing through.' My probing fingers revealed minute traces of gold close to his scalp.

He pushed my hand away and searched the wall to his right as if he were looking for an escape route. My audience still didn't understand. I was enjoying the moment. God, I was good.

'Would you like to enlighten us please, Mister Stephens?' Craig Nash said.

I would have dearly loved to have said, "No comment" but instead, I said, 'Sure thing, Craig.' Adding to the drama, I rose to my feet. 'Perhaps it's time for Cory here to tell us why he killed his brother, Wesley, and then his mum, Patty. Over to you, Freckles.'

As if recognising defeat, Cory sat up straight and said, 'No comment.'

'I need to speak to my client in private.'

'Of course you do.'

Jenny sat there with her mouth open, staring at Cory as if the penny had yet to drop.

'If you don't mind please, detective,' Nash said, rising to his feet.

Jenny frowned and, tearing her eyes away from Cory, she looked at me for confirmation.

'Yep. Little Freckles. Come on, I'll explain.'

'Are you kidding me, Scott?' Bradley said, as we joined him in the surveillance room.

'No. It's true. That's not Wesley in there. It's his brother, Cory. Has been all the time!'

With the sound turned off, we watched Nash in the interview room, who seemed to be having a meltdown while his client sat quietly with his head low. I could only imagine what was being said.

'How long have you known this?' Jenny asked, returning to her senses.

I looked at my watch. 'About two minutes.'

'Let's just stop gloating, eh, and tell us what the hell's going on.'

We headed for Jenny's office. Bradley ducked away to make coffees.

'But the DNA from the body, it was a definite match for Cory.'

'Not only has he been a brilliant actor, he's also been very clever.'

We sat down at Jenny's desk.

Bradley breezed in with three of the quickest made coffees ever. 'What did I miss?'

'Nothing,' Jenny said. 'Sherlock was just about to enlighten us.'

Bradley placed our coffees on the desk, then half sat on the windowsill.

'He certainly had us all fooled, that's for sure.' I was about to take a sip of coffee, but Jenny's knitted brow said, "Don't you dare keep us waiting."

'Okay. Let's start with the DNA. When I arrived at the apartment that day, it was spotless. It had been cleaned from top to bottom. All except that is for the vanity in Cory's ensuite. It was empty except for a comb. Because the hair we extracted from it was so fine and the colour was hard to determine, we just assumed it belonged to Cory.'

'Because you found it in his bathroom.' Jenny took a sip of coffee, screwed up her nose, and shot Bradley with a frown that was as sharp as a slap.

'That's right, when in fact it belonged to Wesley. Cory planted it there, knowing I would find it.'

'So, the sample matched the body we found in the car,' Bradley said.

'Correct. The body was Wesley.'

'Wow,' Jenny said, automatically taking another sip but not tasting it this time. 'But why? Why did Cory kill his brother? And Patty? Did he kill her too?'

Collecting my thoughts, I quietly nodded. 'I believe he did. But let's start at the beginning. Brennan desperately needed finances for the biggest drug deal of his life. He'd already sold off his assets, but still fallen short. The contraband had arrived in the country, so there was no way of backing out. When he learned Patty was living in the caravan park close to The Wasps' nest, he befriended her, and they became lovers—or so Patty thought. Knowing about Cory's past experiences, investing in small businesses, Brennan hatched a plan to get to him, which he did through Patty.'

'Do you think Brennan threatened him or did Cory willingly agree to becoming a partner in the deal?' Jenny asked.

'I'm not sure yet. But one thing that is for sure is that Cory got cold feet, and true to form, he wanted out at the last minute.'

'Like he did with Netty Slater,' Bradley added.

'That's right. But with Brennan, there was no pulling out. If the threats hadn't happened earlier, they certainly would have at that point.'

'So he panicked,' Jenny said, without raising her eyes from the desk.

'Feared for his life. Needed a way out. He'd been estranged from his little brother for years. I'm just guessing at this point, but I reckon, ironically, he was jealous of Wesley's normal upbringing.'

'Jealous enough to kill him?' Jenny asked.

'It seems so.' I took a sip of coffee and immediately regretted it. 'Bloody hell, Bradley. That's horrible.' This was very unlike Bradley's usual form.

'Sorry,' he fluffed up half apologetically, half in annoyance. 'I didn't want to miss anything.'

Placing the cup back on the desk, I continued. 'Suicide was the only option. Well, a faked suicide, let's say.'

'But how did he change his appearance? The freckles, for goodness' sake.'

'The famous freckles were painted on, always were. Without them, the resemblance to his brother was quite uncanny, especially when he dyed his hair. Netty Slater told me he cancelled their training sessions and wouldn't even speak to her. I'm guessing during those few weeks of being incognito, he put on weight. Then, out of the blue, he invites his younger brother to come and stay with him. Wesley eagerly took him up on his offer. Little did he know, Cory wasn't just planning to kill him, but also to steal his identity. I'm guessing that over the next few weeks, Cory studied Wesley—his mannerisms, body language. Remember, he'd been an actor all his life. A much better actor, in fact, that anyone gave him credit for.

'When the time came, just prior to the Schoolies festival, he drove Wesley down to the Bangalow National Park in Northern New South Wales, killed him and burned the body in his car. When he returned to Surfers Paradise, he dyed his hair and Cory Evans was no more.'

'It sounds a bit far-fetched, but it makes sense,' Jenny said thoughtfully.

'A DNA test will prove that's Corry siting in there.'

'Cory thought he was out of the deal.'

'Not only that, but he also thought he'd escaped from the life that had imprisoned him for all these years, which meant for the first time he could walk on the streets unnoticed. Unfortunately, he chose the time of the Schoolies festival to try out his new freedom, only to be mistaken for a Toolie and end up getting bashed. But more importantly, Brennan didn't let go. After Cory's disappearance, he went after Wesley.'

'So, after that, Cory still didn't get out of the deal. And Patty?'

'During his time of impersonating his brother, there were probably only two people that could have spoiled his plan. The two people who would have recognised him—Barry and Patty. So, he was careful to avoid them. But Patty may have seen him entering my office with me. Cory, realising she would have recognised him, had to silence her. Which he did.'

'It would have been just as risky meeting with Cassie, surely,' Bradley said.

'No, she'd never met either Cory or Wesley before. Cory probably saw her as a test, to see if he could pull off Wesley's identity.'

'It won't be easy to prove any of this, but the DNA will be the biggest factor. And if we get Brennan on board, perhaps offer him a little deal, his collaboration will go a long way too,' Jenny said rising from her desk. 'Right. Let's go and charge the little fucker.'

65

Three Weeks Later

Although Cory Evans and Mick Brennan were the key players in the same case, the media split them up. Mick Brennan was the principal of Australia's largest illegal drug importation, and Detective Inspector Jenny Radford was the heroine. Not only did she nail Brennan, but she also removed The Wasps from society. The people of the Gold Coast heralded her as the new saviour, not unlike the way they had me the year previously. Jenny handled it all in her stride—the TV interviews across the national news channels, the recognition by her peers, the accolades bestowed on her.

The Cory Evans murder case, however—according to the media—was purely down to me.

Scotty Stephens strikes again!
The King of the Gold Coast is back!

These were typical of the newspaper headlines. And although I didn't earn a single cent from the case, a renewed interest by the media ensured that there was money to be earned from interviews and magazine articles. It could be said I had become a media tart, but I didn't care.

Regardless of Nash's interference, Brennan's role in the drug haul was unquestionable. He'd literally been caught red-handed loading the contraband from the container to the trucks that he'd hired the previous day under his name. Not so bloody smart after all, it seems.

As suspected, when the DNA report came back, it confirmed the plaintiff was indeed Cory Evans and not his brother, Wesley. It was a no-brainer, a slam dunk and every other cliché I could think of to describe the situation.

The suspects were officially charged and despite Nash's best efforts, they were both detained without bail, awaiting trial.

It was yet another perfect Gold Coast morning, so I walked around Kirra Point and into Coolangatta. Inevitably, I'd end up at the office, but I had a very important meeting first. The final signing of the contract of sale for the house on Ruby Street. It was an exciting day but also a tarnished one. My best mate, Elvis, would normally be present on special occasions such as this, but he wasn't there because he was undertaking the same process 1,700 kilometres away in Melbourne. There was a strange clause that he had added to the contract—a stipulation that forbid me against demolishing the house, or even changing it. Karla Humphries, my lawyer, had dismissed the clause and said she could get it removed, but after giving it some thought, I left it in.

Just over a week ago, I'd travelled down to Melbourne for an impromptu meeting with Elvis. I purposely didn't tell him or his parents of my visit. In my mind, I needed to understand the situation as best I could. To do this, I needed one-on-one time with my old mate.

'Scott?' Mrs Papageorgiou said as she opened the front door to the family home in Essendon. 'What are you doing here?'

'I had some business in town, so thought I'd pop by.' I didn't enjoy lying to her, but it was a necessity. 'Is Nicky home?' I asked, using the shorter version of her son's real name, Nickoladas, that she and her husband fondly used.

'Yes, he is. Come in.' She showed me through the house and out to the backyard.

Elvis was sitting alone at a dated wicker outdoor setting, looking out over the small yard where he used to play as a kid.

'Hey mate,' I said as I approached him.

Elvis jumped as if waking from a nap. 'Scotty?' The usual close-cropped hair had a couple of inches of growth, which showcased his receding hairline. A day or so of greying stubble around the lower half of his face almost rendered him unrecognisable even to me. He'd also put on a fair amount of weight since I'd last seen him. 'I didn't know you were coming to Melbourne.'

'No, I didn't know either until yesterday.' A half-truth. I only decided to come the day before.

'Can I get you anything to drink?' Mrs Papageorgiou asked.

'I'd love one of your special lemonades if you've got one.' A fond childhood memory was of two cheeky little buggers sitting on the swing set in this very backyard, sipping homemade lemonade that Elvis' mum made most days and kept cool in the fridge.

The little old lady disappeared into the house. Elvis' gaze returned to a spot on the back fence.

'So how ya been, mate?' I asked.

'Shit,' Elvis said. 'That's the only way I can describe what I'm going through. And the pile gets bigger and bigger every time anyone asks me how I'm doing or what's wrong.

'Sorry. I didn't mean anything …'

Mrs Papageorgiou returned carrying two tall glasses. She placed them down on the table, then left us. I took a seat next to Elvis and followed his gaze.

'I just wanted to talk to you about the sale of the house.'

Elvis picked up his glass and took a sip of lemonade.

'It's not too late if you wanted to pull out of the deal.'

'Nah, it's gone unconditional.'

'But we can both withdraw if we wanted.'

'Why would we do that?'

'Are you sure you want to sell it, mate?'

'Positive. That old house is just one of the many things I need to eradicate from my life.' He glanced in my direction, and I wondered if I also fell in the same category.

'So why the clause?'

'What clause?'

'The no demo or renovation clause.'

'Is that what this is about? The reason you came down here? What, you wanna just demolish the place, do you?'

'No. Not at all. I just wondered why? If you want to remove the place from your life, why would insist it remains the same?'

He shrugged impatiently, then took a large mouthful of his ice cold drink. I was pissing him off, and that was the last thing I wanted to do. He was in a fragile state at that moment, so I backed off. But I also made a decision there and then. There was a reason for him wanting the house on Ruby Street to remain the same, and although it was possibly a subconscious choice at that time, it seemed important to him. For this reason, I would keep the house exactly the same—the man shed, Elvis' bedroom, the dated kitchen, the bindy infested back yard. Then when Elvis finally got over the illness he was currently going through, I would sell the house back to him at the same price he'd sold it to me. He was still, and would always be, my best mate. It would be the right thing to do.

Karla Humphries' office was about a hundred metres from mine. When I arrived, she was waiting for me with the contract of sale spread across her desk. 'Scotty. Come on in,' she said, welcoming me with a handshake.

I lost count of how many signatures I squiggled on various documents, but when the last one was committed, Karla held out her hand, smiling. Purely ceremonious, but I handed the keys to her as the outgoing tenant. She handed them straight back to me as the new owner.

'Congratulations, Scotty. You purchased what could be Kirra Beach's last prime block of land.'

'Thanks Karla.'

When I stepped back out and into the sunshine, I wasn't quite sure how I was feeling. On the one hand, I was a house owner; on the other, I was a forty-something-year-old bloke who would be living alone in a house that held nothing but great memories but would also act as a reminder of something that I actually wished for. I wanted change in my life and boy, did I get it.

'Be careful what you wish for, Scotty,' my mum whispered.

Could everything that had happened in the last few months really be a manifestation of the thoughts I'd put out to the universe? Tetley's prolonged stay in the UK. Elvis' return to Melbourne. The purchase of the house on Ruby Street. "No, that's bollocks!" Now it was Tetley's voice in my ear.

'Hey Rockefeller.'

The familiar voice snapped be back to the present. Looking over my sunglasses, I saw Jenny and Bradley leaning up against the MINI.

'What are you guys doing here?' They were a welcomed relief from the mixed feelings swirling inside my head.

Jenny pulled out a bottle of Champagne from behind her back. 'You didn't think we were going to let you celebrate alone, did you?'

'What did you have in mind?' I asked, taking the bottle.

'The man shed, of course,' Bradley said.

'Of course.'

We climbed into the MINI, Bradley squeezing into the back once more.

Jenny chatted incessantly during the short drive back to Kirra, but I wasn't taking much notice. My thoughts were with Elvis. Would he be celebrating today? I doubted it.

We turned onto Lord Street from Musgrave, but when we tried to turn into Ruby Street, a police car blocked the road. Beyond that, there were at least two fire trucks. Black smoke bellowed into the air farther down the street, and although we couldn't see where it was coming from, I knew … We knew.

When we climbed from the car, the young constable, who obviously recognised us, didn't stop us from passing.

The roof of the house was already gone. Flumes of water from the hoses did little to prevent the flames twisting and slapping the air with a ferocious anger. The windows and front door were also gone. Just the façade remained, but it seemed to be melting, swaying in the heat like a fighter, hit with a sucker punch, and heading for the canvas.

'I'm going to have to get you to stand back, I'm afraid, guys,' a young firie said.

The Dub was parked in the garage. When the roller door fell in, I could just make out the curved shell of what used to be my beloved car.

The front wall of the house suddenly fell inwards with a crash and among hissing, spitting sparks I could have sworn I heard the throaty laugh of a middle-aged Irish woman. Was this the product of a gypsy curse?

Now there was nothing to see except a burning pile of asbestos. Everything I owned was in that house. Everything was gone. Jenny put her arm around me and pulled me to her chest. Knowing there were no words of comfort, she held me there quietly.

When the flames were finally quelled and the fire trucks had retreated, small flumes of smoke still rose from the pile of ashes here and there. Jenny and I stood in what was once the front yard. Even the man shed was totally eradicated. There was nothing left. I couldn't bear to look at the curved mound where the garage used to be.

'What will you do?' Jenny asked.

'Do you think it's the curse?'

'What? Surely you don't think …?'

'Because if it is, I'm glad it's over.' Although it had only been three weeks since Moe Brennan had vowed her revenge on me via a gypsy curse, and even though I didn't believe in all that superstitious crap, I had to admit, it had been playing on my mind. Kind of like God. You didn't really believe in him, but you're not game enough to dismiss him completely. Perhaps subconsciously I'd taken the curse seriously. So, if the house burning down was a result of the curse, and meant nobody else was hurt, it affected only me.

'There's no such thing as a gypsy curse, mate,' Jenny said.

'I know. Just being daft,' I replied, but why was there still that nagging feeling like the curse was still in place?

'I know what you need to do,' Jenny suddenly said, as if hit with a great idea.

'What's that?'

'Don't you see? The clause in the contract no longer applies. You can rebuild. You've got insurance. You can do anything you like.'

'True.' It was a bit early to be thinking like this, but she had a point.

'You could sell the land. You could subdivide. You could—oh.' The sharp intake of breath was a prelude to an epiphany, I was sure. 'You could build a duplex.' Her eyes searched mine with expectant glee.

A Wesley/Cory shrug was all I could muster.

'I'll buy one side. You live in the other.' Her mind was working overtime. Then she must have realised that she was being a little insensitive. 'Sorry. What an idiot. Come on, you can stay at my place tonight. And tomorrow and as long as it takes.' She put her arm around me.

'Thanks, Jen.' We kissed, and it felt good.

'See this as a new chapter, Scotty. You've got this.'

'I know. It's just going to take some time, that's all.'

'It will. Let's go home.'

As we headed back to the MINI, the fact that I no longer had a home was messing with my emotions. But Jenny was right. I should have been looking at this as a new start.

"Be careful what you wish for, Scotty."

'Yes, Mum, from now on I will.' The picture of two identical white houses joined in the middle suddenly appeared in my mind. Was that Jenny's cat, Nero, sitting on the right mailbox?

How would you rate
this book?

I hope you enjoyed reading *Tarnished*. If so, I would be truly grateful if you would consider writing a review.

Reviews are a very important way of enabling me to reach a wider audience and bringing my stories to more readers just like you.

If you have an Amazon account, you can rate this title and leave a customer review by scanning the QR code below or logging into you KDP account.

Or, alternatively, if you purchased your book from one of the online stores, you can login to your account and leave a review there.

Or if you have a Goodreads account you can post your review at:

Thanks in advance, I really appreciate your support!
Andrew

ACKNOWLEDGEMENTS

As a proud Queenslander, I'd like to begin by acknowledging the traditional custodians of this land which we inhabit, and pay my respects to the Elders past and present.

Thank you to my editor, Julie Guthrie, for your concise edits that force me to work a little harder, of which I am grateful. And a big thank you to the best beta readers ever, Carole Phillips, and Jane McDermott.

ABOUT THE AUTHOR

Andrew McDermott was born in Nottingham, England. A naturalised Aussie he has lived on the Gold Coast Australia since 1989 with his wife, Jane. He is a patron of the Gold Coast Writers Association, and currently resides at Kirra Beach.

Other books by this author...

Scotty Stephens Gold Coast Detective - Book 1

X

The eyes of the world are on Australia's Gold Coast, but for all the wrong reasons. Seven young women have been killed over a two-week period. The cause of death on each occasion was a slash to the throat in the shape of an X.

Detective Constable Scott Stephens is inexplicably plucked from obscurity, promoted to Detective Inspector, and placed in charge of the investigation.

Gold Coast Mayor, ex-AFL star, and billionaire property developer, Julian Monroe, has a lot to lose. Along with his involvement in various multi-million-dollar projects, his long-anticipated cruise ship terminal and casino resort is at a sensitive stage with potential investors.

Scott unearths withheld CCTV footage of the killer fleeing the scene of the last murder. The face of the offender is unmistakable - it's the mayor's son. The only problem is, he has an identical twin.

Scott not only needs to determine which twin is the killer - the brash, up-and-coming AFL star of the Gold Coast Suns, Dillon Monroe, or his brother, Troy - but he also faces a backlash from his employees when he suspects there's been a cover-up.

An explosive climax ensues, around the vibrant streets of the Gold Coast, when the killer's attention shifts, catapulting Scott's plight in a new direction - a fight for his life.

Purchase your copy from all good online book stores or at:
www.andrewmcdermott.com.au

Download the prequel, X'posé, for free at:
www.andrewmcdermott.com.au

Also by ANDREW M^CDERMOTT

FLIRTING WITH THE MOON

High-profile LAPD detective, Joe Dean, loses his career, his family, and his sanity when the twelfth victim of the serial killer – The Moon – is taken from right under his nose.

Twenty-five years later and Joe is a reformed character operating as a private detective. While working on a case, he comes across a book called Flirting with The Moon. Each of the twelve entries is a precise description of The Moon murders, which could only have been written by the killer.

The publisher is tracked down to Sydney, Australia but the only details they have of the author is a pseudonym and a post box number in a Far North Queensland town called, Candle Stick Bay.

Obsessed with the possibility of finally bringing The Moon to justice, Joe flies out to Australia and travels to the remote tropical North to find a tiny picturesque town overlooking the Coral Sea.

While posing as an American tourist, he secretly digs for clues and unearths some surprising secrets about the town and its inhabitants. But as his investigation twists and turns, the murders begin once more, and Joe is forced to confront the demons of his past.

Purchase your copy from all good online book stores or at:
www.andrewmcdermott.com.au

Download the prequel, Hidden Moon, for free at:
www.andrewmcdermott.com.au

Also by ANDREW M^cDERMOTT

THE TIGER CHASE

Dr Elizabeth Smith brings a rare Chinese tiger to the La Zoo, but the tiger is stolen on its arrival. Detective John Dean of the LAPD hates two things in life, strong willed woman, and cats. His worst nightmare is realised when he is ordered to retrieve the tiger with Dr Smith and travel back 2000 miles across America in a station wagon, with the tiger in the back, and a gang of crooks in hot pursuit.

The Tiger Chase is an action-packed story that incorporates drama and humour with a wealth of information about one of the most precious, yet most endangered, species on earth the South China tiger.

An entertaining story about the fight for survival which is sure to raise awareness about the very real threat of extinction facing the mystical and majestic South China Tiger.

Nick Rhodes, Duran Duran

For the first time in history, this most ancient tiger – the South China Tiger, is brought to the consciousness of the western public through story telling. The Tiger Chase has captured the spirit of the Chinese tiger, ancestral to all other subspecies, as well as the culture associated with it. I hope that the awareness it raises would encourage the reader to join us in our fight to save this cultural symbol and protector of nature from the fate of extinction.

Li Quan, Save China's Tigers (Charity)

www.savechinastigers.org

Purchase your copy from all good online book stores or at:

www.andrewmcdermott.com.au

Sign up at the link below to join Andrew's mailing list and receive your free ebooks, his bi-annual newsletter, be the first to know about up and coming titles, and have direct contact with the author.

"I would love for you to be part of my writing community. Your opinion is dear to me and I hope you will enjoy the books in my catalogue and all future releases."

Andrew

X'posé (X prequel)
Hidden Moon (Flirting with The Moon prequel)
Download your free ebooks here:
www.andrewmcdermott.com.au

You can also follow Andrew at:
Facebook: https://www.facebook.com/andrewmcdermottauthor/
Instagram: https://www.instagram.com/andrewmcdermottauthor/
X (Twitter): https://x.com/andymcdauthor

www.ingramcontent.com/pod-product-compliance
Lightning Source LLC
Chambersburg PA
CBHW010427170726
48283CB00011B/3099